W9-CAL-062

sc

DEMCO

SHERMAN'S MARCH

CYNTHIA BASS

SHERMAN'S MARCH

Central Rappahannock Regional Library
1201 Caroline Street
Fredericksburg, VA. 22401

VILLARD BOOKS 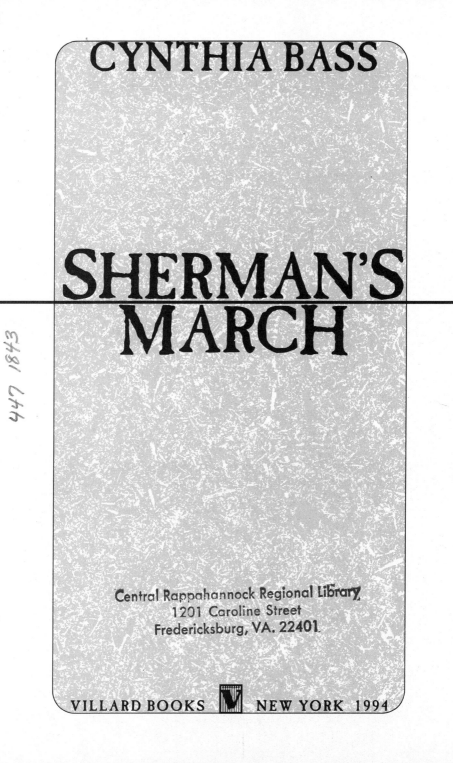 NEW YORK 1994

C4

VILLARD BOOKS is a registered trademark of Random House, Inc.

Library of Congress Cataloging-in-Publication Data

Bass, Cynthia.
Sherman's march / Cynthia Bass.—1st ed.
p.   cm.
ISBN 0-679-43033-4
1. United States—History—Civil War, 1861–1865—Fiction.
2. Sherman, William T. (William Tecumseh), 1820–1891—Fiction.
3. Sherman's March to the Sea—Fiction.   4. Generals—United States—
Fiction.   I. Title
PS3552.A816S48   1994
813'.54—dc20   93-40649

Manufactured in the United States of America on acid-free paper

2 4 6 8 9 7 5 3

FIRST EDITION

Book design by Carole Lowenstein

To Steve

Sherman's March 1: Sherman's March to the Sea, Atlanta–Savannah, autumn of 1864. Considered the first widespread use of civilian warfare. 2: Total war.

CONTENTS

PART I
SHERMAN

SPEAKER:

William Tecumseh Sherman
Major-General, Western Theater, U.S. Army

PREFACE

WHEN MEMPHIS FELL in the summer of '62, I was appointed military administrator. It was an honor I neither coveted nor sought; I am a soldier, nothing more. But since I am a soldier I know how to follow commands, and I undertook readily the task of restoring order to a conquered city. I issued proclamations guaranteeing the safety of the people of Memphis, and promised any citizen with a complaint against our Northern troops an immediate public hearing, with myself in attendance. I signed such proclamations personally, in my own name, William Tecumseh Sherman.

Under my administration Memphis blossomed. Schools reopened; theaters resumed performances; shopkeepers emerged from their cellars to reclaim their countertops—shocked, I'm sure, to find their wares still neatly stacked on their shelves, and their money still safe in its hiding place. I persuaded the city fathers to return to their posts, and urged the religious leaders to open the doors of their churches. In all aspects, in all decisions, civil as well as military, I favored the side of moderation, of reason.

But soon enough I was to learn the foolishness of such policy. At the very moment I was treating the people of Memphis with so great a benignity I was condemned on the floor of the U.S. Senate for insufficient ardor in the face of the enemy, the citizens of that city were setting their hearts against my army. Patrols were attacked and captured on moonless nights, found dying (but not quite dead) in empty fields, bleeding from unspeakable wounds. Rifles disappeared; depots exploded; cannons were examined and found to be jimmied or jammed. Slowly at first, not wanting to know, I began to suspect that those same good citizens who came to me at noon with such politesse were roaming the countryside at midnight, slashing my soldiers' throats with my own stolen sabers, shooting my men in the stomach with my own stolen guns.

In late September I received *incontrovertible evidence* that guerrillas from the nearby village of Randolph had fired upon two of my steamboats. Thanks to my trust and respect for the citizens of Memphis, these boats were unarmed; they could not return a single shot in their own defense. They simply bobbled, helpless and clear in the sights of their unseen enemy.

But I was not helpless. I immediately ordered the village of Randolph burnt to the ground—all save one house, which remained to mark the spot. Then I announced to the people of Memphis that for every boat fired on, I would expel from the city ten families, chosen by lot. I vowed that henceforth any guerrillas caught by my soldiers would be bound, themselves put on boats, and used by my men for target practice.

It has now been two years since I ordered the burning of Randolph. Today Atlanta smolders, an evacuated husk. Every flame, every paneless window, every shell, for one purpose only.

This war must stop. Every day we gnaw one another like two baffled dragons; night falls, and we scoop up stomachs and bury eyes. Meanwhile the real enemies—the civilians—understand nothing. Worse than nothing. They send off their children for us to torture, then call them martyrs, and us barbarians. Cocooned from real suffering by distance and custom, they urge on the slaughter from the untouched shade of their peaceful verandas.

But war has no place for peace. Thus did the teachers of Memphis instruct me. Treated kindly, a soldier responds with kindness; treated kindly, a civilian responds with treason. Thus kindliness in the midst of warfare—bypassing the land between battlefields, sparing the illusion of everyday life—is an error. All it does is hurt your own people, enrich the undertakers, and prolong the killing on either side. War cannot be waged civilly, and still be war.

All that will end this war quickly is more war. Harder war, stricter war, crueler, deeper. Into the occupied zones. Into the cities, into the countryside. War until the people themselves sample its sting—not in their minds, not in their mourning or songs, but in reality. In their own bodies for once, and not their soldiers'. We must take the pain from the battlefield, and bring the war home.

I can do it. I can begin ending the war right now. I have the troops, I have the rifles, I have the cannons, I have the will. I have Atlanta. Give me the rest.

The heart of the Southern Confederacy lies beating before me. Let me wade in that heart. Let me bathe in its blood.

I can make Georgia howl!

CHAPTER
ONE

As it turned out, my pleas needn't have been so dramatic; it was easy to obtain permission for a march through Georgia. After all, both sides had unofficially been living off the land since the second year of the war. Look at Grant, slipping and sliding into Vicksburg, victory possible only because of his famous decision to cut his supply lines and try a little backdoor action in the Yazoo swamplands. What else does "cutting your own supply lines" mean besides living off the countryside? Or Lee. Saint Lee. Invasion of Pennsylvania. Same thing. They stripped the farms bare all the way to Gettysburg; in every town they passed, they seized shoes, blankets, hats, boots. It's true they paid—paid in Confederate money, which is the same thing as stealing, maybe worse, unless you're in the wallpaper business. All I was doing was making things official. So for being a good bureaucrat, I became Attila.

Serves me right.

Apparently it is my strange fortune—or misfortune—to have become famous—or infamous—and I see this could go on indefinitely, so let's drop it right now—apparently it is my strange fate to become best known for what seems to me least important in my life, and least known for what seems to me most. Let's begin with the obvious. "War is hell."

Great point. Nicely put. Wish I'd said it. Almost did. But not quite. What I actually said was both more complicated and less interesting, and if it hadn't been that some whore reporter couldn't fit my whole statement into a headline, my fancy little metaphor would have been forgotten the day I spoke it.

That day was August 11, 1880. It was raining like hell, and probably it's just historian's luck I didn't say rain is hell instead of war is. Or rain is hell on war—something it now appears not even four years of slaughter taught several prominent American generals, both sides. Anyway, it was raining. President Hayes made a speech about something or other. Decent enough man, Hayes, but dull as tea, and he gave one howling damn of a boring speech, and that's not judging by Lincoln either, just by the everyday overblown rot of our current politicians. There were maybe five thousand veterans present at this rally, along with at least ten thousand of their sons. And after Hayes was finished stultifying them silly, they all began calling for me.

I was moved. I admit it. I was also surprised, which I hate; I admit that too. Since I'd been asked to appear strictly as a supernumerary, I didn't have a speech prepared, so I tried to make something up quick. Usually I'm pretty good at that— always proud to be fast on my feet in the verbal department, always amused at how that surprises people, a literate general. But not this time. My mind was an empty plain. I just stood there, listening to the applause of my former troops and waiting for something to come to mind, until finally I realized: nothing ever would. They knew how I felt just as well as they knew their own skins, and I didn't have to embarrass them or myself by reminding them that nobody does what they and I did together unless bound by a love as strong as has ever existed between man and wife, or man and God.

But I didn't know how to say that without sounding as mawkish and stiff as Hayes. So I went for their sons instead—their four-limbed, two-eyed, ten-fingered, unscarred sons, already re-signed to a lifetime's envy of their fathers, and their fathers' war.

I greeted my men: "Fellow soldiers," et cetera. Then I paused, smiling at all those hungry sons. "There is many a boy here today," I addressed them, "there is many a boy here today who looks on war as all glory. But, boys, it is all hell. You can bear this warning voice to generations yet to come. I look upon war with horror, but if it has to come, I am here."

That's what I *really* said. Not quite so historical, is it?—let alone historic. Not so much what war is, but what it isn't—isn't glory, isn't heroics and victory, or if you're unlucky, clean-cut martyrdom. I wanted my boys' boys to understand the burden and boredom of peace is the Kingdom of God on earth, and that other thing, war, is mere red confusion. That was the point I was aiming for. Maybe "War is hell" says it better. But it doesn't say it all.

What happened next was inevitable. That the man chosen by God to play hob with the guts of the Southern Confederacy had come up with a line like "War is hell" was too toothsome a sweet for the journalists to resist. They sniffed Historical Irony the way a hawk sniffs mice. Never mind that when Johnston surrendered I offered a peace more generous than Grant's and kinder than Lincoln's; never mind that I was the only ranking general to criticize Reconstruction. No: I was the rapist of Queen Georgia and the Carolina Princesses; if I said that war was hell, that could mean only one thing. Guilt.

But of course they had missed it completely. Guilt was the last thing I meant, the last thing I felt. I have one regret only regard-ing the March, and that's that we didn't do it sooner. We should have begun that hell the first year; we should have begun the first *hour.* We could've had the South on her knees by Easter, at our feet by Memorial Day—hell, we wouldn't even have to *have* such a thing as Memorial Day if we'd done the thing right. Only that would've left a whole passel of journalists out of a job for the next four years, wouldn't it?

Journalists! I shouldn't get started. Simple-minded, simplify-ing brown-nosing jackals who make the infectious ladies trailing

Hooker's army look virtuous—literary whores never there with their own bodies, but always panting to pump up the empty barrels of their pens with somebody else's blood. Ask them to at least wait till the battle's started before giving away our position and they scream "First Amendment"; tell them that what they consider a good story could ruin a loyal officer's career and they're all Peter Zenger. After what they wrote about Grant at Shiloh, I wanted to Fifth Amendment *them,* and after what they wrote about me at Chickasaw Bluffs, I nearly did. Too bad war is hell on all the wrong people.

But of course it took more than one good quotable crack for history to grant me this weird crown—this strange combination of laurel and thorns. There's also Atlanta.

Yes, I burnt Atlanta. I am the only American general to burn a major American city. Actually I burnt two major American cities (Columbia was the other), although neither were American cities at the time. Still, there's no denying Atlanta burnt. Perhaps not to the toasty Carthaginian crisp portrayed immediately afterward and ever since, but pretty damn seriously.

A few words about that.

First of all, Atlanta was no ordinary city. It's fashionable these days to portray fallen Atlanta as a thriving trade center, a perky metropolis hawking gloves and ribbons and Christmas toys. How anyone can possibly picture this after four years of naval blockade beats me, but that's the myth. Myth, the great scrim of history! The truth is (as usual) a tad less heartwarming. The truth is this: at the time of my incursion into northern Georgia, Atlanta was functioning as chief supply depot for the entire Confederacy. Food, arms, clothes, cotton, linen, men—whatever Jeff Davis needed and couldn't find elsewhere, he could always count on getting from generous Atlanta. She was the ultimate gentlewoman of the Deep South, always willing to give—and if not to give, at least to sell—one more bullet, one more bandage, one more illusion of possible victory to the Glorious Cause.

She was also more riddled with railroads than a whore has chancres.

Another thing. Just as Rome wasn't built in a day, Atlanta didn't burn in an evening. She burnt in bits and pieces, over a long period of time, and she burnt accidentally or at the hands of her own army as often as by my men. In fact, her first great fire, the fire the night she fell, was deliberately set by her own commanders, so anxious to bust out of an approaching Cannae they set fire to eighty carloads of their own ammunition, rather than combine the moral dishonor of abandoning civilians with the military dishonor of abandoning supplies. In other words, Southern gentilesse permitted the Confederacy to desert people, but not ordnance.

Thus did the first scorching of Atlanta occur. And my source for this is none other than the memoirs of Confederate general John Bell Hood himself. *Advance and Retreat,* he called his apologia. Right. Bit more of one than the other.

The second burning of the Gate City took place badly—bad wind, bad timing, and bad luck. After occupying Atlanta for two months and restoring to health and fitness my bloodied army, we prepared in mid-November to begin the Great March. I was very busy the night of November 15—busy with tactical and logistical problems; busy with matters of state (read "Edwin Stanton"); busy overseeing the fate, feet, and stomachs of sixty thousand men. Busy too with the finishing touches on the Special Order— yes, *that* Special Order. Special Order Number 120, my explicit and careful instructions for the March to the Sea.

In any case, I was busy. So when my engineers' staff began burning what was left of the industrial area, and the fire spread, I tried to control things as well as I could; but I didn't stop the war to do it. If perhaps it's been noticed I was less able to assert control here than at other, more apparently challenging junctures in my military career, I only can plead the swarming of more pressing commitments.

Besides, how badly did Atlanta really burn? By early December her presses were back in production, reporters outstraining themselves debating whether I best compared to Tamerlane, Torquemada, the Duke of Alba, or your common water moccasin. Good! Because by then those newspaper bastards were working for *me*.

And now we come to it at last. The crux, the hard clear basis of my final, most enduring immortality. The March to the Sea.

To me it was merely military—a change of base, Atlanta to Savannah. The true purpose of the March was to smash through the Carolinas and hit Lee at Petersburg, where he and Grant had been hacking each other's throats out for months. But history has so garbled and huckstered and gilded the March that by now it's the single most pervasive image in the war's bleak iconography. Smoldering cottonfields, pillaged plantations; kicked-in altars; pissed-in cradles. Bloody wedding gowns. The desecration of Southern womanhood. At best we're remembered as locusts, at worst, rapists: locust-rapists, a rare species, common only in war. I know all the insults, recognize all the images—the real, the possible, the impossibly embroidered, the obvious lies. I accept them all.

What I do *not* accept is that we did wrong. I admit we were harsh; I admit when we had a choice, we were not often merciful (although I might point out we did not often have a choice). I admit we stole. I admit we destroyed. I believe we didn't rape, and I hope not.

But only literally. Metaphorically, I hope we *did* rape. For metaphorically we had every right to. It is not after all on Northern shoulders that the corpses of six hundred thousand American soldiers should be draped. When mourning the stolen jewels and axed pianos of plundered Georgia, mourn them too.

I know I did.

CHAPTER
TWO

WHEN I WAS A CHILD, being a general seemed like pretty hot stuff. Ride a white horse, storm a position, kill your fair share of an undefined host; shed a moderate amount of your own blood; collect in return a reputation for bravery and a reasonable measure of national pride. Toss in a dose of public gratitude while you're at it, and it sure sounded better than being a teacher or running a bank. So off I went. West Point.

Now West Point's always had—and doubtless it always will—more than its share of shortcomings; but during the 1830s it had become particularly woolly-headed regarding its function, which is after all to provide a national military academy. By the time of my matriculation, unfortunately, this function had totally been lost sight of: the National Military Academy I attended was neither national, military, nor particularly academic. It was basically only one thing. It was horrifically boring.

It also was very Southern. Southern cadets were favored in admissions, in coursework, in drill, in promotion, and upon graduation. Our teachers were Southerners, our elders and clergymen too; and the great Southern Ethos—the very few should rule over the great many, and those few should know how to hunt and shoot—was accepted, and taught, without question.

All this bothered me some. But not much: being weaned on the grudging courtesies of south-central Ohio, I confess I was rather seduced by my Southern compatriots—their automatic courtliness, their hot-blooded grace. In fact, it's probably at West Point I first began to appreciate the virtues of the South. Yes. How ironic.

Where I balked at the Point's Southern bias, however, was its emphasis on decoration. Spit-shining boots, stropping nibs. Ironing handkerchiefs. Why iron something you're about to sneeze into? Polishing buttons till the brass ran silver. It wasn't enough to be clean. You had to look absolutely *bridal*.

I never could feature that cleanliness-Godliness crap. Nor could I feature the mindless and endless roll calls. God, were they endless! I understand the need for drill and discipline as much as the next man—as much as the next *ten* men (ask my soldiers)—but never will I understand why you had to take roll every two hours when there was no way someone could possibly leave the premises, nor anywhere someone could possibly go had he left. But like everything in that army (or anyone else's), 10 percent of what we did made sense and 90 percent made generals.

Still, I remained at West Point. I stayed relatively clean, I showed up at those roll calls I felt made sense, I skipped the rest. I made plenty of friends who later became enemies, and plenty of enemies (most remained so). When it was all over I wound up ranking fourth in my class academically—though booted to sixth on account of disciplinary demerits. Deep are the roots of those cracks about "military intelligence" being a self-canceling expression!

Was I a good student? Depends on your definition of "good." Or we can use *my* definition, wherein "good" means the sort of student teachers loathe at the time but remember with tearful reverence about twenty years later, when you father an industry, discover a planet, build a railroad, cure scarlet fever, make one million dollars. Or win a war. These days my West Point professors have run out of adjectives describing my brilliance; you can't find anyone who doesn't remember me as a second Marlborough, a new Themistocles. It's like being reborn: all my classroom challenges, all my disputations and disquisitions, all my big-mouthed rebellions and argumentations (a rebel amongst Rebels, hahaha) have been officially forgotten, wiped off the board by the great eraser of public approbation.

In reality, though, I was a pretty good student at a pretty bad school. Let's take a for-instance. West Point, a strong believer in doing the classics (classics being what you read in a class), was naturally wild for ancient history; deck out with a military spin and we're talking Hannibal. Now Hannibal was undeniably brilliant, steadfast, and cool under fire, and he had one hell of a sense of duty (plus one hell of a group of politicians he had to answer to—the Carthaginian city council sounds like our Department of War in utero). But phenomenal triumphs though he achieved, Hannibal did, well . . . *lose.* Though nobody ever mentioned that.

So I did.

What good is victory? asked Cadet Sherman—who got 78/100 in this course—what good is victory, if you lose the war? What good is bravery if all you accomplish is death? What good is nobility of character if your side, in the end, is defeated, and not even by someone as brilliant as you but by a cropful of vulgar and loud-mouthed nobodies who must somehow have known something you didn't?

Well, you'd think I'd accused Jesus Himself of funking it. Hannibal, I was informed, in tones of both censure and ice, was the world's greatest general; *nobody,* I was loftily reminded, could fail to appreciate his brilliance. You could if you lived in Carthage, I answered; if you happened to be a Carthaginian counting on your general to win the war, you just lost your bet. You're missing the point, Cadet Sherman—Cannae was the greatest victory won by the bravest of soldiers led by the noblest of men.

(Hmmm. Nobility, bravery, victory . . . loser. Sounds like Robert E. Lee.)

Classics aside, we studied chemistry, engineering, physics, natural history, and a very limited style of applied Higher Mathematics, so-called. Arithmetic, really: if two cavalry companies need seventy horses for twenty days, how many horseshoes will two regiments use over one summer? (Answer: too many. Don't lug around that many horseshoes—you'll lame your horses and need *more* shoes. Dismount your cavalry whenever possible and use them as infantry. P.S.: Attention, future brigadiers! This isn't the proper answer—just the correct one.)

We also received instruction in geography, grammar, moral philosophy (whatever the hell that was: I never attended), theology (!), etiquette (!!), and art. Art didn't mean art history, it meant drawing, and I enjoyed that class quite a bit, though we never drew maps or learned anything useful about cartography; in fact it was only on duty in Florida, when I drew a map with a bridge the same size as an alligator, that I stumbled onto the concept of drawing to scale. We were also minimally exposed to Spanish and French (just in case we went to war with one or the other). Unfortunately, here too our education proved useless, as the Spanish they taught at West Point turned out to be totally different from the Spanish they spoke in California or during the Mexican War. And I'll get to the French part later.

In addition to the above, we spent hours learning to prance around like idiots during cavalry practice. The Southern boys were especially good at this.

(Except for the best horseman I ever saw. He was a freshman the year I graduated—a Northern boy, Illinois, shy as a squirrel and about as talkative. His given name was Hiram Ulysses but things got balled up—you know the army!—the first day he registered, and he got recorded as Ulysses Simpson. Later he worked out how to become the only man in America to lick. Robert E. Lee, but he never could hit upon how to correct his registration. He remained U. S. Grant for the rest of his life.)

It wasn't till late in our last year at West Point that they actually got around to imparting any real military education. Even then it was at best simple rudimentary tactics—just enough to get you thoroughly confused when you were attempting something possibly useful. Take the lesson on "Usage of Bridges." It was really more history than anything military: we looked at sketches of Moti Heath, Garigliano, and the North Bridge at Concord; we wrote down the year; and we wrote down who won. We never learnt *why* they won—or, more importantly, why not.

Nor did we learn how to actually *build* a bridge: how to find matériel in hostile countryside, how to fit it, how to measure its strength. Nor were we ever taught how exactly to defend one (Cub Run Bridge at Manassas), or cross one under enemy fire (Burnside's Bridge at Antietem), or even anything so basic as getting the goddamn War Department to issue them (Burnside again, before Fredericksburg). Once the war started, we found out the whole country was practically nothing but streams and rivers traversed by bridges: but all we had learnt at West Point about bridges was how not to get wet crossing one.

Dead, but not wet.

Napoleon was our hero and idol. As might be expected; he was after all the only man to have done anything militarily interesting since Frederick the Great. Marengo! Egypt! Ulm! Austerlitz! Jena! What magnificent triumphs! Or Trafalgar and Moscow and Waterloo—hell, what fantastic defeats! Even the battles he botched, we loved. *There* was somebody, by the way, who knew how to live off the land, at least until Russia. (Which reminds me of Jeff Davis's promise to the Confederacy when we started the March—that we would starve like Bonaparte on the outskirts of Moscow. To which I replied: "No snow.")

Unfortunately, however, worshipping Napoleon turned out to be one of those bad ideas that, like so many errors in wartime, seem incredibly stupid in retrospect: that is, once they fail. Take, for example, Bonaparte's much-adored, much-imitated, all-conquering (at least for a while) battlefield strategy, the Grand Attack.

Essentially the Grand Attack is just what it sounds like—a massive frontal collision of your men versus theirs along a flattened, continuous front. As history shows, the Grand Attack *was* grand for Napoleon, in an era of smoothbore rifles with a range of, if very, *very* lucky, two hundred yards absolute maximum. It wasn't so grand for us.

Or grand in a different sense. For with both Union and Confederacy using cannons you could actually *aim,* and rifled muskets instead of smoothbores, and minié balls—accurate beyond *eight hundred* yards, and piercingly lethal—le Grand Attaque rapidly degenerated into le Grand Firing Squad: great if your goal was to thin out your population, totally ineffective as battlefield tactic. A new technology, without our realizing, had shifted advantage the other direction: defense, entrenchment, encirclement, turning, flanking. In other words, trying to get the hell out of the way of the bullets.

This seems obvious, right? Right. Now name all the Civil War battle plans based on tactical defense.

You can already stop. With the exception of Yours Truly (sixth-ranked at West Point, remember?), Joe Johnston (my chief opponent, and the South's greatest general), and a couple of other unsung and unloved mavericks, nearly all the generals, Union and traitor alike, consistently plotted offensive warfare. Yes, even the Man himself: in spite of his much-praised so-called "defensive-offensive" crap, Lee was the offensive warrior par excellence.

But this wasn't our only Napoleonic error. Seems our French got a bit muddled too.

Napoleon's main principle of attack was based on having his troops what he called *réuni* before dispatching them into battle. By this he basically meant not having his men scattered half-assedly up and down the line but rather available and ready to reunite at the first sign of an enemy's weakness. Unfortunately, however, West Point French, never too swift, translated *réuni* in rather a different sense. We learnt it to mean literally "be united"—that is, to be one massive unit of (what else?) offensive warfare. Our term for this was "concentration."

And Christ, did we concentrate! Both sides, both theaters, Grant, Lee, Beauregard; McClellan, Hooker, Hood. Even me, at blood-skidded Shiloh: right into the teeth of those new killer rifles, a pure concentrate of idiocy, one line of about-to-die children after another after another. We concentrated our bloody hearts out. Our soldiers', too.

But let's face it: when you really get down to it, Napoleon was a lousy model for reasons far more basic than changing technologies and language gaffes. For Napoleon, like all geniuses, broke all the rules, and this only works if you're a genius yourself, which most of us aren't. Certainly I would never advise anyone to weaken his right the way Bonaparte did outside Austerlitz—or Lee outside Chancellorsville, for that matter. Because even though Bonaparte won, and Lee did too, how many of us are Bonaparte or Lee? In my opinion, the best thing to do in war is to concentrate on winning, not on getting a prize for originality on the battlefield.

In fact, the best way to win a war may not be on the battlefield at all.

Which brings us to Special Order Number 120, my instructional guidelines for the March to the Sea. Yes. There were guidelines. I wrote them. Yes.

CHAPTER
THREE

W̶E HADN'T BEEN more than a month in Atlanta before realizing the unwisdom of resting our laurels and asses in an occupied city. John Bell Hood, the Confederate idiot Jeff Davis had replaced the great Joe Johnston with, kept prodding us with deadly little battles designed to lure us back toward Tennessee—back, that is, to exactly the same territory we'd already bled ourselves dry on during the entire summer. Obviously this wouldn't wash. But what was the alternative?

The alternative, once articulated, was stunningly simple. Too bad I can't burnish the brass a little by saying the plan for a "March to the Sea" arrived via cherub-infested reverie, or in grateful response to a long-invoked prayer; but actually it came in response to a telegram—a whole series of 'em, in fact, each saying basically the same thing, i.e., congratulations re Atlanta, and what can the country expect for an encore? It was clear I'd better come up with an idea fast, before the flurry of polite "suggestions" hardened into policy; and with something spectacular, before the drama of our latest victory faded from official recall—a process which usually takes noncombatants about seventy-two hours. It was equally clear I had to come up with something *that would work.*

For something strange was happening that autumn of '64—something militarily most abnormal. The North was winning the war, that was without question. But the South wasn't losing. The plague of stalemate was leeching the land.

So I sat down and made a proposal. Let Hood go back west, if that was what he so badly wanted! We would go eastward instead. A bracing dip in the occupied Georgia surf. Atlanta to the Sea.

"General . . . about the mail . . ."

I looked up from the same pool of papers I had been drowning in since before sunrise. By now it was nearly sunset. "I thought we made a decision about this yesterday," I said sharply.

"Yes, sir, we did. Only since then I've been doing some thinking—"

"Nice luxury, that. Used to do it myself from time to time."

Major George Nichols—my aide-de-camp and a good man but serious, serious—frowned.

"I'm sure you do more thinking about this army, sir," he said, "than the rest of us put together and multiplied."

" 'Put together and multiplied'?" I repeated. "Sounds like one of those Academy formulae, to calculate fodder for pregnant mares or some such foolishness." I pulled some papers from the bottom of one pile and jammed them on top of another. "What exactly about mail were you thinking?" I asked him.

"That it matters more than you realize, sir. Receiving it, I mean. I believe morale might suffer without it."

"We're running the Union army here, George, not the Post Office Department. Though sometimes it's hard to say which one's the slowest."

George didn't laugh. He never did, which may be why I liked him. He just frowned harder.

"If the men knew they had some kind of base," he said, "either they were marching from, or marching toward—"

"Well, they definitely know where they're marching from, George. They're marching from Atlanta."

I should add that this conversation took place in mid-October—took place, that is, nearly two weeks before I received an official go-ahead for the March, nearly three weeks before I formally informed my officers what we were up to, and *nearly a month* before we actually started moving. Yet so irresistibly does the passionate tide of rumor swamp every army that on even so early a date George was able to query:

"March from Atlanta, yes, sir. But against Hood . . . or Lee?"

Unlike some generals, I've never believed in lying to my officers. There seems no point—after all, they're really only extensions of you, in place simply because you can't be everywhere at once (something I have some difficulty remembering). Besides, with everything we were trying to pull together, he must've intuited the truth. For the heart—instinct, insight, divine intervention, luck (call it what you will)—never serves its host more efficiently than in war. Never needs to.

"How're we doing with the evacuations?" I asked, changing the subject.

He took out a leather memorandum-book and flipped to the proper pages. Each page was covered with long red columns of scratched-out figures.

"We've made some progress, General. It's slow. You can't really rush the wounded. That is, I suppose you can, but—"

"—But you don't," I said. "You're quite right, George. This is one war where we're not going to abandon our soldiers the instant they become casualties. It's important all officers understand that. It's equally important they understand the *only* permissible slowdown in this army is for right-of-way to the wounded."

George nodded but just made a tick in his notebook. I must already have made him that speech. Probably several times.

"Tell me about those wounded," I said. "Numbers. Conditions. Problems. Prognoses."

"Several dozen, sir. Mostly ambulatories en route to Chattanooga. Some prisoners awaiting exchange. The usual cases of flux. No influenza, thank God. No measles. No mumps."

"George, don't waste my time telling me what there's none of."

He flushed. "Yes, sir, I mean, no, sir. I won't. There's also some men—the worst ones—I mean the worst wounded, the bad ones . . ."

George seemed to be having some trouble speaking. Lots of folks do, around me; maybe it's this habit I have, of not only talking fast but *listening* fast: that is, I tend to interrupt. (I mention this so it doesn't seem as if I spent the war surrounded by a corps of stutterers. I didn't. I spent the war surrounded—this is important, and true—by that war's greatest warriors. Not Grant's armies. Not Lee's boys. Not Sheridan's. Mine. Is this prejudice speaking? Possibly—for what is prejudice but funneled love?; and what is love but the crowbar of history? Consult my prejudices; you may find them the best advertisement for impatience this side of the French Revolution.)

George was still floundering on with his sentence about the worst men. What he meant, of course, was the men *worst off.* In war the best men are always the worst.

"Think maybe we'll drop by later," I said. "At the hospital. See the boys."

George looked away. "I think I'll skip that, if you don't mind, sir," he said. "I'm starting to have a little trouble stomaching—"

I interrupted him once again. "I know it can drag on your stomach," I said. "But you've got to remember, your stomach isn't your soul."

"They're hard to separate sometimes," said George. He let the pages of his notebook ripple through his fingers. He added, "Maybe I've just seen one battlefield too many."

I tried to look sympathetic, but it was difficult. I've never felt I've seen too many battlefields—only too many hospitals. Men in battle—they're brave, or they're cowards, or maybe they're even dead, but at least they're *something,* they've made an effort, they've had their say. It's when they're lying in a bed, or on a floor, or awaiting the dubious aid of some leechcrafting barber-cum-surgeon who knows about as much medicine as my grand-mother's cat—that's when war becomes truly sickening, truly an assault on the stomach and soul.

But being a general means being a generalist. You don't just send men into battle; you're supposed to be there when they come back out. Besides, how could I know for certain it was the South, or God, or those goddamn J. P. Morgan explode-in-your-own-face rifles that had gutted my boys? Maybe I did it myself. Let's face it—you make mistakes in battle just like in chess or marriage; sometimes you get away with it, sometimes you pay, and sometimes other people pay for you.

So I performed hospital duty with the ardency of a nun. My boys appreciated it; my enemies called me hypocrite. This being a stunning compliment compared to most of my sobriquets, I let it go.

Anyway, on with the war. George and I reviewed various details of supply. Shoes, blankets, canteens, morphine—we needed everything, and Georgia, herself low on all necessities except food and fodder, all else having gone (willingly or not, who knows? *Now* they say no, *then* they said yes) to support Lee's army, was no help whatever. Our needs therefore required we lean on our own War Department. This was rather like leaning against a bolted, double-locked, tripled-chained iron door; eventually it might open, but Christ, what a grind till it did! Still, it was all we had, and they *were* on our side, more or less. I dictated a few letters.

And received a few. One was from Secretary of War Edwin McMasters Stanton.

Stanton, that loathsome toad! It's always surprised me he had not, in civilian life, been a journalist. For certainly he had all the qualifications: he was quick to panic and public to share it; he howled at defeat but casually accepted victory; he professed a great love for the Union but didn't give a blown nose about the state of the Union army. After the war was over and Lincoln safely pushing poppies, he decided he'd always worshipped his ex–Chief Executive; but at the time Lincoln needed him most, Stanton was amusing the Washington nabobs by referring to the

President as "the original gorilla." As the following letter shows, Stanton should never have been granted a voice in the war, still less the impossible-to-ignore bellow attached to the post of secretary of war. But as much as war is hell, so much more is it politics.

Stanton's letter:

To Major-General W. T. Sherman,
commanding Military Division of the Mississippi,
October 12, 1864:

General:

Your request to abandon your primary base at Atlanta and make for the sea continues to be taken under enthused consideration. Much has been made here of your recent successes [*no thanks to you, Sir!—W.T.S.*], and all of us congratulate you with o'er-brimming hearts.

General Grant, as you surely know, continues to engage the Rebels in siege outside Petersburg. Victory on this front appears inevitable but protracted, making progress in your theatre so much the more appreciated, and its continuance so much the more to be urged.

You have, my dear General, at all times my tremendous respect and affection. [*Right. I have a tremendous respect for rattlesnakes too. But that doesn't mean I enjoy their company.*] But this war, more than any other in human history, involves more than individuals. That is to say, it is a *moral* war, a war for a Principle, this being the most sacred Principle of all, that is, human Freedom. Deep within your Lion's Heart you of course agree. [*No, but . . .*]

General, two rumours hopefully misapprehended concerning your convictions have come to my attention. Let us address both.

Item one is your attitude toward the First Amendment.

Sir, surely you need not be reminded it is both proper and guaranteed by law that journalists report the news as they see fit; and in these times, the war *is* the news. I know you harbor an intense dislike for our friends of the Fourth Estate, due I suspect to that ridiculous "insanity" business of 1861. [*Oh,*

might that be when I labeled this war both abomination and holo-
caust, warned it would drag on for years, and predicted the death
of a half-million soldiers, and The New York Tribune *called me*
a madman, and I nearly lost my command?]

However, as we are all brothers in Christ, and the whole
point of Christianity is to let bygones be bygones [*funny, I*
thought it meant just the opposite], it is time you make an attempt
to forget that incident and show yourself willing once more to
cooperate with the Press.

To this point, General Sherman, I *most strongly* urge you
desist refusing interviews and also refrain from advising your
fellow officers to do the same. At this moment in history our
Army needs the Press more than the Press needs this Army.

I want no more reporters turned from your camp. This
includes illustrators and photographers; also foreigners. The
South has garnered much favorable overseas publicity simply
by permitting English and German correspondents to ride
with Jeb Stuart. I would like you to consider doing the same.
[*Fine by me; let 'em ride with Jeb all they want. But no horse of*
mine risks laming just to haul some cowardly, critical, lying re-
porter's fat noncombatant ass!]

The second rumour, General, equally grave, perhaps more
so, concerns your public pronouncements regarding Slaves.
Sir: you have claimed that the North, in its heart, cares no
more for the Negro than does the South. You are additionally
reported as stating that white Northern soldiers will refuse to
fight side by side with Negroes, and that after the war they will
refuse to live so. You have further criticized Northern efforts
to recruit Negroes for armed service, on the grounds that it
breaks up the black family and thus mimics Slavery.

My dear General, on what do you base these heretical state-
ments? And more to the point, on what do you base your right,
in the midst of the war's greatest crisis, to *share* them?

Well, this was about as far as I got with Stanton's letter before
flinging it aside. I wasn't even sure which part of the letter galled
me the worst. That black business maybe . . . all right, time's
passed, you tell me. Was I right, or was I?

Besides, what difference does it make whether I was or wasn't?

The March hadn't even begun, and already I'd liberated more slaves than any other commander in the entire Union army. By the time the war was to finish, every black baby boy not named Lincoln or Freedom or Emancipation was named General Sherman. How many Negro babies named Edwin Stanton you ever run into?

Ah, but if Stanton were here—as if I'd let him!—he would argue that isn't enough. The deed does *not* speak for itself, Stanton would say; it has to be done *in the right spirit*. Well, why don't we ask those ex-slaves about that? Ask if they'd like the freedoms they've got, or would they maybe prefer going back into bondage till someone more loving than Tecumseh Sherman comes down the pike? Somehow I think that's an opportunity they'd prefer to pass up.

As for the journalist issue: I will not back down on that. When the Founding Fathers spoke of freedom of the press, they meant freedom of a *responsible* press. They were envisioning Tom Paine. We got Horace Greeley instead.

To hell with freedom of the press. If we hadn't had to worry about those damn photographers dragging dead bodies into everyone's parlor, we could have fought the war right and won ten times faster.

Just before I tossed Stanton's letter I caught one final sentence. In it he "wished to express Mr. Lincoln's deep gratitude that your triumph in Atlanta *preceded* the National Election." That *really* had me quivering. I loathe politics: in spite of (because of??) one senator for a brother and another for a father-in-law, I've never voted. Certainly I would never arrange a military encounter for something as ephemeral as an election—even the election of as great a man as Mr. Lincoln. For politicians come and go as the whim of the people dictates; but soldiers come and go by the will of God.

Which is probably why we admire soldiers, then elect politicians who kill them off.

"George," I said to Major Nichols, who had been with me long enough to know the best way to deal with my rages was to go off and admire the scenery till I settled down, "George, stop looking at that goddamn sunset and come back here. The fire's out."

George returned, notebook still handy. "Would you like me to take a letter, sir?" he asked. He didn't look too enthused.

"How about a 'g' and a 'd'? Dear Mr. 'G--d--n' Stanton . . . nah, forget it. Stanton's master for the time being, even though he cares as much for this army as Jeff Davis does for his slaves; and no dignified letter of protest from an upstart general's going to change that. Just have somebody send a cipher that I received his latest and yours et cetera. Now let's get something to eat."

George snapped shut his notebook with a bit more alacrity than the prospect of your average dinner in the Union army might seem to call for. I suspect the reason he looked so eager was that, with food in my mouth, I couldn't talk, thereby giving his ears a much-deserved rest. Poor old George! He probably entered the war with far more exalted visions than of winding up aide-de-camp to the North's most garrulous general. I really should have paid more attention to him—or better yet, less; let him off the hook a bit, let him rest. But the truth is I've never been able to stand within two feet of anyone without starting a conversation. (And the additional truth is Poor Old George didn't do so poorly, after all: less than six months after the war was over, his *Story of the Great March* already was published in the thousands by *Harper's*.)

So we decided—okay, *I* decided—to grab a bite. The next question was who with, officers or men. Though it didn't really matter; deep within enemy territory, surrounded by guerrillas, scouted by hostiles and supported by one tenuous, overburdened, sniper-targeted thousand-mile supply line, whatever reached us was either canned or dried or evaporated or condensed, and pretty democratically atrocious regardless of the rank of the consumer. Had this been the Eastern Front, of course, things would've been different; Grant's army was awfully hierarchical, had been since McClellan, and the officers in the

Virginia theater actually had *menus,* whereas the closest we in the West ever got to a choice was salted beef jerky versus oversalted beef jerky versus no jerky at all.

I chose this time to mess with the men and motioned to George, taking care, though I knew at least five thousand of them personally and by name, not to seek out any of them. For well I knew that nothing, not even defeat, so demoralizes an army as perceived favoritism. I walked up to the first fire I saw.

"Evening, boys," I said. "Mind a little company?"

We shuffled through the requisite charade, them bobbing up at the same time George and I were trying to sit down. Finally we all got settled.

"How's dinner tonight?" I asked. "Any mothers going to be out of a job?"

Everybody hooted and started talking at once. As I expected: in war, food, not death, is the primary subject of conversation.

One of the soldiers waved a forkful of dried potatoes. "Reckon not even my mama could help these sorry babies," he said.

Another soldier feigned surprise. "You mean they ain't good?" he asked. "Well, hell. I was about to urge my sweetheart to write General Eaton for the secret recipe."

General Eaton was U.S. Army commissary-general; the hoots redoubled.

I munched a potato. Interesting. Four years ago the mention of anyone's "sweetheart," in any context, would have had all of them silent and half of them weeping. Now:

"Charlie, you're pointing your lady toward the wrong general. She shouldn't consult Eaton; she should be writing Fightin' Joe."

Definitely no tears; just smirks, and extended nudges. Not for why you might think. "Fightin' Joe," you'll remember, was Joe Hooker's nickname in those halcyon months just before Chancellorsville—Chancellorsville, where he entered the history books by being on the opposing side of Lee's greatest victory while simultaneously answering Julie Capulet's eternal query: "What's in a name?" As punishment for that Virginia debacle he was shipped out West; that is, to me.

(Hooker, of course, also achieved another kind of immortality by officially recognizing the prostitutes trailing his army—"hookers," get it?—though I've always had my doubts about that one: unless gonorrhea flushes the face and destroys the liver, Joe's chief addiction was liquor, not ladies, by the hour.)

But these snickers were about neither dalliance nor incompetence. They were about me.

About three months earlier, during the fall of Atlanta, bushwhackers had murdered my able subordinate James MacPherson (first in his class at the Point but an admirable soldier nonetheless). I promptly recommended Oliver Howard to Washington as his replacement. Howard was—is—a good man, even if quite the abolitionist (when all this was over, he founded that black college, Howard University), and he and Hooker were just about neck-and-neck in seniority. . . .

Well, maybe not. Maybe Hooker led. But I chose Howard anyway. Not because I thought him faster or brighter than Fightin' Joe (neither was either), but because Hooker was just such a pain in the butt to be around for more than five minutes.

And what made him so painful? Certainly not losing to Lee—if I held that against every Northern general, I'd own a grudge the size of both Virginias. No, what made Hooker so problematic were the battles he *won*. He simply could never stop talking about them.

At first it was funny. Then it became annoying. Then it became very annoying. Finally it became worrisome, as I began fearing that so much pride *in* victory might indicate surprise *at* victory; that is, lack of confidence. Once having feared that, I found myself less than confident in him myself—and he was out.

When Hooker discovered he'd been bypassed in favor of an abolitionist-prohibitionist-congregationalist, he about had a kitten. He trotted out all the arguments he could think of; and when he saw he was getting nowhere, he tried to outflank me with every connection he'd garnered since gaining his majority. I couldn't help thinking: Christ! If only he'd used half this much energy on Lee!

It's possible I made the above observation aloud.

At any rate, very soon after, Hooker left his headquarters without authorization (and not for the first time) and appeared at my own. Not a smart idea. In fact, the worst: the last thing anyone angling for advancement should do is ignore his current responsibilities while claiming readiness for more. I felt compelled to point this out to Fightin' Joe.

"Let me get this straight," I said. "You abandoned eleven thousand men in the middle of battle—to come ask for command of eleven thousand *more*?"

"Come off it, Cump," Joe said. "This battle you say we're in the middle of, we've been in the middle of since June. I didn't 'abandon' anything."

"Interesting point, General. I might even agree. But there are plenty of other generals who might not. There are plenty of other generals, *General,* who might welcome command of those men you say you didn't abandon, but somehow aren't with at the present moment."

Hooker clutched his presentation saber and gasped, "Are you threatening me, sir?"

This from a man I had known since West Point, almost three decades before. Old Joe always did have a taste for theatrics.

So also, in my own way, do I. "Of course not," I said. "I never threaten. Especially not fellow officers. And most especially not fellow officers with whom my friendship goes back even longer than does my friendship with General Grant."

It was Grant, of course, who eventually replaced Hooker and got us to finally kick ass in the East; Hooker despised him for this, and now his face, ruddy to begin with, darkened to almost the same color as the red Georgia soil. It was interesting, the way Joe's flesh matched dirt; but not interesting enough to warrant two more corps.

"Joe," I said, "you're a good man, more or less, which is all you can say about anyone, more or less. You bit it with Lee, but hell, he was so hot at Chancellorsville, he *deserved* to win. You just caught him on a good day. What I'm concerned about here has nothing to do with that."

"Glad to hear it," Hooker mumbled. Then he couldn't resist

adding, "Chancellorsville wasn't just 'one good day,' by the way. You weren't there. It was three long days of hard work."

"Correction noted. Three days." I didn't point out it was three long days of hard work whose outcome was determined in the first two hours, when Hooker made more bad decisions in less time than a cow needs to give birth. Worse yet, too often he made *no* decision—the deadliest decision of all.

"What I mean to say, Joe," I continued, "is you've done damn well since. You saved my neck at Lookout and Resaca"—he hadn't, but somebody had, and the Almighty wasn't standing before me at that moment griping about command structure—"and I'd like to think you'll be there when it sticks out again. It's not an insult to say a man can command a corps but not an army. A corps commander's job is harder than an army commander's anyway. He has to deal with the everyday details of actual combat, real field battle, whereas an army commander—"

Blah, blah, blah. I could continue this speech for hours—had, from time to time, when similar situations came up for similar Hookers. It's one of those observations that's both true and untrue: that is, commanding a corps *is* in many ways more difficult than commanding an army, but that doesn't matter. When it comes to commanding, only the tip of the feather in the hat on the head makes any difference. Only the top counts.

Hooker fingered his saber. I'm no mind reader of geniuses, but I'm not bad with dolts; I knew he was rubbing my aforementioned gratitude against his guess that the recommendation likely hadn't gone through yet. Now he said:

"Yep, that Lookout Mountain. By God Almighty. That was really something."

He spoke in a tone of such creaking nostalgia you'd think we were a couple of half-dead cronies recalling a cherished memory of fifty years earlier, instead of a botched, bloody action that only took place last November.

"Yep, we really pounded 'em," he tacked on. "Yes, sir, we did."

Yes, sir, we did. Only, unfortunately, one could make the same claim in reverse: they pounded us too.

I could feel myself getting impatient, and wondered how much this impatience had to do with Hooker in general and how much with Hooker *as* general.

"Joe," I said, grabbing some papers, with a mind to actually attend to them as an alternative to Hooker, "Joe, let me be honest here. I'm not putting you in command of that army and that's that."

Our Lookout Mountain camaraderie melted like butter on biscuits. Hooker bared his enormous front teeth.

"That's not quite that," he said. "I've got friends in Washington. And you've got a lot of enemies."

"I don't give a bat's tit about your friends. Let me tell you something, Joe: my enemies like me better than your friends like you. It's called winning."

Joe immediately threw a perfect salute. "Then I trust you will accept my resignation," he said.

They say nothing but death happens fast in the army. I'd have to add: nothing but death and the opportunity of throwing away garbage, especially garbage you've been hauling around for the past eighteen months. The idea that Hooker thought he could threaten me with a surprise resignation angered me even more than the idea that he was willing to throw in the towel at this, the hour of his country's greatest need. Alas, poor Columbia, if she has to rely on her Fightin' Joe Hookers for succor!

I saluted right back, Pointman to Pointman. "So long, Joe," I said. "Don't let that door bump your ass on the way out."

And later, when the press came snuffling around, smelling blood in the air and demanding the scoop on their favorite dipsomaniacal son, I didn't kick them out the way I usually would. Instead, I greeted them with a shy smile and a puzzled shrug.

"Gentlemen," I said, "General Hooker has left my service. You must draw your own conclusions."

Needless to say, their no-evidence gossip and shark-shaming speculations crucified Hooker, and that right there was the end of his field command and his career.

Adieu, Fightin' Joe! It was this my men were sniggering at over their charred spuds. Soldiers love to watch officers fall from grace, and the further the fall the more the enjoyment. I daresay in their hearts they might not have wept overmuch for me, either. It's one of the few real freedoms a soldier gets, daydreaming the public humiliation—or better yet, death—of his commanding general. I used to do it myself.

On we gnawed. In addition to the potatoes there was condensed milk—"condemned milk," the men called it—dried (very) beef, and coffee beans, which some of us still went to the bother of actually grinding; others, this group included, just munched them whole. After chawing a couple of mouthfuls, your pulse started pounding between your toenails, and your mouth felt as gritty as Bluebeard's death. For dessert we shared a can of glazed quince.

"Well, boys," I said, when we'd all finally finished, and I had lit a cigar, and they'd all rolled their tobacco or filled their pipes or loaded their cheeks, and the few that didn't smoke or puff or chaw had located licorice and horehound drops to suck on, "well, boys, thanks for dinner. So fine a meal I can hardly stand it."

"That's what the hospital's for," somebody said.

"Well, I'm heading there now, matter of fact. Maybe I'll see what the docs might be offering by way of a tonic."

"Best not to mention your stomach, General," a corporal advised. "Tell a doctor an organ ails you, he'll likely remove it."

In view of the syphilis rumors, this comment led to some thoughtful shifts of position. I noticed George watching me with a meaningful grimace. George always believed I should take opportunities like this to ask the men if they had any complaints, any specific problems they'd like to bring up. Whereas I always believed the opposite: in an army everyone has complaints, all problems are specific, and if anything's that important, I shouldn't need to coax.

So I puffed my cigar and let it go out and asked for a light and puffed a bit more. And sure enough, one by one, concerns appeared.

"General, you reckon we're ever gonna see new boots?"

"Boots? Damn your boots! General, you reckon we're ever going to see new socks?"

"General, this knife couldn't cut a marshmallow. You think you might circulate a whetstone?"

"General, this here toothbrush was falling apart back at Bloody Shiloh. Now it's got about three hairs left."

"And you, Pete, got about three teeth left!" said a companion.

"My point exactly. One toothbrush, General, one lousy toothbrush—that's all I'm asking."

"Son, I'm sorry," I said. "I can supply you the louse, but not the toothbrush."

Loud boos. A black-haired man with captain's bars cleared his throat and said: "General, what about ink? Any chance you could cadge us some ink? I'd even pay for it."

"Yeah, with my money," said Pete. "General, whatever you do, don't play a friendly hand of poker with this Nicholas Whiteman here, or you'll soon be minus that handsome flannel shirt you've been sporting since Chickamauga. No offense, sir."

I gnawed my cigar. The one they called Whiteman didn't blink. He was a good-looking man, thirty or so, with storm-deep blue eyes and a comfortable smile—the kind of package supposedly only the South produces.

"What's the need for all this ink, Whiteman?" I asked. "You're not some kind of a goddamn journalist, are you?"

The captain grinned and shook his head. "God hasn't yet damned me that deeply, sir," he said. "I'm just trying to maintain memories."

"You and everyone else. George here's maintaining memories too. He keeps a diary and writes in it every night." George blushed. "George, give Captain Whiteman here a bottle of ink."

George wrote himself a note to do so. Whiteman closed his eyes and intoned, "October nineteenth, eighteen sixty-four, year three, day one-thousand-something. Dear Diary. This evening I asked the Scourge of Atlanta for a bottle of ink. He requisitioned me one. It was easy. Tomorrow I'm returning the ink and requesting a discharge instead."

I shook my head. "Request denied, Whiteman. Military necessity—we need gambling men. But feel free to badger George here for another bottle."

"How about a bottle of another kind?"

I chuckled and rose. Alcohol was a touchy matter in my army—even more so now that half of it was commanded by a teetotaler—and of course it was touchy overall anyway, on account of Grant and was he or wasn't he? A great many generals in my army drank (this major-general included), but those who didn't, *seriously* didn't. Same with religion. Nothing like war, apparently, to convince you for certain one way or the other.

"Anyone of you got any messages," I asked, "for the boys in the hospital? We'll be shipping these fellows north as soon as they're able. Anyone got a friend you want 'em to look up when they're home?"

A few names were mentioned; George wrote them down. Whiteman smiled.

"What's funny, Captain?" I asked.

"I've been wounded three times," he said, "and each time they took one look, gave me a bandage, and escorted me back to the front. Why can't I do it right?"

"Cheer up, son," I said. "We're stuck in the middle of Georgia in the middle of the South in the middle of the war."

I relit and repuffed my cigar, and brushed some dirt off my trousers.

"Believe me," I said, "you have not yet begun to die for your country."

CHAPTER
FOUR

THERE'S LITTLE IN LIFE much grimmer than visiting hospitals. Personally I prefer graveyards. Though you know what they say: catch a field hospital right after a major battle, you can have both.

The field unit I was visiting now contained the remains of the battle of Allatoona, held two weeks previous. Allatoona, in northern Georgia, was a fortified mountain pass abutting the Western & Atlantic Railroad. By October of '64 that track was my sole supply line into Atlanta, and therefore cherished beyond rubies: it was at that moment my favorite little railway in all the world. So when John Bell Hood hurtled into the pass with his usual moronic élan (that man should really have spearheaded the Charge of the Light Brigade, not a Confederate army), I naturally ordered John Corse, one of my bravest and quickest generals, to slam in after him.

The Rebs held a clear manpower advantage, three to one. We held the advantage of heavy fortifications (plus of course the additional advantage of not being commanded by Hood). The result was predictable slaughter—each side lost *one third* of its men, a worse day, percentage-wise, than even Antietam—and a major Union victory.

At one point in the battle, when smoke and fog had so blotted out daylight that Corse and I could communicate only by signal flag, I sent a message urging him to hang on and saying I'd try to get there as soon as possible. What I signaled exactly was:

"Hold Allatoona. I am coming."

Pretty basic signal-flag correspondence. Not exactly Shakespeare. But a reporter had sneaked in somehow; and after it became clear Allatoona was a Northern triumph (only the South invents myths for its defeats), the story went out that what I had said was: "Hold the fort, I am coming." For some reason that bogus little phrase was instantly seized on, and the expression "Hold the fort" slipped at once into the national vocabulary. It lives there today: "Hold the fort for me, honey, I'll be right back." It even became part of a goddamn hymn:

> Ho! my comrades see the signal
> Waving in the sky,
> Reinforcements now appearing,
> Victory is nigh.
> Hold the fort, for I am coming,
> Jesus signals still!
> Wave the signal back to Heaven,
> By Thy grace we will.

Well, the history of war is the history of getting things wrong. It's a shame those journalists didn't catch Corse's signal back: "I am minus one cheekbone and one ear, but can beat all Hell yet." I'd like to see them make a Sunday-school hymn out of *that*.

Anyway, after holding the fort, and winning the battle, and burying our latest dead, we set up a field hospital for our survivors, and theirs too. That meant about six hundred men, crammed into twenty tents and attended by maybe a dozen doctors and the assorted handful of hookers and addicts and angels who made up the nursing staff. I remembered how after

Vicksburg we'd tried to arrange the tents in order of severity of injury. Unfortunately, just about every soldier in every tent died.

Now I stood fingering the flap of the first tent I came to. Within was the usual hell.

Civil War medicine. You hear a lot. Most of it's true. It wasn't only what little we knew; it was also what little we had. We knew for example that patients did better in a clean environment; we couldn't provide one. We knew they did better if their food wasn't wormy; we couldn't control that. We knew unpolluted water was healthier than water that had been spit in and shit in and waded through and shared with horses; but we couldn't always find a battleground next to an aqueduct. We did what we could. It was seldom enough.

The first thing that hit when I entered the tent was the smell. It wasn't terrible, it was just . . . pervasive. Until you visit a field hospital you don't really notice that blood has an odor: sweet, slightly oak, slightly winey, like lemonade left to steep in the sun. These lemons had been steeping for two weeks; the blood on the bandages and the ground, and in the bedpans, had the color and ooze of raisins. Lemons and raisins: these were the first things I always noticed when doing hospital duty. Also the only two items I religiously avoided eating.

There were odors of healing too. Coffee and tobacco, the soldier's manna; limes for scurvy; beef tea for strength. Quinine that made your eyes water and your nose run. Turpentine that seized up in your throat. And over everything the heady, whorehouse fumes of tincture of opium, blue in the bottle and numbing as snow in the mind.

I leaned over the first cot. Most of the men were on the floor; you had to be pretty shot up to merit a cot. On the other hand, you couldn't be so shot you were going to die, or why waste the cot?

(Heartless, yes. Sensible, also yes. It was, by the way, a system the patients themselves devised; among the many things soldiers don't kid themselves about are survival statistics.)

I've mentioned this was two weeks after Allatoona. That meant the man I was looking at now had received his injury fourteen days ago. Since then, I gathered, it had been a race between modern medicine and gangrene. Which one was winning? Ask yourself—which one's been around longer?

"Yeah, they tell me one thing one day and another the next, General," the patient said. A scrap of paper over his head identified him as Farlowe—Eddie Farlowe. "First they said it was no worse than a stubbed toe. Then they said it was no worse than a hangnail. Then when it turned musty and they had to whack it off, they told me no big tragedy: lots of men got only nine toes. Some of 'em even are born that way. You reckon that's true?"

It was obvious from the flatly drawn sheet along Farlowe's right flank that by now that toe, and a good deal more, was mere memory.

"I can see where that might be true," I answered. "Back home I had a teacher born with six fingers. We used to wonder what poor bastard had to even things out by getting four."

Only then did I think to check Farlowe's hands; luckily, they were still intact.

"The hell of it was," I added, "he was the man they had teaching us schoolboys arithmetic."

Farlowe shook his head. "A fella like that," he said, "you'd think he'd take up the piano."

"Or milking," I said.

"Or weaving," he said.

"Or telegraphy," I said.

"Or sharpshooting," he said.

That shut us both up. Then:

"Where's home, General? Where you learned your arithmetic."

"Ohio, son. Lancaster. Downstate. Where's yours?"

"Lancaster, too. Only mine's in Pennsylvania. Lancaster, Pennsylvania. How about that, sir?"

"Quite a coincidence, Ed. Two Lancaster boys. Your Lancaster anywhere near Gettysburg?"

"Not really, sir. Tell you the truth, I never heard of Gettysburg until, you know, Gettysburg. I didn't even know it existed."

I nodded. Neither had I. It's surprising how often that's true in warfare. I bet Napoleon never heard of Waterloo either, until half the armies of Europe showed up there.

"You ever hear of Allatoona before, General?" Farlowe asked.

"Actually I did. I used to live in the South. Fact, when the war started, I was offered top command of the Confederate army. How's that for irony?"

Farlowe looked shocked. Which wasn't surprising: mention of my possible Rebel leadership always buffaloes people, as though Lee were the only Union general dangled the traitor's bait. Though maybe this shock came from learning that even with his commanding general knowing of Allatoona, the battle was still so ferocious he'd lost his leg.

I stood up. "You take care now, Eddie," I said. "You're going home soon. And when you get back to Pennsylvania, don't let those Gettysburg veterans rag you that you missed the main fight. You tell them Tecumseh Sherman says those Eastern battles are all puffed-up political garbage. The real war is here."

Farlowe leaned himself up and shook my hand. "I'll tell them it was an honor, sir," he said, "to serve with you."

Comments like that, while I can't deny finding them thrilling, embarrass like hell. I mumbled something about the honor being all mine, et cetera, and hurried on.

The men in the next three cots were sleeping. The man in the fourth was having some kind of conniption, and a nurse had one hand clamped on his pulse and the other over his mouth. I walked to another line of patients.

The first man I saw was in gray.

He was lying on his side, chewing an apple. If he were much older than twenty, I was a virgin. When he saw me, he spat.

He said: "It's you."

"In the flesh," I replied.

"What an honor." His voice was bitter as pitch.

"Yeah, that's what they all say." I bent down. "What's your name, son?"

"Franklin Tate." The voice was a snarl.

"Where you from?"

"Why? You aiming to send my mama the death notice? Don't

bother, General. She's from Atlanta. She's probably already dead."

"I'm sorry to hear that," I said.

"Say, that sure makes me feel better. Before you leave, maybe you wouldn't mind finding the guy who shot up my knee and see if he's sorry too."

There are certain conversations it's best to resist. Alas, they're too often too interesting to. I lowered myself to the floor, leaning onto my own (unshot) knee.

"Franklin," I said, "I'd love to find the soldier who iced you. I'd give him a medal."

Tate's eyes flashed. "You really are one son of a bitch," he said.

"And you," I said, "are one classic horse's ass. What the hell did you think was going to happen? What the hell did your mama imagine, sending you off? I'm not the reason you're lame and motherless. Who started this war? Did I declare war on myself? No, you pride-benighted bluebloods declared war on me."

"Didn't take you long to accept though, did it, General?"

"Too long for my taste, Franklin. We should never have pussyfooted around that first year, trying to avoid civilian hardship. That was Lincoln, not me. You want to know what I really think?"

I noticed two rows of patients had jerked themselves up into sitting positions and were now listening, wide-eyed and open-mouthed.

"I said, you know what I really think?" I repeated.

"I already know," said Tate. "You think this little debate's going to impress the hell out of your soldiers."

Right the first time. I was surprised, and must have looked it, for Tate smiled grimly before adding: "By the way, General, thanks for the compliment, but I'm not a blueblood. I don't even believe in slavery."

That got me going again.

"You know, Franklin, that doesn't surprise me. The way I hear it, not one single Southerner supports the Peculiar Institution. Lee hates slavery; Stuart hates slavery, this great genius

Hood hates slavery. . . . I guess it's all just been one big mistake. I guess when you people said you were prepared to dismember the greatest, freest, kindest, and most forgiving nation ever conceived on this planet for the sake of slavery, we thought it meant you *owned* a couple. Our mistake."

Tate, in no position to move much, glared at his apple.

What happened next is what makes me believe soldiers are truly the only compassionate beings in this sad, dreary universe. Eddie Farlowe—and to be honest, one really would have to say what was *left* of Eddie Farlowe—Eddie Farlowe of Lancaster, Pennsylvania, leaned himself up on an elbow the Rebels miraculously had left intact. Calling across the cots, he said:

"General, all respects, sir, but this fella ain't in shape right now for a fair fight. You ought to back off, sir."

Then the soldier next to Farlowe, his wounded neck so infected he appeared lynched, also sat up, and said, "Yeah, Uncle Billy, Eddie's right. You want to take this Reb out in the nearest alley, that's fine, but you oughtta wait till this cruel war is over."

I glanced over at Tate. This not being country melodrama, he didn't look especially moved by this soldierly solidarity, or even too mindful it had occurred. But then, I probably didn't look particularly chastened either. For such is the nature of war: you struggle so hard to show neither pain nor fear, you wind up unable to show anything. Doesn't mean you don't feel it, though.

"You get well quick, son," I told him, and stood up. He didn't say anything back—just turned to the man in the bed next to him, who was crying, and had been since I'd entered. I patted the crying man's foot. Fortunately he had one.

I noticed a doctor was watching me, standing near to what passed as a medicine chest (two bottles of opium, four of rum, and a pile of green lace handkerchiefs, probably from a brothel, now used to bandage and gag). He was bearded and dirty, and wearing a suit so bloody it looked as though he had been walking through . . . well, let's just say he looked as though he had been walking through a field hospital two weeks after a battle and leave it at that. The only way I could tell for certain that he was a doctor and not, say, somebody's father or one of those nosey red-hot photographers or Sanitary Commission troublemakers was the expression pasted across his face. It was the same face you see with all professionals—doctors, lawyers, West Point administrators. They all have that same demeanor, that same self-loving self-assurance: lesser beings have once again hopelessly balled up the universe, and they've got the only cure. Hold the fort. I am coming.

"Hello, son," I said.

He scowled. Doctors have one of those jobs you're supposed to address them by—like priests, or professors, or senators, or presidents. (Or generals.)

"General," he said.

"Good job you're doing here," I said, gesturing around the tent. I'd seen cleaner pigsties, but what the hell, you've got to say something.

"Thank you," he said. "You too."

There was a hiss in his voice that assured me this wasn't a compliment. I sighed. It's funny when noncombatants, whether through passion, inertia, or fate, get linked to a war; they tend to become either virulently against that war (doctors, reporters) or violently pro (politicians, the clergy). In neither case do they become *educated*—simply opinionated. And as expressive of those opinions as a cat in heat.

"I've said it before," I said, "I didn't start this war."

He bristled. "I've said it before too," he said, "General Sherman didn't start this war, but he's sure determined to get his money's worth before it's finished."

Then he opened an opium bottle and took a deep whiff.

Outside of an operating theater, I'd never seen anyone do that before. His face flushed; his eyes turned clouded and dreamy.

"I hope," I said, "I'm correct in assuming that's not standard procedure before amputations."

"No, General, it's not. Standard procedure before amputations is to wipe off the blood from the previous amputation if you've got a spare minute and to get the address of next of kin."

"With you operating," I said, "that might be a wise precaution."

He smiled and took another draught of opium. When he smiled I saw he was still pretty young. Which surprised me: maybe because doctors are always saying they can save lives—something only *they* still believe—I'm accustomed to thinking of them as always old, and myself always as younger. This one wasn't much older than Nicholas Whiteman, that blue-eyed captain who'd wanted the ink.

He stuck back the plug on the bottle and wiped his hands on the vest of his suit. The material was rigid as cardboard from stiffened blood.

"Sorry," he said.

"What about?"

"All these corpses. I know you'd like to be able to use these specimens again. Saw you talking to Eddie Farlowe there. Sweet kid. He's dead. So's the boy next to him with the neck. So's the Southern kid. So's the weeper. They're all dead. They won't even make it back to Tennessee. If the gangrene won't get 'em, the pneumonia will."

"You don't have much faith in your profession," I said.

"That's because I've got so much faith in yours," he replied. "Look, those boys are lucky. They'll be dead soon. Their families will revere them and name nephews after them and nobody'll ever remember one aggravating trait they ever possessed. And if there's a heaven, they'll all sit around and jawbone pridefully how bravely they fell—heroes all. Let me show you some other heroes."

Can somebody please tell me why I followed him into the next tent? I know, I know. It's part of what generals do between battles.

The first thing I saw was three men, sitting atop barrels. They didn't look too bad; their skin was rosy enough, their eyes weren't bandaged, and they all still possessed two arms and two legs. When they saw me their eyes showed recognition, but there were no greetings. No curses either; only a weird mumble. The room smelled sweet—a tender smell, dimly remembered, like mothers and babies.

I realized the smell was milk.

"We're weaning them," the doctor said. "They all got shot in the jaw. Two we got out the bullet and one we didn't, but the cheekbone was shattered in all three cases, and our surgery wasn't exactly up to snuff. They'll never be able to open their mouths again. They're like old men with cerebral hemorrhages, only they're young and perfectly healthy and they get to live this way forever. Other than rum and water and milk and a moan every now and again they're never going to kiss or say or taste or swallow anything else for the next fifty years."

I looked at those three sets of lips, each parted just wider than the width of a straw. I said, "I see."

He gave me a smile. "Well, one good thing," he said, "at least they'll never complain about it."

He pointed to another man. His leg had been hit but appeared to be healing. "Hi, General, hi, Doc," he chirped.

"Hello, son," I said.

"I'm going home soon," he said brightly. "I did my bit and I'm proud of it, but I sure am pleased to be going home, I surely am."

The doctor said quietly, "Bet his family won't be. We operated once and his leg got infected. It wasn't bad enough to amputate so we dosed him with morphine and cut off the rot. He got infected again. So we dosed him again and cut him again and he got infected again. Eventually he cleared up, but in the meantime we'd given him so much morphine he got habituated to it. So now he's going to be using it every three hours for the rest of his life. He's got a wife and three kids and was fixing to be a minister when he enlisted. Now he's fixing to be a morphine addict instead."

I didn't say anything.

"And here's the *spécialité de la maison*," he said, taking my elbow and leading me to a corner away from the milk drinkers.

"An escapee from Andersonville. And lest you suspect I'm a Southern sympathizer, I'm pleased to report the Rebels in our Northern prisoner-of-war camps look just as bad. Leander?"

He was thin as silk. He was thinner than the bars supporting his bed; thinner than a needle; thinner than light. His eyes appeared loose, too large for their sockets. His wrists were nothing but vein and pulse.

"Hello, son," I said.

He opened his mouth. It was toothless and blistered, the gums dark green. The doctor reached for his pulse. I knocked aside the probing fingers. The pulse was distant but steady as autumn rain.

"Leander," I said, "listen to me. You recognize me, don't you? I'm your commanding officer, and the fact you've had the misfortune of having summered in a prison camp as a guest of Jefferson Davis doesn't change that. You're still a soldier in my army and I expect you to recover because the war isn't over and your brothers are still dying. They need you and we're expecting to use you again. You understand what I'm saying?"

His eyelids fluttered, open and shut. Christ knows if he even heard me. Christ knows, at that point, if *Christ* even heard me. It didn't matter. That doctor had heard me. I'd heard myself.

CHAPTER
FIVE

I WROTE THE ORDER that altered the face of modern warfare on a windy November evening.

I was entertaining a lady at the time. Lydia Harter, the famous Charleston belle Lydia Angela Dantley when first I met her (twenty years ago), now Mrs. General Daniel Harter with a husband on Lee's staff and three sons in Beauregard's army, had brought me a present—a packet of genuine tea.

I sniffed it zealously. I really don't care for tea, but after four years of nothing you miss everything, even things you don't like.

"This stuff must be rarer than God's grace," I protested. "Why don't you save it for a real guest?"

She smiled. "And what guest," she asked, "could be any more real than the conqueror of my adopted city?"

So we sipped and we gossiped, and I issued commands and found her a napkin, and generated directives and gave her a spoon, and dug up some sugar and got George to track down a can of milk for her and a wedge to open it with. Meantime I was writing and crossing out and rewriting what was to become

Special Order Number 120, my gift to history—no, to historians. Outside, over her shoulder, the thinning trees of occupied Georgia sashayed and whispered in the autumn breeze.

I'd heard such breezes before. I'd lived in the South two times, first for six years right after West Point, then more recently as headmaster of the Louisiana State Seminary Military College, just before the war. Both times I had loved it—not only the land (it's astoundingly beautiful), but also the people (they are too). It's always been my impression that Southerners are a remarkable bunch—remarkably charming, remarkably hospitable, and remarkably loyal (I mean of course to their friends, not their country). Once the war started, this point was proved time and again: it turned out I had charming, hospitable, and loyal friends in virtually every city I conquered.

Most of these friends were women. Some I had known on their own, others through their husbands—former Army comrades, now dead or in enemy armies. They all remembered similar things: picnics and dances of two decades ago, midafternoon walks, midnight confessions, comments and compliments I'd made as a first lieutenant so in love with them and the world and myself that I'd say almost anything, just to hear myself talk.

Lydia launched our conversation as such conversations always were launched—by Dorothée Beaumains in Memphis, by Loretta Cowper in Meridian, by Mary Louisa Gordon last August in Dalton. Do you remember? Remember when? Remember?

"Do you remember," she asked, "how much fun all of us used to have just being together?"

"I remember," I said. "No matter what we did we always enjoyed it. I guess that's because we were young—"

"No," Lydia said; "we were special."

"Everyone's special at that age," I said. "That's what being young means."

"Then we were all very young," she said, "because I remember we were all very special. You most of all, Bill."

I must say that's how I remembered it too. Being special, I mean. Myself and all my friends—we moved in a universe where nothing mattered besides ourselves. We were beautiful. We were young, energetic, immortal—even Bill Sherman was young, even he was beautiful.

And acts of love were of special beauty. For me falling in love was as simple as lifting one's face to the sky on a winter's day; up you looked, there was another woman, as fresh and different as the newest snowflake. Back home I had an understanding with a pretty Ohio woman whom I loved devotedly: but I wasn't *in* Ohio, and devotion lies in the heart of the beholder, not in the eyes. And the air of the South has a special beauty when you're not out there killing its citizens.

"Double-check those railroads," I said to George. "Half these reports say we cut all of them and half say we're still using them. Which is it?"

George made a notation. "Why didn't you refugee when Atlanta fell?" I asked Lydia.

"This is my home," she said. "I need to be here so my family will know where to find me."

"Mind signing a deposition to that effect? Your newspapers have the city in flames."

She stirred her tea the way some women flutter a fan—a gesture to show grace, the twist of a slender wrist disguised as practical movement.

"It isn't like you," she said, "to pay much attention to what folks think."

"I don't care what they think. I care what they say."

Lydia smiled. "But isn't it really to your advantage," she asked, "to be seen as a pyromaniac?"

Lydia caught on fast—always had. Fact is, she caught on one hell of a lot faster than Stanton and his War Department fogies. Strike enough fear in the hearts of your enemies, you just might avoid striking so many hearts.

George passed me some papers. I noticed one I'd already signed. On the bottom, in red, George had written and circled the question: "Don't you think she might be engaged in Espionage?"

I grunted. Sometimes George could be a tad bit Stantonesque—that is, querulously unimaginative. For the truth is that unlikely as it was that Lydia was a spy (perhaps not unlikely, actually: most Confederate spies were female, the men all being at, or under, the battlefields), the best thing for me would be that she *was* a spy. For surprise was never my intention. Word of our coming was meant, like fire, to spread.

"Don't worry about it," I wrote back to George, and said to him aloud, "I want you to make certain Mrs. Harter has a guard placed outside her home. I don't want anything happening to her personal belongings when we move out."

A real spy might have asked when we were moving; Lydia just added more sugar to her teacup. I imagine it was the first sugar she'd seen in months; and like me with her tea, desire fed on rarity.

I desired Lydia. Not exactly her body (although that too); but looking at her I felt a terrible ache, less of need than nostalgia of need. When would it ever again be possible to have time for desire? Had it really only been forty-two months since I had regarded a human body as anything but a potential corpse?

"I see some of the boys packing extra coats," I said to George. "Tell them to forget it. Officers too. No extra anything."

George wrote it down. "That goes for food too," I said. "Three days' rations. Period."

Now Lydia did look puzzled, and did ask.

"Three days' rations?" she repeated. "You're moving out and that's all you're going to take?"

"I hope to depend," I said, "on Southern hospitality."

Lydia, when we were younger, had been one of the most hospitable of Southerners. Pre her husband, pre those enemy children, I used to visit her home; and eager as I would be to be alone with her, I barely could wrench myself away from her parlor, so enamored was I with her family. Her mother, palely cool as the water lilies in her private pond, as graceful as willow. Her brothers, spirited and confident as colts. Her father, warm, always calm, always welcoming, and so amused by my youth and gawkiness he didn't even bother to hide his amusement. It was almost insulting how unalarmed he was when I would arrive to escort Lydia on one of our unchaperoned outings; he would hand her her shawl and kiss her forehead, and I always felt he could barely restrain kissing mine too.

"George," I said, "check all the units for ambulatories. We can't have any injuries slowing us down. Even minor ones."

"I've checked," he said.

"Double-check," I said. "I don't want anyone showing me how tough he is. This isn't the time for heroics."

On the top of the paper, under "Special Field Order 120," I wrote:

1. For the purposes of military operations, this army is divided into two wings viz.: the right wing, Major-General O. O. Howard commanding, composed of the Fifteenth and Seventeenth Corps; the left wing, Major-General H. W. Slocum commanding, composed of the Fourteenth and Twentieth Corps.

2. The habitual order of march will be, wherever practicable, by four roads, as nearly parallel as possible, and converging at points hereafter to be indicated in orders. The cavalry, Brigadier-General Kilpatrick commanding, will receive special orders from the commander-in-chief.

I tapped pen against paper. Lydia and I alone on those shadow-kissed Charleston nights was a memory sharp as steel. Lydia had not been the first girl I ever kissed, but she had been the first *woman*—the first female I kissed who knew more about kissing than I. (I never was one for brothels; you're not supposed to talk in whorehouses, and I never could trust myself to keep quiet.) She also had not been the first woman to whom I made love. But she was the first woman to make lovemaking *atmospheric;* that is, she made love differently depending on the weather.

On warm nights we would ride far, far out of town and embrace in wet meadows that smelt of hay, and take our time. On rainy evenings we'd rush into stables (including her father's), tear off each other's clothes, fling them over saddles and buckets, and hurtle through everything. My head on the ground, pebbles digging into my skull, or buried in her hair, I would hear behind me the uneasy stirring of sleepy quarter horses surprised into resigned voyeurism.

One September we made love in the snow. Yes, snow in September (everything about the South is perverse, and you can start with its weather). I spread my coat (lightweight wool, brass buttons, pale silk lining, all courtesy of the peacetime army) on that unbelievable snow, and took her hand and laid her down, facing me and that mistakenly winter sky. She sat back up to remove her hairpins, twenty at least, and each one she stuck into the snow like a tiny wicket. Then she laid back down. Somewhere along there she had managed to loosen her basque without unbuttoning her blouse, so while her breasts were visible they remained inviolable, carved beneath layers of lace.

We kissed. Her lips were cold, then immediately warm. Her blouse contained twice as many buttons as any Northern woman's, and they were fitted into such tiny buttonholes, it probably would have been easier for me to sew each of them on than ease each out. But we weren't in any hurry—well, we were and we weren't; we were impatient to get to the next step but at the same time we could happily have spent five hours right here, had only they been the previous five. Eventually she was exposed beneath me, covered with flakes of snow and tiny remnants of lace and a few loose buttons and the marks of my kisses. When I finally entered her, it was like entering a vial of cider, she was that sweet and warm.

"And how is your wife?" asked Lydia.

The hazards of tender memory! I slashed myself free from its tightening bonds.

"My wife flourishes," I said. "And your husband?"

"He says he's fine," she said. "His letters sound tired."

"We're all tired," I said. But only to be polite, for actually I wasn't—hadn't felt tired since the war had started, in fact, and I'd found what I really was good at. "Your sons are well?"

"All well," she said. "Peter—the youngest—was wounded at

Drewry's Bluff, but it turned out not to be serious. He lost an arm."

George made a snorting sound—not exactly sympathetic, but not indifferent either. "I imagine it's serious to Peter," I said.

"What I mean is," said Lydia, "he survived."

I studied the first two paragraphs of the Special Order. I didn't find war tiring, but it *is* tiring to live in a country strewn with missing limbs. It was my honest intention (said before; bears repeating; no one believes it; to hell with them) that by marching through Georgia I meant to effect the eventual end of that bloody landscape. Yet that, I knew, lay in the future: in the meantime, more legs, arms, lungs, intestines, must litter the hayricks and meadows of our pitiful nation. I wrote out the third paragraph:

3. There will be no general train of supplies, but each corps will have its ammunition-train and provision-train, distributed habitually as follows: Behind each regiment should follow one wagon and one ambulance; behind each brigade should follow a due proportion of ammunition-wagons, provision-wagons, and ambulances. In case of danger, each corps commander should change this order of march, by having his advance and rear brigades unencumbered by wheels. The separate columns will start habitually at seven A.M., and make about fifteen miles per day, unless otherwise fixed in orders.

"Shall I assume you too have children?" Lydia asked.

"Six," I replied.

Lydia's smile was hard to interpret—was she relieved her husband had given her only three offspring, or regretting not marrying me and reaping a doubled total? Or was it merely the politeness of all mothers (a behavior foreign, in my experience, to fathers) discussing the fruits of union, happy or not?

"They are all well?" she inquired.

George hit his notebook against the side of his chair.

"I live for my children," I said. "They are all well."

In the old days—the very old days, I mean, with Lydia in Charleston—I would have explained further. For the truth is, I did not really live for all my children.

I loved, of course, each of them. But for five of them it was an undifferentiated love: I gladly would die for them all, but stuck in a room with any of them I ran out of things to say after about ten minutes. (How unlike my soldiers, with whom I could always talk, but had no intention of dying for.) They were their mother's children—four beautiful daughters and a shy second son named after my father. The only child I really would say I *knew* was my beloved and firstborn son, my namesake, Little Willie.

But by now I had not seen Willie for over a year. A year!—so long in a child's life. Can he possibly miss me as much as I daily miss him?

The last time I saw him was a year ago. I already said that. My wife had brought three of the other children, and him, to visit my camp after the fall of Vicksburg. Willie, nine years old and sturdy as birch, was the only one of my children really interested in the war; to the others it was only their father's job (some fathers are farmers, some are laborers, mine's a general). He took to camp life like roses to sunshine.

Willie, my little rose.

How you would hate that metaphor!

Articles four and five of the Special Order were the key to the March. I was about to release sixty thousand healthy veteran soldiers, virtually foodless and extremely well armed, into a civilian population. Granted that population was defended by an excellent and war-hardened cavalry; still, cavalry isn't infantry, and civilians aren't anything. There was going to be—

Lydia smiled prettily. Lydia could deal with sixty thousand Yankees on her front porch. How about her sisters?

How did I want them to deal with us? I didn't want them weeping, but they had to weep. I didn't want them suffering, but they had to suffer. I might want to let them escape the war, but they were the ones who had started it; now only they could stop it: they and I, together, a strange marriage. I had to make their cries loud enough to reach their stone-deaf government; desperate enough to convince their generals, ready to die in the last ditch, not to fill up that ditch with the bodies of women and children.

My men had taken to Willie with an enthusiasm too time-consuming not to be genuine. They called him Sergeant and saluted whenever they saw him; when he giggled they threatened to promote him to lieutenant-general (outranking me). They mocked his red hair and asked, scratching their heads, where they had seen hair that color before (my own hair of course being red as the Devil's nightgown). They managed to get hold of some blue material and tailored for him a sergeant's uniform complete with chevrons. Then they howled at him for too-rapid advancement and demanded he tell who his friends were in Washington.

"You must not run in Cump Sherman's crowd," they told him, "or you'd still be a private digging fenceposts."

Willie ate it all up like cream on raspberries. He never could, poor pup, come back with a fast-enough answer, but his replies were so sweet they were better than wit.

The day we were to set sail from Vicksburg, the men presented him with a scaled-down, double-barreled shotgun. He became so excited his high-pitched thanks sounded like bleats in the deserted campgrounds.

Evacuating Vicksburg was much harder for me than leaving Atlanta. The main thing was I'd never faced such a business before, and the details astonished me by their simultaneous importance and pettiness. Bandages. Government forms. Compassionate leaves. Sick leaves. More forms. Salt rations. Tobacco rations. Flour rations. Long-winded missives from Stanton, each with a dozen demands disguised as questions. Letters of sympathy. More forms. Charts showing graves.

Also, I wasn't used to performing militarily in front of my family: of having to present the face of a leader and a father at the same time. Eventually the press of my duties forced me to choose, and I left my wife and my children to care for themselves.

We already were on the departing steamer when my wife

realized Willie was missing. She began screaming. Immediately I dispatched three men to search the boat; twelve to search the shore; another dozen ran back, on their own, to our empty camp. No sign of him anywhere. Mrs. Sherman and I stood paralyzed on the deck.

Every time we heard shouting, our hopes soared; each time we heard the empty reports, our fears redoubled. His sisters began whimpering. His mother began reciting all the places he might have run to. My heart shriveled. Each favorite hideout was the same place a Rebel sharpshooter would choose. I pictured a little boy with a shotgun and thought: Oh, my God, what have I done?

And that was when I realized we must make war so terrible— so terrible its memory stops even the concept of future wars.

They found my son and he was alive. Alive, alive, alive: God still moved in this universe. Willie, feeling unwell, had sat under a tree to rest. He had fallen asleep and not heard the sounds of departure. My men brought him back to the ship, and I listened carefully to his explanations.

"How could you not hear the ships' whistles," I asked, "and all the men calling you? How could you not hear your mother? Or me?"

Willie yawned. "I'm tired," he said. "I'm sleepy. I'm sorry. I'm tired. I'm sleepy."

"Well, we'll talk about it later. Give me a kiss and promise not to worry me like that again. Go rest over there."

I pointed to a stack of blankets on deck. Willie trotted obediently over, lay down, and fell asleep, curled within himself like a kitten.

Four hours later he still was sleeping. Six hours later I carried him below deck. He was still asleep, and breathing rapidly.

Twelve hours later the doctors informed me the swamps of Vicksburg had given my child typhoid.

By the time we reached Memphis, my angel was unconscious. I summoned doctors, who could do nothing: without a wound, there was nothing for them to bathe or swab, nothing to cut off. Forced to weigh the needs of one hundred thousand living soldiers against one dying son, I tried to tend everyone; I was studying maps of Chattanooga while laying cool rags on Willie's forehead when one of the doctors leaned over and touched my arm. He took the rag and the map from my hands and softly informed me my son was dead.

Article Four of the Special Order read:

4. The army will forage liberally on the country during the march. To this end, each brigade commander will organize a good and sufficient foraging party, under the command of one or more discreet officers, who will gather, near the route travelled, corn or forage of any kind, meat of any kind, vegetables, corn-meal, or whatever is needed by the command. . . . Soldiers must not enter the dwellings of the inhabitants, or commit any trespass; but, during a halt or camp, they may be permitted to gather turnips, potatoes, and other vegetables, and to drive in stock in sight of their camp. To regular foraging-parties must be entrusted the gathering of provisions and forage, at any distance from the roads travelled.

And Article Five:

5. To corps commanders alone is intrusted the power to destroy mills, houses, cotton-gins, etc.; and for them this general principle is laid down: In districts and neighborhoods where the army is unmolested, no destruction of such property should be permitted; but should guerrillas and bushwhackers molest our march, or should the inhabitants burn bridges, obstruct roads, or otherwise manifest local hostility—

I closed my eyes for a moment and tried to picture what I was describing. All I could see were funerals. Lydia's, Willie's, the boys in the hospital, Rebel boys. I hoped for, but could not imagine, anything else.

—then army commanders should order and enforce a devastation more or less relentless, according to the measure of such hostility.

I opened my eyes and looked once more at Lydia.
"My children live in my heart," I said.
She said, "Like all children."
And I said, "Yes."

So. Did I write the Special Order to end the war, or to avenge my son? Or to avenge my soldiers, or to save their lives? Or to destroy the South, or to save her from destroying herself?

I remember I thought I wrote it to hasten peace. But that's only memory; what actually happened may have been different. What actually happened may have been worse. What really happened may have been terrible.

If we remembered the past as it really happened, we'd probably kill ourselves.

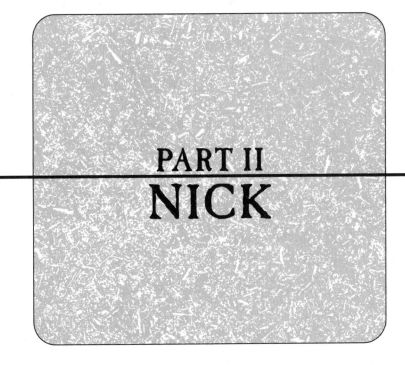

PART II
NICK

SPEAKER:
Nicholas J. Whiteman
Captain, XIV Corps, U.S. Army

CHAPTER
SIX

BEFORE I JOINED the infantry, before the army, before the war, I liked reading history, and daydreamed a lot about living in interesting times. The Renaissance always attracted me, for some reason; in fact, for Reason itself, for being the birth of reason and the so-called modern world. The Crusades also beckoned, with an opposite lure; they seemed like a chance to really cut loose, to seize a lance and a banner and a kiss from an undistressed damsel, and then go crazy. The Greeks sounded good too; so did the French Revolution. What struck me as boring was peacetime America circa 1860.

But of course I was wrong. History is interesting because historians do good laundry: they twist out the water of everyday life till all you've got left is Richard the Lion-Heart and Lucrezia Borgia. No wonder it's interesting! But when you're splashing around in that water yourself—and they can name it crusade, revolution, or American Civil War—you'll find you spend most of your time bored nearly beyond belief, and longing for something to happen more interesting than what they call "history" turned out to be.

I mentioned all this—history, Renaissance, boredom—to Pete. Pete was my sergeant, even though he was thirty-four, six years older than I, and a professional soldier, something no one has ever praised (or mistaken) me for. Why Pete was a sergeant while I was a captain was something both of us often noticed (though he—no surprise here—noticed more often than I). It was just the Way of the Army.

Now Pete rolled his eyes. "Nick," he said, "you're bored this one single second, and you right away get in your usual lather about the Crusades and the Renaissance and how nothing interesting ever happens to you. But this isn't boredom at all. You have no idea what real boredom is."

I was bored right then, so I bit. "Okay, what is it?" I said.

Pete said: "You're dead."

That shut me right down. I don't care to speak much of death—not out of superstition, exactly, but more for the same reason married soldiers don't talk about infidelity (their wives', that is). Why wonder, why torture yourself—why tug God's sleeve with your fears and confessions? Surely you'll live longer if He forgets you're living at all.

We broke for lunch around noon. In view of all that's about to happen, I'm obliged to report we dined from our knapsacks—hardtack, what else?; dried beef; dried fruit; and dried potatoes. Afterward we ate coffee, and I played a little poker with Charlie Delancy, a private from Indianapolis and an apprentice boot-maker before the war. I won a pair of new boots, should the war ever end and I find myself in Indianapolis. Then we marched some more, halting just before sunset.

We were quicker than usual making camp that first evening—care to guess why? We found relatively flat ground without too much trouble (actually no trouble at all; there were over fourteen thousand men in XIV Corps, and they'd flattened things out pretty nicely), and there was sufficient fresh water and plenty of trees to be diarrhetic behind. But our real time-saver was dinner. We didn't make it.

Not that we couldn't. We still had food—not much, but some; we'd left Atlanta with three days' rations, and all we'd eaten was lunch. So it wasn't that; we weren't starving. No. It was the Special Order.

Forage liberally. A devastation. More or less relentless.

I looked around me. There were fifty-some men in my company and not one willing to make eye contact, not only with me but with one another. Instead we all were watching the men of the other companies, to see who was going to do it—*Forage liberally*—what they were going to do—*A devastation*—and how they were going to do it—*More or less relentless.* And I thought, well, if it's going to happen sooner or later . . .

Forage liberally. A devastation. More or less relentless.

"If it's going to happen sooner or later," I said, "it might as well happen now. Charlie, Pete, Tim, let's see what they're serving for supper at the nearest farmhouse."

Pete and Charlie scrambled for rifles and candles. Tim Rice, who was too young to vote but already had lost both an eye and a brother, shook his head.

"Nah, choose someone else, please, Captain," he said. "I don't like the idea of robbing civilians. I don't believe in it."

Pete said, "You believe in eating what we bring back?"

"Drop it," I said to Pete. "Tim, do what you feel like. Three's enough anyway. Pete, Charlie, let's go."

"Maybe Charlie don't want to go either," said Pete. "Maybe he too don't like the idea of robbing civilians."

Charlie was checking his cartridge belt. "No, I like it, I like it," he said.

Great. We all liked it. We started to walk.

For the first hour or so, all we saw were more soldiers, doing exactly what we were, which was trying to get away from each other. It reminded me of Halloween night at home in Decatur, crawling around in neighbors' yards and hayricks, anxious to do some mischief but not wanting to do it where it'd already been done. Then we rounded a little path and followed it up a low hill and back down again. The voices of the other boys fell slowly away.

I looked around. We were alone. Alone and in darkness and silence so total it swallowed our candles and even our breath.

"It's awful quiet here," Charlie whispered.

"You scared, Princess?" snickered Pete.

"Nope. Just . . . not used to it. Ain't been this still since the war started."

Five slow minutes passed. An owl hooted and a breeze rustled. A cloud parted. The moon appeared. The silence and blackness rolled away like a painted curtain before a play.

We were standing in front of a lighted house. It was small and squarish, surrounded by dead roses with matted thorns, and built out of darkish brick, with a cupola and a single smoke-scented chimney. It reminded me of a church or a schoolhouse, and set out here where I expected plantations and slave pens, it looked homey and inviting, the way churches and schools always look till you get inside.

"Go around back," I whispered to Pete. "See what they've got in the garden. Watch out for dogs."

"Go around *back?*" he repeated. "Hell, Nick, what for? We're armed, we can march right up the front porch."

"They could be armed too. Just see what they've got in the back to eat."

Pete fumbled for his rifle and stuck on his bayonet.

"Put that back!" I said. "What do you want to do, gut someone's poodle?"

"Hell, I don't care if I gut someone's *gut!* We don't have to creep and crawl around like this."

Debate time. "We're not hurting anybody if we can help it," I said.

"Nick, what's got into you? These are the sons-of-bitches who gave you that nice scar down the rib cage! Who shot out Tim's eye!"

End of debate. "Just do what I tell you," I ordered. "We're here to get food, not slaughter civilians."

Pete jammed the bayonet back into his belt. "I'm sure this ain't what the General had in mind," he hissed as he tiptoed away.

Now Charlie looked like he too had a problem. I asked what it was.

"I don't know. This is weird. Maybe we ought to go back and just eat what we got at camp. Maybe we ought to be doing this during the day when at least we can see."

"Don't worry so much," I said. "We'll be done here before you know it. Come with me and we'll see where their barn is."

We started to the side of the house, toward a little shed. I bet it's their smokehouse, I thought, and at that my mouth immediately commenced slavering. Bacon! Fresh ham! Smoked Virginia ham! Well, smoked Georgia ham, but what the hell, smoked anything that was *supposed* to be smoked, as opposed to smoked hotcakes, or smoked beets, or smoked rutabagas, sounded delicious. I wondered if somewhere behind those bushes we might find a henhouse, and if maybe that shadow behind the porch might be a churn. . . . We could bring back the boys an entire breakfast, something most of us hadn't seen since the bombing of Sumter. It occurred to me that in over three years nothing I'd tossed in my stomach had got there by choice.

I was standing there salivating, keen as a hound, when suddenly the entire front porch was flooded with light. Candles, lanterns, a piney torch—it looked like Atlanta all over again. A man's voice called:

"Who's out there? I'm armed! Who's out there?"

Charlie instantly fell to the earth, jamming cartridges into his Spencer; I could hear its familiar *click-click-click*, gobbling the bullets. I had my Springfield and a loaded Colt.

"Cover me," I whispered and slid to a tree. I trained the revolver toward the porch.

"We're soldiers!" I shouted. "We're armed too! And we're hungry!"

"Go be hungry with somebody else!" the voice shouted back. "You bastards have already been here!"

"Been here already?" I yelled. "That's hard to believe!"

"What do I care what you believe! There's nothing left here except bullets, and if you want to swallow one you just take one more step!"

"That's a bad idea! I've got fourteen boys here and we've been slaughtering Rebels since Shiloh! We just burnt Atlanta and we're ready to do you next! You shoot that weapon and the best I can say for you is, you'd better have fire insurance!"

The man said, "Rebels? You been slaughtering *Rebels?* Who are you anyway?"

Then I heard a raucous, familiar laugh. I wheeled around, astonished; Pete was running along the side of the house, rifle dangling, a hunting spaniel dancing between his legs and his arm around an elderly lady who looked about as ferocious as my Aunt Kate. About as wide too.

"Nick," he shouted. "Don't shoot! And call off your fourteen men all named Charlie! These folks are Union!"

Charlie, still on the ground, said, "Huh?"

"They're Union, Chuckie! Same side as you, remember? Nick, get away from that tree! You look like you think you're Robin Hood!"

I stepped away carefully, into the light. The man on the porch took a few steps forward. Then he jumped off the porch and into my arms, almost knocking me over. As if on cue, my revolver discharged, nearly hitting the dog. The woman shrieked.

"Goddamn that gun," I said, "it's got a mind all its own. Pete, what's going on?"

The man still had his arms wrapped tight around me; I shook myself loose. "What's going on?" I repeated.

"We are all brothers," said the man.

"Sure we are," I said. "But I'm keeping these guns loaded anyway."

"There is no need," said the man. He held out to me what had looked from the porch's shadow like a shotgun. It was a broom.

"We're Mennonites," he said.

It didn't look or feel like a trap—and in war that's pretty much how you judge, looks and feelings, because none of the so-called training ever covers what really happens. Still . . . I walked over to Charlie and whispered for him to get up slowly and stay ready. He planted his rifle into the earth and slid up its side like a snake up a stick.

"Okay, you're Mennonites," I said to the man. "Prove it."

He smiled. He really did; managed a smile with all those pointed guns. Then he handed me the broom. "We're Mennonites," he repeated. "And we mean to protect ourselves the best we can. Wheeler's men already have been here once."

Wheeler? Joe Wheeler was chief of the Confederate cavalry. "You're trying to tell me you need protection," I asked, "from your own people?"

"They're not our people," the woman said. "We're Christians and they're slave owners. You are our people."

Well, that's one drawback to a civil war: everyone looks alike. The man glanced at the broom and continued.

"Wheeler's riders were here two days ago," he said. "They wanted my son. For the Rebel army. He's only fifteen, but these days that's old. We told them the truth; that we were Mennonites, that he couldn't fight—wouldn't fight. They said it didn't matter; they'd make him a guard in a prisoner-of-war camp. They said a few months of that might even change his mind. And when he told them it wouldn't, they threw him onto a horse and rode away with him as if he were a sack of flour."

"Too bad you don't live up North," remarked Charlie.

"We did. My first son was seized by the Union army. They called it conscription."

By now the woman and Pete were whispering to one another. I overheard the words "bread," "eggs," "apples," and then we all began moving together—first to the stairs, then to the porch, then to the woven rush mat just outside the door. And then we were in the house.

The strangeness of all that had already happened paled next to the strangeness of being within four walls. The house seemed tiny to me; the walls pressed against me as though they were melting; the ceiling was three feet high; the floor rose to my knees. The air after four years of living outdoors felt thinned, lightened, like the air when you wake with your face in a pillow, the lifetime ago I had slept like that.

And the rooms! The furniture was wood—plain, spotless, polished; the floors too; the white walls sparkled, the windows glowed. Dried flowers in vases; fresh greens in a basket; one rug on the floor, the color of faded roses; a Bible on a table, black with faded gold letters. A pair of scissors. A mahogany box. A shawl.

I stared and stared. Real life was so beautiful! I had forgotten.

"Come to the kitchen and let us feed you," the woman said.

Their kitchen was large and equipped with sufficient pans, platters, dishes, and goblets to stock a small restaurant. There was chicken simmering in one pot. There was a ham bone cooking in another. There was half a turkey resting on a cutting board. There was bread. There was pie. There was milk. There was cider. There was cake. There were cookies. There was no hardtack anywhere. Everything looked fresh. Everything smelt like heaven.

"What can we offer?" the woman said. "Have you time to stay for a meal? Or should I make sandwiches? You must have other men; will they need food too? Some of these pies? Some fruit? Let me run to the henhouse and see if any more eggs have dropped. An omelet? Soup?"

I can't recall a woman ever speaking words more seductive. Everything she mentioned I wanted ten of, and yes, I mean I wanted ten pies, I could eat ten chickens; hell, the way she pronounced those vanished, familiar dishes, I could down twenty. She even made unlaid eggs sound appealing.

Yet I knew, even before she was half out the door, what I would have to say. I didn't *want* to say it—the truth is, at that moment, after her enumeration of home-cooked treats, I wanted that meal more than just about anything I'd ever wanted in my life. But just as her right hand hit the doorknob, I saw for a second a Union soldier in the Southern home of a Northern sympathizer, and all the ways he could possibly play his part.

And I knew I was supposed to act with goddamn honor.

"We can't take your food," I said.

As soon as I said it, I started to wonder how many times Pete was going to stick me over this; Charlie too. But neither of them said a word, and in fact the surprised-looking faces weren't my men's. The woman said, "But we want to feed you. We want to help. We don't want you going hungry."

"Ma'am, we don't want to go hungry either. But it's not our intention to starve people out. And your family's got a lot better chance of starving than we do."

The man grinned. "You boys act like this every place you show up," he said, "it won't be us doing the starving."

"That'll be my problem," I said. "I've made my decision and we're sticking with it."

"Suits me," said Charlie.

"Yeah, okay by me, too," said Pete. "There's lots more houses in Georgia. And if it turns out they're all full of people like you, well, we oughtta be home by Christmas."

Interesting, isn't it?—how the goal's always Christmas, whatever the war. Still, you read certain phrases in the papers enough, you hear them repeated on parade and in prebattle sermons, you start to employ them even if you don't believe them: so now the kitchen was full of nodding heads, mine included, all intoning that we did indeed hope the war would be ended by Christmas, maybe even on Christmas Eve.

"New Year's Day, on the outside," said Pete.

Everyone laughed: mutual delight in each other's compassion matched only by joy at each other's wit. We—Pete, Charlie, and I—were still chuckling when we left. Our good deed had stupefied us into self-satisfied simplemindedness. Georgia was full of good people. We were among the best.

And so we kept walking. Eyeballing stars, we fell into an argument as to exactly what, besides the Big Dipper, was overhead: Pete thought he could spot Orion, Charlie insisted it was Ursa Major, I reckoned it might be Venus. I made the mistake of confessing I never could see how the Greeks had conceived the constellations, and Pete launched into a rambling explanation I was pretty certain was wrong. We tried to remember how the zodiac worked and what signs we were born under. From the polestar we knew we were headed north but couldn't tell by what, west or east; we were deep in that midstage of exploration when you realize you're lost but you aren't yet worried about it.

We came to a path. Southern paths are subtle: usually you first notice them when they swallow your ankle. This time it was Pete who stumbled and swore. We took to the left and followed the soft sunken earth, and slowly it led us, with the twists and stops and mistaken dead ends of a fairy-tale road, to an unlit cabin.

"This time no botches," I said. "Pete, you check the back. Charlie, you and I try the window. And listen, you two: let's can the surprises. We can't spend all night on this nonsense."

Pete nodded and disappeared. Charlie and I blew out our candles and tiptoed to the window—or what had looked like a window. For once again things turned out not to be what they seemed: where I had thought there was glass, there was only a square of gingham, hanging over a cutaway hole in the cabin wall.

I lifted the cloth. A woman's voice said, "Vincent? Is that you, Vincent?"

"It's not Vincent," I said. "Ma'am, are you alone?"

"Who's that? Who's there?"

I'd heard fear before but never that much: her voice rose and fell from octave to octave in just four words. Feet moved in the unlit interior and I raised my revolver, but nobody came to the door, and behind the curtain the blackness remained. I nudged Charlie's arm and he slipped to the door. I saw the door had no knob; either it locked from the inside or just needed a push.

He pushed. The door opened.

Nothing met him: no voice, no light, no Vincent, no woman. Also no footsteps. Charlie stepped carefully into the room, his extended rifle circling the air just ahead of him like a sniffing dog exploring a clearing. I could hear his steps and his breathing, but nobody else's; if the woman, or anyone else, was inside, she was more skilled at skulking than he.

Maybe I could do better. "Charlie," I hissed. He came to the cutout window. "Go around back," I whispered, "and check on Pete. I'll take the house. Okay?"

Charlie nodded. He looked, maybe, a little relieved. Then he left, and I entered.

Once inside with the door softly closed, I immediately started to wonder: was I alone? Alone in the darkness, or watched from it? There really was no light at all, outside of the moon coming in through the cloth of the window, and the glow it cast was worse than nothing, because it created shadows. There was a very slight breeze, and it keened at a weird, high pitch through the beams of the ceiling and walls. I moved one foot forward and then another, trying to advance at least as far as Charlie had done with safety.

Then I stopped. Beyond where I'd seen him step, I had no idea who or what might be next.

I made out the shape of the top of a table, but I couldn't see its legs. It occurred to me that my own legs were highly visible to anyone hiding beneath. Gripped by a sudden recollection of my brother once lurking under my desk and jumping me in my bed, I grabbed my rifle in both hands and thrust it under the tabletop, sweeping from side to side. No resistance, no pressure—just dust, which I couldn't see but felt, rushing up to my nose. I held my breath, praying not to sneeze. Both ears popped as the unsneezed air gurgled in my throat.

I shuffled forward another few inches. I was getting used to the darkness by now; I could see all four walls, pillowed by shadow so they appeared soft and rounded, like murky clouds. Anyone standing amidst those corners would blend perfectly into that softness, while I stood straightly vertical, a target as clear as a tree. I listened for breathing. I heard nothing, not even my own. I cleared my throat.

"I hold in my hands a repeating rifle," I said—this wasn't true but was all I could think of at the moment. "My finger is on the trigger. That means that even if you shoot me it's going to fire"—also not necessarily true—"and somebody else will get hit too. So come out without shooting and we'll all save our skins and our bullets. We're not here to hurt anyone."

Nobody answered. I raised my rifle and aimed in the direction of one vague corner, then another, then the third. Suddenly thrilled by impatience, I lunged into all three corners, slashing the air with the stock of the probing Springfield like I used to stab scarecrows in bayonet drill. All I felt was the bouncing rebound of wood against metal.

There remained one more corner. Furthest from the window, it was steeped in shadow, near what looked like the frame of a second door. If anyone wanted to watch me, it would be from here.

I noticed then I was sweating. Not merely sweating, but sweat falling like rain, soaking my hair, wetting my lashes, bathing my hands so my grip on my rifle felt slickened with lard. All I would have to do, I realized, to stop this sweat, this uncertainty, all these questions, was to fire into that corner. Either I would hit nobody, or I would shoot somebody who wanted to do me the same. Only—only maybe I'd shoot someone who only *wanted* to shoot me. Maybe they couldn't. Maybe they weren't armed.

I slid myself toward the unseen corner. I was so intent on that final dark quadrant I didn't even notice the wall until suddenly something was clawing my face—then I swung, hitting the wall so hard the stock of my rifle trembled and the whole house shook. When I calmed down enough to realize I'd gotten snagged on a nail—just a nail on a wall hooking a picture—I was so embarrassed I bent over to pick up the picture and hang it back. I thought I was seeing stars from the impact, but when I looked closer I realized not.

The wooden frame held neither painting nor photograph. The stars dancing before my eyes were the stars and bars of the Rebel flag.

I stared, astonished. Seeing that framed Confederate banner in the home of a civilian, something chosen by her to be part of her day, of her life, and knowing what stood behind it—those cannons, those mines, those endless rifles that had shot me three times, killed Tim's brother, slain my soldiers, destroyed my country—made me, for a moment, almost queasy with rage. That she should take comfort in a symbol of so much bloodshed! On the other hand . . .

On the other hand, the comfort she had taken had been in her own home. Which I was at this very second invading.

I unhooked the frame and skidded it into the fourth, last corner. I might not be ready to shoot an unseen civilian, but I wouldn't mind breaking his—or her—toes. But outside of a thud and a fresh handful of dustball, there was no reaction: the dark little room was completely empty. No threat at all.

So where was she? This Vincent-lady, where had she gone? My fingers brushed against the back door I'd expected to find, and I started to push it open. But something convinced me not to—some sound outside that really wasn't a sound at all, just a shift in the range of silence. I walked quietly across the room and out the door I had entered, and I moved around the side of the house and into a mud-splattered patch of turnips.

I couldn't spot Pete (what else was new?), but Charlie was clearly visible, bent over picking roots and sticking them into his shirt. His face bore the bland contentment of all happy gardeners; he might as well have been trimming petunias for the state fair. He was as oblivious to me as he was to the woman standing beneath a shaggy oak, taking unhurried aim at the back of his head with a musket as long as a crutch.

I walked up behind her and stuck my Colt into her neck.

"Please don't shoot him," I whispered. "I really don't want to deal with it."

Her head jerked and she opened her fingers; the musket fell to the ground. Charlie looked up, astream with turnips, and grunted in shock. I kicked him the musket.

"Christ, Charles," I said, "you're the original Trusty Sentinel. A few minutes more, you'd be learning if heaven's extending its quota on Union soldiers." I removed my Colt from the woman's neck.

"But—but—where'd she come from?" he asked.

I said "The house" at the same moment she said "*My* house"—an interesting distinction. "Who's Vincent?" I said. "Your husband? Your son?"

She said: "My dog."

Charlie was juggling a couple of turnips. Now he stashed them into a pocket to free his hands, which he put on his hips.

"Vincent!" he exclaimed. He didn't sound suspicious, the way I felt—he just sounded affronted. "Strange name for a dog," he said.

She said, "I didn't pick it for your admiration."

There were so many things here I just didn't like. Everything, in fact: this woman who aimed so calmly and spoke so haughtily; her home, bare as an icehouse in summer, and us with our mission to forage the state; this Vincent character. Was Vincent really only a dog with an unlikely name, or was it some kind of code? If so, to be heard by whom? *Had* they heard? Were Forrest's raiders this far east? Were Hardee's men this far west? What about Wheeler? What about Hood? Or was Vincent for real, and a Doberman? And where was Pete? I really wanted this over with.

"You seen Pete lately?" I asked.

Charlie wasn't even listening. Instead he said, "It just don't sound right, a dog named Vincent. Now when I was a kid, my dog's name was Freckles. On account of he had some. You had a dog, Nick? What'd you call him?"

"As a matter of fact," I snapped, "his name was Charlie."

Charlie gaped; the woman snorted. "That's your name, isn't it?" she said to him. "Well, it figures."

Just then Pete strolled out through the back door.

"Hey, what's going on?" he said to Charlie. "I thought you were inside."

"I thought *you* were out here," I said.

"Ain't nothing out here," he said. He noticed the woman. "Who's she? Another Union sympathizer?"

"Sympathizer!" the woman said. "You folks break into my house, frighten my dog, steal my turnips, and you ask for my sympathy? You're with that devil, aren't you? You're Sherman's men."

All of a sudden I felt giddy, almost wounded, with confusion and hunger. We'd started at dawn, we'd marched fifteen miles, we hadn't had dinner; we'd already encountered a pile of food that we hadn't taken. We were lost, mapless enemies wearing the wrong color uniform and with zero ideas what to do next.

"Take it easy, lady," I said. "We're not asking for sympathy, we're just asking for supper. Give us what you can spare and we're out of here. I promise."

"You've already got it," she said, and pointed at Charlie. "It's in his coat."

"Hey, don't look at me," he said, "I only took turnips."

"That's all there is," she said. She turned to me. "You ought to know. When you were rampaging around in there, you didn't ambush a ham or turkey, did you? Didn't shoot up a nice loaf of bread? Bucket of cider? No, of course not. There's no food here. Never was to begin with, 'spite what you people think, if you call what you do thinking. And with my husband dead and my son too probably, well . . . I've got turnips. Got some cherries too, but they're mostly worms. Sour. Tossed up all night. You're welcome to them."

Damn! Once again this wasn't working, and I couldn't say why not: whether it was the assignment itself, or my men, or these people, or me. Or maybe this was the kind of duty you didn't *want* to be able to carry out well.

"Charlie," I said wearily, "give her back the turnips."

"Hell, Nick!" exclaimed Pete.

"You heard me, Charlie. Do it."

"Nicholas, listen," Pete said urgently. "He gives her those turnips, she has more food than us. I mean, we at this moment have *nothing*!"

"I got one of Vincent's bones I suppose I could offer," she said. "But it's pretty chawed."

"Lady," I said, "are you really as poor as you say? And you might as well tell me the truth; we're not the only soldiers who'll find you, and they won't all be as patient as me when you pull that stunt with the musket. Are you really alone out here with nothing to eat?"

"Why should I tell you anything?"

"Because," I said, "if you really are starving, if it's really just you and your dog with nothing but turnips and cherries and it's already the middle of November, I'll have to—"

Pete and Charlie were listening with great curiosity.

"You'll have to . . . " she prompted. "If I'm really this poor and haven't just hidden all my syrup and eggs under the floorboards, you'll have to—"

I dug in my pocket and found a greenback. "Here. Take this."

Of course she said no. Could've predicted it. *Should* have. "Please," I said.

"I don't want it," she said.

"Take it anyway," I said. "You can—you can buy Vincent something with it. A blanket."

"He's got a blanket."

"Get him another one."

"Can't. He'll have more blankets than me."

"Jesus Christ!" I grabbed her right hand, slammed the note on her palm, and curled her fingers around it. Then I scooped up her musket. "Here," I said, "you sold me this."

"I'll starve without that," she said. "It's a hunting rifle."

"She's got you there, Nick," Pete said.

"She nearly got *me* here," Charlie said, patting his neck. "She tried to kill me," he said to Pete.

"So why's Nick paying her off?"

Nick didn't know why he was paying her off, Nick at this moment didn't know anything; self-knowledge had fled from his brain like hares from a fox. All he knew was at that moment he'd be willing to fight another four years if he could get him a guarantee the only Southerners he'd have to encounter from here on out would be back on the battlefield, where they belonged.

We stood there, all of us, several stalemated seconds. Behind me I could hear a faint rumble as Charlie dribbled turnips out of his jacket. Her fingers, tightening further into the fist I had forced them in, squashed the dollar into a tiny ball. When she finally stopped squeezing, I was ready for her to do something dramatic: throw the money into my face, toss it over her shoulder, even cram it into her mouth; but I wasn't prepared for her simply to extend her arm and open her hand and offer me the money back. I took it, and it felt so much like a transaction, so like I was being paid for something and had to give something back, that I gave her the only thing I could spare. I gave her her musket.

"Just don't use it on anything blue," I said. "Try sticking to wildlife."

"I'll stick to whatever's a threat," she said. And that was that.

Only not quite: as we trudged away, sharing a turnip (Charlie having observed with his usual zeal the private's first commandment, freedom of interpretation), we heard a rustle in the bushes ahead of us. Before we had time to do much except fall to the ground—Charlie and me—or fumble for weapons—Pete—a cat sped past, jumping through hedges and wild roses as he raced to the tiny, turnip-bestrewn garden. I watched as the woman leaned down and gave the animal a pat on the head.

"Vincent," she muttered. "My baby. My sweet kitty."

I couldn't believe it. I couldn't believe *her.* Civilians! Even when it didn't help them, they lied.

I don't know how long we marched after that. Charlie was afire; if Vincent was a surprising name for a dog, it was an absolute twitcher for a cat, and he couldn't drop it, no matter how much I wished he'd try. Then he began describing what I'd looked like with my gun at that woman's neck—"Here's Nick looking more jumpy than *she's* looking"—and Pete started mumbling how maybe next time we went foraging we ought to have a little bit more of a plan.

"Hell, yes," I said, "next time we'll only go places we've got invitations."

"Don't be so touchy," said Pete, "I only meant, you know—"

"Take it easy, fellas," said Charlie. "We're all just tired."

"Oh, *I'm* not tired," said Pete. "I *love* wandering around since before nightfall with a commander who's so obviously in command. I'm completely confident Nick's only been fooling around and any second now he'll be finding food for fifty people in the middle of an occupied country in the middle of the night and getting it back to camp in time for us to get some sleep before we go through all this again tomorrow. I'm not tired at all. Just curious.''

We were approaching another road. This one ran parallel to a rocky stream, and beyond the tangle of bushes and stones we could make out a house with cirrusing smoke from a double chimney. Somebody somewhere must have opened a window, for as we stood there watching, a clock in the house struck midnight.

Midnight! We looked at each other with rolling eyes. We'd been wandering around nearly seven hours—seven hours, for one goddamn turnip. I couldn't tell if the idea was really my own or whether my mind was just echoing Pete's voice, but I finally decided: enough was enough. No more. No more sneaking around, no more requests, no more mistakes. No more presents; no more standoffs. We were going in armed, and we weren't going out empty-handed.

We marched, three abreast, to the front door. There was a massive brass knocker in the shape of a swan, and Charlie was about to drop it against the wood when I lifted my rifle and pounded it into the door. The resulting boom was gratifying: it sounded like noise from a real war.

Footsteps moved toward the door, and a girl called, "Who is it?" She sounded wary and sleepy at the same time. I rammed the door once again.

"Union soldiers!" I yelled. "Open up! Now!"

She opened the door. She was black, short, expressionless, and about twelve years old, her face and body a shifting fusion of child- and womanhood, the same as my brother's daughter the last time I'd seen her. I shuddered: the sudden thought of my wide-eyed niece being sent by herself to confront soldiers at midnight with nothing to protect her but a wax-choked candle-stick sickened me.

I said, "Don't be afraid, miss. Where's whoever's in charge?"
She didn't answer.

"You're not here alone, are you?" I asked.

She still didn't answer.

"Look, miss," I said, "you can trust me. We've already seen smoke from two chimneys. Where we come from, that means more than one person's home."

"And where *we* come from," said an older voice, female, from behind the door, "we don't call the servants 'miss.' " She spoke with the calm asperity of a spelling-bee judge.

"Well, where *we* come from," I said, "we don't call the slaves the servants." I nodded to Charlie and Pete. "Come on, we're going in."

And it was as easy as that. The woman who emerged from behind the door was white, and if she and her slave were not the only two souls in the house, we never did meet any others. Not that we looked very hard: I asked right away to be shown the kitchen and pantry and garden, and having seen each I at once . lost all interest in anything else. It seemed there wasn't a lot of food and there wasn't that little either. I asked the woman to make me and my men something this very instant, and she turned to the girl and repeated my order, word for word, even using my intonations rather than her own.

The girl moved from cupboard to stove to table with the speed of a dervish, and in only a minute or two presented me with a plate of sandwiches. I took one, passed the others to Pete and Charlie, and thanked her.

"Oh, you're *very* welcome," the woman snapped.

I took a nibble. It was chicken—actual, real chicken, not canned, not spoiled, not raw, not burnt, not adulterated with sawdust and gravel and handfuls of salt. It tasted like a miracle, that chicken—as fresh as the Fourth of July, as tender as peace. She also handed us each an apple and a glass of milk. We took all of thirty seconds to consume the whole meal.

After that we fell into a pattern; I gave the woman an order and she repeated it to the girl, and the girl did whatever I asked; then I'd thank her and the woman would icily say, "You're very welcome." I figured for fifty men who'd been waiting since sunset for supper we needed twelve loaves of bread, two dozen hens, and as much sugar and coffee and salt as we could carry. I wished we could take some eggs too but suspected they wouldn't survive the journey all the way to the front door.

"Some of that honey, too, please," I said. "And some of those cookies and some of that tea."

As I named foods and amounts, I wrote everything down on a scrap of paper, and when it was all neatly tucked into burlap bags, I handed the woman the list. I don't know why; partly it seemed more legal that way and partly it seemed more threatening.

Then we all stood and looked at each other. I wanted to say something to the girl but had absolutely no idea what: part of me wanted to tell her to just walk out of there, part of me figured she had enough people telling her what to do. And part of me couldn't decide which was better for her, staying here, where the rules were manifold but at least known, or joining us, where the rules were being made as we went along and where it didn't feel all that safe even to me, let alone to a woman, let alone to a girl, let alone to a black girl. Eventually she left the kitchen to resume her post by the front door, and we walked past her, laden with yeasty, sweet-smelling booty packed as if for a gigantic picnic, without saying anything at all.

CHAPTER
SEVEN

HOWELL COBB was one of the earliest and most ardent of Southern Confederates. It was his open letter to the people of Georgia that galvanized her secession. It was at his express suggestion that Andersonville prison was established. We reached Cobb's plantation on Tuesday. It was day six of the March.

I'd gotten a little smarter by then. I no longer marched with only two people, for one thing, and I no longer marched at night for another, and most important I no longer marched with no idea where I was going. When I went foraging now, I took at least two dozen men, plus horses, wagons, maps, and a compass. And like anything new, after awhile it stopped feeling new at all. It just felt normal.

Better than normal, in fact. Those first six days of the March were like six birthdays in a row, or six Christmases, six Fourths of July. It was like being on a mammoth pleasure excursion—a party with no adults. We ate when we wanted. We slept when we felt like it. If we wanted to get away from the main sweep of the army, we did—as long as you caught up before nightfall, nobody cared where you'd caught up from, or what you'd been doing. It was understood that if you took food, either you took enough for your men or you took nothing at all. It became a point of honor always to bring back something.

One time, instead of dinner we requisitioned flowers. We climbed over a back fence into a garden, spared the turkeys, ignored the pumpkins, turned our backs on the pigs and chickens and eggs; instead we grabbed armfuls of dahlias and wild roses. We wove the dahlias into wreaths and stuck the roses into the mouths of our rifles, and when we came back to camp that evening we trailed bees for forty-five minutes. We trailed bees another time too, when we ventured into an apiary. In Madison a sergeant in Company D broke into a dry-goods shop and stole their dressmaker's dummy, whom he christened Lily and outfitted daily with fresh hats, brooches, and gloves.

We were proud of ourselves. We were living off the land, foraging liberally, carrying out the letter and spirit of Special Order Number 120, and it was turning out to be neither difficult nor dangerous nor especially hard on the conscience. For the first time since the start of the war, I could feel the string loosen; for one whole week, I woke up reasonably sure I would remain unshot until sundown. The General, I most strongly believed, was strategically, tactically, and whatever else you might care to call it, a genius.

Then we arrived at Cobb's plantation. And afterward Georgia didn't stand a chance. Not a chance.

"This is incredible," Charlie said, as we passed the wide, open drive curving up to the house. "It's the size of a palace. I've never even seen churches this big."

"I bet my whole hometown," Pete declared, "has less rooms than this."

Charlie said, "I bet Tim's whole *county's* got less rooms than this!"

Tim Rice, my reluctant forager, didn't respond—just turned

his opaque blinded eye, first on the house, then right to the sun:
the heat, he'd once told me, felt good on the socket. The rest of
us kept right on staring. All around me I could hear murmurs of
surprise and startled appreciation. The size of the house; its
quiet, its beauty. The perfection of its proportions, its echoes of
ancient glory. Its nimbus, in the middle of all this chaos, of
flawless, shimmering grace.

The entire Cobb household had obviously departed—recently, probably, and in some haste, for we could hear the neigh-
ing of all the horses they'd had to abandon, and the barking of
dozens of dogs still caged in a long double kennel on the side of
the house. Small groups of slaves—ex-slaves, really—were mill-
ing about, some on the porch of the house, some on the curve of
the road or beside the well. A larger circle stood near one of the
fenced-off fields. They seemed to be holding some kind of meet-
ing—I could hear that special way voices murmur when opinions
are many and varied—but as soon as one of them noticed me
watching, the whole group fell silent.

"C'mon, Tim," I said. "Let's go for a little stroll." I began
walking, Tim trailing behind. We started toward the knot of
people standing beside the fence.

It was then that I noticed the gates. They all were locked from
the inside—the field side—which seemed utterly weird, as if the
intention were to lock people out, not in. And all were locked
with extraordinarily complicated devices, bulky assemblages of
metal and wood and string looped into configurations I'd never
encountered, not even on ships. On the other hand, the fences
themselves were only about four feet tall.

We stopped to inspect one of the massive knots. Tim said, "I
used to make knots like this. It's to keep in the cows."

The *cows*? I rattled the lock. The whole arrangement seemed
freakishly inefficient—even supposing you needed a key or scissors to spring the lock, what was to prevent somebody from
vaulting a fence only four feet high? Vault it, hell—what was to
prevent anyone from just *climbing* over?

I checked behind us, back to the line of soldiers, to see
if anyone was watching us. Some were—Pete was, Charlie

wasn't—but most had already drifted off the main road and were approaching the house. Tim and I proceeded along the fence line. A black woman, maybe about forty, separated herself from the group of slaves and walked up to join us.

"Good morning," I said to her. I gestured to the gates, to the locks, to the fields, to the house. "What's going on here?"

She stared right into my face, then swiveled her head toward Tim. The first eyes she encountered—mine—left her impassive, but when she encountered the netted tissue of Tim's dead iris, her own eyes softened. Or maybe not—almost immediately she shrugged her shoulders and looked toward the ground.

"I asked you to please tell me what's going on here," I said.

She said: "Nothing's going on here."

"That can't be exactly true," I said. "Surely you're not in the habit of receiving General Sherman's army every day of the year."

I thought for a second I noticed a sneer—just a flicker of swift contempt. But her voice held no sneer at all when she said, politely, "Oh, we receive lots of folks here. Family friends and army friends. Mr. Cobb—he's a general."

I said, watching her carefully, "Mr. Cobb—he's an idiot."

This drew no reaction whatever, except from Tim, who said, "Oh, hell, Nick, you think they're all idiots. Ours too."

"Where *are* the Cobbs this bright November morning, anyway?" I asked her. "I notice they haven't exactly come out to greet us."

She said, "I wouldn't know. Now if you'll excuse me, I've got things that need doing. . . ."

"What things? What could you possibly still need to do?"

She didn't answer. I felt frustration and confusion—that dreamlike sense, so common in wartime, of not understanding, not even *beginning* to understand—wash over me.

"Look, what's your name?" I demanded.

"Alice." A total lack on her part of desire to ask the obvious next question—"What's *your* name?"—and a complete resignation to continue with the interrogation. Now I realized she was older than I first thought—almost my mother's age. I couldn't imagine my mother giving a stranger her first name only.

"Alice what?" I said.

"Alice Cobb," she said.

Tim whinnied with surprise. "Alice *Cobb!*" he exclaimed. "Alice *Cobb!* Nick, how about that!"

She nodded. "That's right. Before, I was Linda. Linda Kennedy."

Tim stared at her, baffled. "How come you changed?" he asked.

"The usual. They already had a Linda. And Mr. Kennedy, of course he didn't care. This way he could use the whole name again."

"Very wise," I said. "Saves wear and tear on the memory. Saves on ink too."

It was meant to be sarcasm, but of course it faltered: Tim didn't recognize sarcasm, and Alice didn't either, or if she did she had schooled herself carefully against acknowledging it.

"Alice," I said. She looked back at me, with that same perfect deference. "Alice, exactly what do you think's happening here? I'm a Yankee soldier—a captain in the Union army. You hear what I'm saying?"

"Oh, I hear," she said.

"Well, pardon me for sounding like a goddamn fool," I said, "but aren't you even a tiny bit pleased? You know what our being here means, don't you?"

She was silent. And so, not only *sounding* like a goddamn fool but feeling like one as well, and using a phrase I never thought I'd be using and therefore had never realized until it came out how pompous it'd sound, and how paternal, and how theatrical, and how moronic, I said:

"Alice, you're free."

She looked out at the field and along the line of the road and up to that beautiful house. She looked at the locks on the gates. She said, "Well, that's fine. But I'm happy here."

Then Tim, whom I'd never heard raise his voice, even when

the bullet went through his eyeball, screamed, "Well, Jesus Christ!" And it wasn't blasphemy—it was a prayer. "Jesus Christ! Then what the hell are we doing here?"

"Couldn't tell you," said Alice, "you'd have to—"

She was gazing calmly at his flushing face, then she glanced at his boots. She frowned. She looked up, then at his boots again. She looked at me. I watched her eyes—*felt* them observing my legs in their faded blue uniform; *felt* her follow my muddy left foot as I kicked at an itching blister on my booted right ankle. Felt them look back and remember other shoes, other feet, other legs. Felt her connect.

She pushed back her hair.

"There's not a Confederate ranked lower than general," she announced, "who's still wearing boots." She stuck out a hand.

"Welcome to Georgia, Captain," she said.

In real life (prewar) (they're already talking about prewar vintages, why not a prewar life?), in real life I'm a professional draughtsman. My speciality's medical, but I can draw anything: I've sketched brides and babies and trees and gardens; I've diagrammed ships and bridges; there was even a stretch where I drafted tombstones—where to put the name and date, where to stick the inscription. Occasionally I've even prepared etchings for illustrated versions of the classics. Once I did part of *The Divine Comedy*. I started to read it—I always tried reading what I was drawing, to get some idea what was supposed to be going on—but I couldn't understand it, and eventually the editor just told me the story. He said in the section I was preparing, the poet Virgil was giving Dante a guided tour of Hell.

I got Alice instead.

The moment she shook my hand, the rest of the slaves in her little circle had resumed talking; now they were scattering, some toward the house, some toward my soldiers, others along the drive or beside the fence. Alice, nodding her head to both of us—hello and good-bye—started to join them; in fact she already had when she noticed Tim, who had absentmindedly wandered over to one of those odd knots. She watched him reach over the gate and begin fingering it. Then she walked back to join us.

"I've watched that knot being tied every morning," she told him, "and untied every night. I bet I know that knot better than you know your own mother. I've dreamt about it so often I see it when I'm not even looking."

Slowly the knot unraveled. Tim said, "My mother's passed. But I know what you mean."

She said, rather coolly, "Do you."

He said, "I keep seeing my brother getting shot out of the eye I can't see out of."

I stared at him. I never knew that. I felt, suddenly, horribly guilty and responsible, even though to the best of my knowledge both he and his brother were doing exactly the opposite of what I'd ordered when they'd been hit. Alice, on the other hand, seemed quite unmoved.

"It's not the same thing," she said, Tim's fingers decoding the knot. "You're picturing something that happened. I've been picturing something that *wasn't* happening."

"Alice," I said, "is it all right if I ask you a question?"

"You've done nothing but," she said.

I blinked, then asked anyway, patting the grainy pine of one of the fence's four-foot-high logs. "Why didn't you just jump?" I said.

"Jump what?"

"The fence. It's not high. Why didn't you just take a little running start and sail on over?"

"What for?"

"Well . . ." I floundered, "to be free."

"I wouldn't be free. I wouldn't even be dead. Oh, I did my share of fence jumping, Captain, back with the Kennedys. They had this same setup, where you're locked in but it's real easy to get out. It's so they can identify the leapers."

"The leapers?"

"Folks who still got enough bounce to jump. There's really only one way for them to tell, and you always end up telling them yourself. So: you leap. Then they know, and they go after you, and you run, and they run—well, they've got dogs, they've got lights, they've got guns, and let's face it, they're a lot healthier. They run you down. They don't kill you when they catch you, because what's the point of killing something you paid good money for? They just fix it so you'll probably think twice before trying again."

She lifted her skirt to her knee. A scar ran up her right calf. She said:

"I ran away twice from the Kennedy place. The first time they just beat me, which wasn't too different from what happened a lot anyway—at least that time I knew what it was for. Usually they'd whip you and about five days later you'd figure out why— you'd served coffee when they claimed it was tea they'd asked for, or you'd laid out somebody's cape when really they'd wanted their shawl; or you'd laid out somebody's light pink shawl when they were expecting the dark pink one. Or maybe you just didn't look happy enough. They were real big on you looking happy at the Kennedys'."

She gave me a wide, dead-eyed smile full of teeth. "Like this," she said. She dropped her skirt.

"The second time I tried it they broke my leg. Long as it's splinted, you still can make coffee, and it turns out you still can do plenty of other things too. When it healed in about three months, why, they broke it again."

Tim had finally stopped fiddling with that damned knot. Alice said:

"That was a bad time. Not just them breaking it but sitting there waiting for them to get around to it. They sat me down on a bench and told me what they intended to do and had me lay out my leg. Then they—the field overseer and one of the Kennedy boys—they started in rolling tobacco and downing a few drinks. Then they fell into conversation about some white girl and they even asked me if I thought she was pretty. And after about an hour or so one of them picks up my leg like it's some-thing left lying around and he guesses he'd better do something with it before somebody trips on it and hurts himself. And he just takes it and breaks it over his knee. Just snaps it apart. And then he starts cursing, because he'd given himself a bruise doing the breaking.''

She suddenly reached out and gave the knot one last tug. It fell loose. Quietly she reached over the gate and without any fuss pushed it, from the inside, wide open. She didn't look pleased or triumphant doing it. She didn't look anything.

"Come along if you want," she said, "I'll show you around."

She started up the road toward the house, Tim and I trailing along. A few slaves, half a dozen at most, joined us. There were a couple of murmured "thank-you's" and "bless-you's" and a little weeping, but really not much: the general feeling seemed to be, what took you so long? I was surprised; I'd expected jubilation or, at the very least, a strong indication of gratitude. But since so much of what I said to Alice seemed to be either wrong or insulting, I said nothing.

Not Tim. He said, "I'd've thought people would act a little more happy, seeing us."

"They're sick of acting happy," said Alice.

"I didn't mean act," he said, "I meant, *be* a little happy."

"Oh, they are. That's exactly what they are—a little happy."

Tim shot me a she-still-doesn't-understand look and started again. "But isn't this what you've been waiting for?" he asked. "Sherman? Emancipation? The Yankee army?"

Alice kept walking. "It was for a while," she said. "We got pretty worked up when we heard you were here in Georgia. But then nothing happened. Then we heard about Atlanta, but still nothing happened. Then we heard you were marching this way, and we figured something would *have* to happen, and it did."

She veered off a little to the right; we followed.

"One morning last week," she continued, "a whole troop of men rides up. Real pretty, all in blue—matched your eyes, Captain. A bunch of us run out to meet them. Turns out they're Wheeler's cavalry—Rebel cavalry. Guess they'd killed enough of you boys to deck themselves out. They start whipping and beating and running their horses through us—right *through* us. Told us the whole Yankee army had sunk in a swamp outside Atlanta and the war was over."

Tim said, "You believed that? That's crazy! There's no swamps outside Atlanta! Now Vicksburg—Vicksburg's got swamps. Nick, you remember—"

Alice smiled at him. It was the first time I'd seen her really smile, and I wondered how come it looked so familiar; then I realized it was the same way I smiled at Tim—protective and exasperated. "It's too bad we didn't have you here," she told him, "to set us straight."

It's too bad you didn't have me either, I felt like saying; her "You came into Georgia and nothing happened," I've got to admit, riled me. It didn't exactly line up with my recollections— the fog-banked horrors of Missionary Ridge; our every-mistake-you-can-make frontal assault at Kenesaw Mountain; the endless, debilitating boredom of besieging Atlanta, and its bloody, final chaotic fall. *Something* had happened before we'd gotten to Cobb's plantation; it just hadn't happened to her.

I started to point this out—to argue our path to her life hadn't been slow on purpose, or because nobody cared; that it had been arduous, hourly, daily bedeviled by loss, bestrewn with lungs, intestines, kneecaps, and befouled with blood. I'd managed to open my mouth to offer this little speech when Alice said: "Here's where my daughter died."

We were passing beneath a tree, a beautiful, spreading cedar, glossily green. "At least," said Alice, "I believe she was my daughter."

"You believe," Tim repeated. "How could you not know?"

"I was sick for my first three babies," Alice replied, "and they all died. So when I had the next one they gave her to somebody else to nurse. Then I got sold and wound up here, and later on she showed up and she was from Mr. Kennedy's too, and she'd been told to look me up—that Mr. Kennedy had sold Mr. Cobb a woman who might be her mother. So maybe she was and maybe she wasn't. We both liked to think she was."

"Did she look like you?" Tim asked. "I mean—that'd help you know, wouldn't it?"

"Nobody ever thinks anyone looks like them," Alice said, "least of all children. She looked like an angel to me, and I sure don't look like an angel, so maybe she wasn't. When she died I worked hard to pretend she wasn't and that turned out to be hard as pretending she was. So there you are."

"How did she die?" I asked. I knew I would hate the answer, whatever it turned out to be, but it seemed like the only thing I could possibly say.

"An accident," said Alice. "It's always an accident. Lucille—that was the name she had when she got here, so that's what I called her—Lucille was standing under the cedar, because Mr. Nash, the overseer, was talking at her and he liked to stand in the shade when he talked. Anyway, this man on a horse comes dashing up the front drive here, and Lucille kind of gives a start, and Mr. Nash tells her, 'Stand still when I'm talking to you.' And she did. Not because she was so taken with what Mr. Nash was telling her but because that was about the first time she'd stood in shade all summer, and I guess it felt so good she didn't feel like moving. So she just stood there and let that horse charge right into her. Even Mr. Nash jumped but Lucille just kept her ground and let it happen."

Tim said: "Oh! You mean she committed—"

Alice said, "The horse lamed himself hitting her. They had to shoot it, because it was taking longer to die than Lucille did."

By now we had passed the tree and were approaching the house. Alice said, "You know, I've never seen this place straight on like this. When I came it was nighttime and we rode in along the side. There was me and four other women from Mr. Kennedy, and two men from down the road someplace, and six babies from somebody else. Those babies just wouldn't stop crying. Finally one of the drivers pulled over and he stuffed handkerchiefs into their mouths."

"You're not supposed to do that!" said Tim. "My sister's got twins and she says you just have to let them cry. Stick stuff in their mouths and they're likely to choke, she says."

"She's right," Alice said.

"Alice," I said.

"You want me to shut up," she said.

"No, but—" I didn't know what I wanted. I didn't want her

not to talk, but I wanted what she said not to be true. I knew about slavery: in fact, I thought I knew all about it—I'd seen a production of *Uncle Tom's Cabin,* and when I was passing through Boston, I'd picked up a copy of *The Liberator.* I was convinced it was evil, but I'd always thought it dramatic evil—violent atrocity, biblical villainy. Not this scroll of capricious cruelty, of mistakenly strangled children and cordially broken legs. Not these day-to-day morsels of casual torture. I said, pointing to the house, "You ever been inside?"

"No. I was an inside at the Kennedys' till the first time I tried escaping. But I was always an outside here."

"Want to now?"

"Not especially."

By now dozens of former slaves were passing in and out of the front door. One woman was wearing a brocade scarf, a man was carrying a clock; everyone else was taking food—honey, molasses, salt.

"Where're the Cobbs through all this?" I asked.

"Oh, Mr. Cobb's off somewhere warring. The ladies and children, they refugeed."

"Refugeed?" It was the first time I'd heard the word used as a verb.

"Took off for greener pastures. Least, less blue. I understand they told the housefolk to keep an eye on things till they got back." I thought I saw the outer glimmer of a smile.

"What do you intend doing now?"

Before she could answer, Tim said, "You can come with us! Lots of you are. There must be, what?—at least four thousand since Atlanta alone. You could join us and, like Nick here says, help make history."

"No, thanks," said Alice. "Whatever making history means, I aim doing the exact opposite. I've got one thing more I need to do here and then I'm lighting out on my own."

By now we had slipped past the front of the house, which was no longer being entered and left by black faces only. For as more and more Alices spoke to more and more soldiers, and word naturally spread of whose home this was, the lighthearted martial discipline of our first six days swiftly melted away. Nor did the presence of so much money and beauty do much to stop the process. The opposite, in fact: the existence of all that expensive loveliness in the middle of all this cruelty seemed to give instant and automatic permission to keep pushing further. This was looting, all right, but *justified* looting. This was a step beyond.

I understood that when a group of my men walked by, carrying a skillet of still-smoking pancakes. Instead of eating the hotcakes or rushing them back to our mess, or even just leaving them out so if they didn't eat them somebody else could, they were picking the pancakes up by their crispy edges, holding them to the sunlight, frowning like critical jewelers, then carefully hammering each pancake into the doors. I gawked: all that exquisitely polished and beveled wood, each section fractured by a hoecake and a five-inch nail. But I didn't stop them.

Alice said, "A friend of mine got beat for eating a pancake that'd been left out for the birds. They beat him so bad they accidentally broke something and he couldn't stand up straight. So they gave him some opium so he could, and quick sold him to somebody out of state."

Her stories were wearing me raw. "Must've been a real surprise," I said, "when it wore off."

"Yeah, for both," she agreed. "Master gets a field hand who can't walk. That must've been a surprise. Slave gets a taste of opium, which from what I understand is about as close to Heaven as a black man gets in this world."

We passed another cedar—taller but less wide around, and invisible from the front of the house. "That's where they whip you when it's hot and they don't feel like walking all the way into the woods," Alice said. "Though it generally puts them into a real mood, because Mrs. Cobb scolds about whipping so close to the house where somebody might get hurt."

On a nearby bench was a heavy horse blanket and a coil of rope. I imagined the rope was to bind with, but the blanket really threw me. I asked Alice; she shook her head.

"Nah, that's not what any of that's for. They never tie you

around a tree; that's too dangerous. They tie your arms up in the air, to a bough, so they don't accidentally break your spine. That blanket and rope, they're for the tree. They don't want the bark all scarred."

"You must hate the holy hell out of these people," I said softly. "There must be no curse you haven't put on them."

"From what we keep hearing," Alice said, "*you're* their curse."

Tim, to my surprise, said, "I hope so."

By now we were nearly around the back of the house. "I'm not what you'd call *fond* of them," Alice continued, "but no, I don't hate them. Hate drains you, I've noticed, and I sure don't need any help there. But there's one thing I want to do that'll go a long way toward filling me up. You can stay if you want but I'd just as soon you leave."

Put that way, of course, I decided to stay. As soon as we turned the corner, I saw all those kennels I'd noticed earlier—cages that as Alice had kept talking I'd begun to imagine were slave quarters, and was now relieved to discover were kennels after all. They were filled with hunting dogs whose Latin nomenclature I'd long since forgotten, although I still remembered what their lungs and arteries looked like and how perfect and clever the grip of their jaws.

"Pick me a dog," she said to Tim.

He looked at me. I didn't want to protest; I figured this was her version of foraging liberally, and in a world where soldiers were stealing corsets and crucifying pancakes, a female slave planning a life on her own would do well to travel with a dog at her side.

"Go ahead," I told Tim. "Do it."

"Why should I?" he protested. "I don't want a dog. Wouldn't be fair, making a dog march like we do."

"Just *pick* one," said Alice.

Tim was getting that mulish look that was his way of saying what Pete so often said, only more loudly—he didn't get it, he didn't like it, and he wasn't about to do it. I shrugged and pointed at random to a tawny bloodhound.

"He chooses that one," I said.

"Can't say I recognize him," Alice said, "but he'll do."

She glanced at me. Then she deliberately walked over to Tim's right side—his blind side. His left eye was fixed straight ahead, bleakly observing the dog he didn't want but, for obscure reasons of Abolition, Disunion, and Emancipation, somehow was getting stuck with. Suddenly she lunged, grabbing his brother's prized Colt-Root repeater out of his right hand. He tried snatching it back, but he couldn't quite see her.

And I, who could see her perfectly, what did I do? At first I fumbled for my revolver, but what was I going to do, shoot her? So I jammed it back into my belt.

"Don't do anything stupid, Alice," I said.

She lifted Tim's rifle, released the hammer, aimed, and fired. The bloodhound exploded.

Shooting cues people as well as kills them; as soon as the shots went off, I could hear shouting and running. Alice meanwhile kept firing, five more bullets from a rifle that kicked so badly, by the time she ran out of bullets I could see from the hang of her hand she'd injured her wrist. A half dozen hounds lay dead or dying. Twenty or so soldiers burst into the yard, some from around the side, others from inside the house. At least that many slaves ran close behind them. When they saw the dogs, the soldiers grew silent and the slaves applauded.

"What's with the shooting?" asked Pete.

"I tripped," I said. "You know—shoddy equipment. Rifle went off."

"Six times?"

Alice stepped forward, rubbing her wrist. "Nobody tripped," she said. "I shot those dogs. Give me another gun and I'll shoot six more."

Pete looked baffled. "What for?"

"I can't even remember," said Alice, "how many mornings began with seeing a friend lying out in the yard with a dog mouth around his leg. They'd just leave them like that, on the ground—us passing by and them watching us and us watching them. And the dog waiting for someone to tell him to let go."

"Maybe it would've made more sense," said Pete "to shoot the owner."

"Might have," said Alice, "but I didn't have a rifle till just now."

"Speaking of which, Alice . . ." said Tim. She handed it back.

I knew what was going to happen next, and I didn't do anything to stop it. And it did happen: as soon as Tim reloaded and began firing, every soldier in that yard started shooting. They—we—didn't stop until over a hundred dogs were dead.

And we didn't stop there either; we killed every dog we came across for the rest of the March. And we razed Cobb's plantation. And we freed every slave. And we burnt every stalk of corn and every fence rail and every barrel, and we wetted the ashes and scattered them into the fields. And the war went back to being a war again.

CHAPTER
EIGHT

IT WAS probably ten days into the March that I recognized I was frightened. Terribly frightened, in fact, and had been ever since we had left Cobb's plantation. And the more destruction we wrought, the worse it got. Not fear of the enemy, or fear of death. Fear of . . . It was like being strapped as a child into a carousel. You were supposed to be safe, protected, assured, having a good time; but instead all you could think of was this endless, entangled circling. I felt entangled now: this March, this South, this war, history. History could not possibly let the South get away with slavery; history would not possibly let us get away with what we were doing to the South. Somehow or other, we'd both have to pay.

That evening I got the order I'd been both expecting and dreading. We were to march down the flank of the wing to take our position at the back of XIV Corps.

I hated the rear. I'd hated it when I'd been wounded and sent there for patching, and I hated it even more now. I hated its chaos, its forced inertia, its sense of always just missing the genuine action. I hated the rutted roads it inevitably inherited. I hated its late-morning starts and concomitant last beddings. I hated its garbage; I hated its duties; I hated its taps. I hated being in the position of always having to catch up on shots somebody else was calling.

And of course, in my present mood, I hated it because it felt so exposed. I was positive out there somewhere . . . *there* . . . just beyond our field of vision . . . armed bushwhackers stood in polished silence, gauging our every move.

I volunteered for guard duty. It seemed pointless not to: I felt too tense to sleep, and surely I'd find more solace in watching than imagining being watched. At midnight Tim came by to spell me. I told him to go back to sleep. He protested, I insisted, and we argued back and forth in whispers that seemed to me ungodly loud. Finally, unwilling to tell him the truth—that I was just too jumpy to entrust my safety or anyone else's to anyone but myself (a mangled position combining the sprightliest altruism with a particularly loathsome species of cowardice)—I allowed he could stay, but I would stay too. Given that kind of skewed permission, he took his position and soon fell asleep.

For over an hour I sat there bathed in Tim's soft, steady breathing. But not even that relaxed me. In fact, the opposite: Tim and Charlie, even Pete, seemed inexpressibly precious— sweet, defenseless, innocent, and doomed.

The night progressed, growing colder and colder, with that bone-nipping chill Georgia autumns still managed to startle me with. The Sunny South indeed. It was at least fifty yards to the next guard, which seemed to me far too great a distance; for all I knew the man was asleep, or for that matter, dead, and calling to find out which would cause just the racket I didn't want to make. As the minutes tapped on, I strained to discern some sign of life from any of the guards strung along the perimeter. A cough, a flickering match, a curse, a belch—anything would be acceptable. Anything that could convince me that with the exception of me and the still-asleep Tim, the entire line of pickets had not had its collective throat slashed.

I touched my own throat. Everything seemed intact. The muscles were where they had started off. My fingers didn't come away covered with blood.

I stared off into the darkness. I'd always believed I'd survive this war. I still so believed. But I was starting to realize I wouldn't go out the same person I had gone in as, and this bothered me—in fact, it goddamn depressed me, right down to the ground. So much of war is just making acquaintance—first getting the names straight, then the families, then the fears, habits, terrors, and dreams. Then they get sick, killed, transferred, or promoted, and you have to start in with a new batch. And it's easy work and relatively brainless, and it keeps you from worrying, and you can repeat it indefinitely as long as you don't lose track of your own stories, your own feelings.

Which I was beginning to. Lose track, I mean. I felt opaque, on edge, undependable. And I missed Nick Whiteman. Christ knows he wasn't much, but I'd always felt I could count on him for at least one thing—he'd never surprise me.

The night deepened, and a breeze started in; it freshened soon into real wind, and the woods seemed to come alive. I remembered reading how early this spring, when Grant had chased Lee through the Wilderness brambles, the forests had somehow ignited, trapping thousands of wounded and roasting them whole. Now I heard clicks and murmurs and snapping branches in the woods that stretched out before me in one vast black shadow all the way back to Atlanta. Was it fire, was it footsteps, was it just the natural order? Or was the South finally so desperate she'd commit on herself any small tortures we'd missed?

I stood up. Leaves flitted past my face like moths chasing a light. The trees moved and moaned. The air was a palette of black chalk.

Shoes crunched. I froze. I tried to remind myself it wasn't unusual, footsteps in camp—people always wandered around a lot, and besides I wasn't sure if these really were footsteps anyway, or—

Somebody touched my shoulder and a hand covered my mouth. The voice in my ear was so steady and quiet it gave the impression of coming out of my own head.

"Captain Whiteman. Don't make a sound. Have someone relieve you and come this second."

I don't know which acted sooner, my mind or my body. My heart heaved into my ribs, my arms both jerked, one toward my gun, one to shake myself free. At the same time the touch of a hand on my mouth in that mud of darkness was so unexpected, so completely unanticipated, my first reaction was that it wasn't even a human hand—that it was the paw of some swamp- or forest-bred monster, emerged from the night to cripple and murder. My second thought was, who—human or monster—would address me by name before doing me in?

"Who is this?" I whispered.

"Bert. Bert Morris. You don't know me. You also outrank me but I got orders. Wake up this kid and let's go."

I removed his hand from my face. Bert Morris. Actually I did know him; he was in fact one of the leading legends of XIV Corps. Suicidally heroic, homicidally effective . . . I'd always been happy we'd never met.

"Orders from who?" I asked.

"Nichols," he said. "Sherman's aide. Move it. This is official."

I leaned down to Tim. He awoke with a startled cry.

"Shut him up!" Bert hissed.

I mumbled to Tim to take my place. He nodded sleepily. "You able to stay awake?" I asked. "I can find Charlie—"

"There's no time to find somebody else," Bert snapped. "Come on!"

He tugged me up and we began walking.

We walked for at least ten minutes, until we had reached the edge of the picket line. I heard the rush of a stone-bed stream; I had drunk from it earlier, when this outstretched night was still yesterday afternoon. I watched Bert manuever through the darkness. He was younger than I had imagined him—younger than Charlie, maybe even younger than Tim. I stumbled over a root. Maybe you had to be young to be any good at this.

"So what's going on?" I asked.

"Keep walking," he said, "there'll be light in a couple of minutes."

"I asked you a question. Don't make me pull rank."

"You'll see in a second."

He jerked me left, and without any warning we entered the forest, deep into pine. I smelt the sharp, unmistakable odor of freshly erected latrines. Voices murmured, and I could make out a faint glow of light amongst the trees.

Suddenly somebody shined a lantern right into my face. I recoiled, flash-blinded. The world turned a painful pink. Pine needles, excrement, mumbles: I struggled to blink through the blur of voices and smells.

When I could see again well enough to focus, I could almost have opted for staying sightless.

There were three bodies. All corpses. All Union. Two of them dangled from trees, arms bound behind them, hands tied with twine, and more twine wrapped around the base of their throats. Twine, I thought, watching them—as if watching could make any difference—twine. Not even rope, twine. Oh, God, it must have taken forever. You couldn't even tell what had finally killed them: whether they'd died of strangulation or broken necks. Their swollen faces lolled on their shoulders like ailing roses.

A few feet further into the woods, a third soldier was hanging. He was barefoot, coatless, and upside down. His throat had been slashed, and thickening blood still dripped down his mouth to his wide-open, sightless eyes. His hair was so bloody it glistened, glued red to the earth. A sheet of paper was pinned to his chest.

" 'Death to Foragers,' " I read aloud.

Just beyond the lanterns, somebody cleared his throat. Someone else sighed.

"Thanks very much, Captain," said Major Nichols. "We've already read it."

Standing near Nichols were maybe a half-dozen other members of Sherman's staff, a couple of soldiers, and behind them, huddled, a trio of captains whose names I didn't know but whose faces I recognized, the way it is when you see people daily but seldom talk. They all looked embarrassed—no greetings, no eye contact, nothing but tugged mustaches and hands plucking blindly at buttons and belts—and very tired, as if at the end of a long race they'd been ordered to run another. I looked at their dazed expressions until, slowly, I made the connection. Each captain was one of the dead men's commanding officers.

"Over there," said Bert. "Yours. By the stream."

I don't want to know, I don't want to know, whichever one of them it is I don't want to find out. I thought I was just thinking this but I must have said at least a portion of it aloud, for a redheaded man next to Bert muttered a few words of sympathy. Nichols nudged my shoulder with the edge of his sword. I walked the six steps to the stream.

It was Charlie. Of course. Who else would it be? Who else was so stupid, who else was so blind? Who else would wander off into the woods without taking somebody with him? Who else would leave his gun behind him but grab for protection his awl? Who had he thought might attack him—a band of Secesh cobblers? Of course it was Charlie. Who else would so totally forget or ignore everything I ever had warned him about?

He had tried to resist. That was obvious. And they must have known his resistance was useless, because they'd never gotten around to shooting him. Indeed, they'd gone out of their way to make his death as nonmilitary as possible. As a message. A warning. A jeer.

Ah, Charlie. You started the day as a soldier and ended it as a corpse, but not the soldier and not the corpse you had the right to envision. Instead you suffered the brutal, inventive death of a newly evolving creature—a species identified only last month, in the mind of a Union general. Forage liberally. . . . My poor young, dumb, judgmental Indianapolis bootmaker. You still owe me money.

Everything they did to you they did to a forager, not to a soldier. That's why they took so long. And that's why they never shot you. Instead they broke you. Legs, ankles, fingers, wrists— whatever you might have used to ride with, to run with, to seize with. And perhaps they would have stopped after one broken wrist or one fractured ankle, but probably someone looked into your pockets and found something you'd stolen, and you didn't have the sense or debating skills to point out it was all the General's brainstorm so leave me alone. I wanted to think they at least had proceeded quickly, but I knew enough osteology to know you can't break that many bones that fast without dropping your victim off the side of a cliff, and there were no cliffs nearby, just this pine forest that swallowed everything—footsteps, echoes, screams. Oh, Christ. How it must have hurt. How it hurt me just looking at him.

I noticed Bert standing beside me. "Poor kid," he said. "Goddamn bastards."

"Don't call him a kid," I said, "he was probably older than you."

"You get how they finally killed him?" he asked. His voice was almost admiring.

"I assumed he'd passed out," I said. "From the—from the pain. And somehow his death just followed."

"Nah," said Bert. "Look at his mouth."

I leaned down. Seen up close, Charlie didn't look like a kid at all; for the first time ever, he looked full adult, with all the dignity of a man who had died in the line of fire and duty. His lips were swollen and his neck sharply arched, as you would expect from someone who'd had no fingers or hands or forearms to resist what had been jammed into his mouth and halfway down his throat. I tugged on the ball of paper. It came out slowly, tightly wadded and wet, streaky with spit and blood. It was a copy of Sherman's Special Order.

The other three captains and I buried our dead. The redhaired lieutenant who had tried to be sympathetic—Dan, as he politely introduced himself—walked me back to camp. Dan explained— not that I'd asked, just to fill air with conversation, to move things along, to prevent thought—that his men had been assigned guard duty on the lip of the forest, where the road met the creek. He said there'd been people up half the night, relieving themselves, fetching wood, getting a drink; but at some point all had become quiet. Then Bert, who had been off watch since midnight and was supposedly sleeping, heard a noise. He had sprung into the woods, yelling and firing his revolver—his normal reaction to anything, Dan said—but it had obviously been too late. Equally obvious, it had been a planned and deliberate ambush.

Word of the deaths spread through the corps with the speed of cholera. Everyone wanted revenge, but no one was sure how to get it. We had been picking up occasional Rebel stragglers since leaving Atlanta, for the most part with total fraternization, but suddenly the friendship and sharing stopped; they went back to being the enemy, and a double guard was placed on their ranks.

The men of my company (and that includes me) reacted to Charlie's death as much with bafflement as sorrow. It wasn't his death per se that hurt us—we were used to death, death marched and ate with us, death was our first lieutenant. It was his manner of dying. Charlie had, in effect, been executed, and such a death threw us; it lacked the dignity of the battlefield, the tragedy of the infirmary, even the irony of disease. Instead it made him a martyr. For anyone who had known Charlie, this was so unexpected as to be nearly unbelievable, and we mourned because we had lost him twice—lost our friend Charlie himself, and also an accurate memory.

Soon Charlie and the three hanged men weren't our only martyrs. A foraging party of fifteen came back one twilight two men short. A dozen others went out to find them and discovered both bodies in a ditch, naked, purple, and forcibly drowned in six inches of water. The following daybreak four guards were discovered smothered in their own blankets. The next evening three more men failed to return; so did their search party. The next morning we found the bodies of all but one.

Actually we didn't find the bodies themselves. What we found was their skeletons. The sole survivor told us the victims had been captured at gunpoint, herded into a barn, then burnt alive. Two boys who tried to bolt had been shot at the door, then tossed back inside, mortally wounded. He said they said they were sparing him so he could tell what had happened, and would go on happening, so long as Sherman continued his war on civilians.

"Some of them were in uniform—straight cavalry," he said. "Some were civilians themselves. They each of them knew the Special Order by heart—said some Union paper published it and it's been reprinted all through the South. They claim that by taking the war off the battlefield we forfeit any expectation of mercy in this world or the next, and while God'll take care of the latter, they believe they'll deal with the former themselves. And they say they'll burn all of Georgia for the chance to blister one Yankee, and the people of Georgia'll gladly hand them the matches. They say we'll never get out alive."

That night somebody tried to strangle one of the Southern prisoners. I wasn't sorry. The prisoner survived. I wasn't glad.

By now it was late November. Foraging, daily becoming riskier and more savage, acquired a new dimension, concerned more with people than food. Meanwhile our nighttime losses, even on full alert, mounted, the deaths of our boys growing increasingly violent and baroque. We'd strike. They'd strike back harder. Us. Them. Them. Us. Both sides teetered and balanced as the fulcrum of our seesaw grew slicker and steeper.

When dawn came on day thirteen of the March, we were told not to break camp and ordered not to ask questions. The resulting rumors were chilling: epidemic in the forward ranks, fire in the rear; the death of Lincoln; the General's death. Of all the above, only the last one touched me; we'd already gone through the first two items, and number three seemed unlikely to make any difference—the war by now had its own personality, stronger and more bloody-minded than any statesman's. But the idea of being stuck out here in the middle of nowhere (worse than the middle of nowhere: the middle of Georgia) with no supply line, fantasy maps, guerrillas everywhere, a restive contingent of captured Confederates—that idea bit bad. I was sure that without the General's guiding genius we would die here, slowly, violently, and without honor.

Around noon a terrible rumor started spreading, and officers rode down the line reminding and cautioning us not to move. This happened again at one and at two. At three o'clock I was summoned by courier to come see the rumor in person. It turned out to be true.

The rumor was land mines.

When I got to the site of the mines I was startled to see the three nameless captains from the night Charlie died; someone on Nichols's staff, I concluded, must have thought we required further proof of Southern perfidy. As it turned out, my logic was good but flawed.

The mines had been sown beneath a field less than a hundred yards from where the head of the corps was now halted. Apparently the line had just been about to swerve in that direction when some scouts noticed what looked like the carcass of a large animal; alarmed that there might be wolves nearby, one of them grabbed shotgun and knife and rode into the field to investigate. Less than a minute later, his horse exploded and he was thrown six feet into the air. Only luck, God, or a meaty rump had saved him from extinction. After returning (very cautiously) to the main line, the scout had unloaded his rucksack.

Its contents remained here now, on the road, still covered with dust. They didn't look real. They didn't look fake either. They just looked . . . unexpected.

They were the right hand, some fingers, the thin mustached face, and a chunk of singed torso of a Union soldier.

"Poor bastard must've blown sky-high," the scout muttered. "There's bits of him scattered all over. I ran out of room."

"Anyone recognize him?" somebody asked.

Nobody did—that is, nobody did by name. Of course all of us recognized him otherwise. He was any of us who would have stepped in that field before him. He had saved us all. He was our latest, and greatest, martyr.

Another hour went by with nobody moving forward, for the simple and obvious reason that backward was the only direction anyone knew for certain was safe. It was an eerie feeling, as the late November sun entered its evening dip, to look at one's shadow and realize that shadow might be lying over a detonator.

It began getting windy, and leaves and a few loose branches fluttered into the field and the road ahead. When nothing exploded, an officer directed a few of the boys to fire the field, one shot at a time. Ten minutes passed, then a connection—a boom like a cannon, only with no echo; just a crash, and the shaking earth. We exchanged sickly grins and rebuttoned our coats against the chill.

Then I heard it. It sounded like hooves, but it couldn't have been, because no one with any sense would be riding that fast under these conditions. But as it grew closer and closer I realized it had to be a rider: nothing besides a horse makes that elegant, rhythmic, distance-devouring sound. I wheeled at the same moment everyone else did.

Cigar clamped in his jaws, red hair flying, face sweaty and eyes on fire, it was the General, galloping full speed and swearing as he drove through the line.

His mouth was so twisted with rage, his words came out stuttered, expelled, as though he were spitting stones. His spine was rigid, his forearms shook. In art, in nightmare, on the very worst day of my own real life, I have never, ever, seen anyone so riddled, so completely consumed, by anger. Officers trailed after him like discarded chunks of a flaming comet.

He leapt off his horse.

"Where is he?" he demanded. "Where's the body of this poor goddamn hero?"

Major Nichols stepped forward. "Right over here," he said. "It's not a whole body, sir. More like—maybe a half. Maybe less."

Sherman glared at him. "I didn't ask for fractions, Major," he said. "I asked for the corpse."

"Yes, sir." Nichols cleared his throat, and the little circle of wide-eyed soldiers surrounding the shattered torso parted. The General strode to the remains and looked down.

He looked and looked. At first I thought he was looking because he was one of those people who found grotesquerie hard not to look at; then I thought he was looking because he was praying and wanted to keep his eyes on what was left of whom

It was useless. I had somehow become the only man in all XIV Corps available for this particular duty.

"You," said Nichols to me. "Step forward."

I stepped forward. I could feel the relief of the others flow through the air, as gentle as snow; and their compassion flutter, as sweet as summer. How warm, how comradely, how dear the brotherhood . . . on the other hand, nobody offered to take my place. God damn the South, I thought. I straightened my coat. God *damn* them.

"Pick up the body," Nichols commanded.

I stooped down. God damn the North too. What was the point of electing these clowns if they couldn't handle something so simple as winning a war? As preventing my death?

I lifted the torso. It was cool, heavy, and stiff, like a leather hassock.

"Take him into that field, please, Captain," Nichols said softly, "and bury him."

I figured the likelihood this was the last time anyone was going to hear from Nick Whiteman again, ever, gave me the right to speak what was on my mind. Shifting the body from shoulder to shoulder, I said:

"Yes, sir. And who's going to bury me?"

Nichols looked stricken. As for the General, he glanced at me holding the body and facing that field of unknowable risk, and his face turned the color of spoiled plums.

"Captain!" he bellowed. "Put down that body! Get away from those mines! What in the name of Moses and all the plagues do you think you're doing?"

I put down the body with utter zeal.

"But, General," Nichols protested, "you just said—"

"I said bury him!" Sherman roared. "I didn't say kill one of our boys just to bury another! We could be here forever that way!"

"Well, sir, then who—" Nichols asked.

Sherman said: "Fetch the prisoners."

Nichols jumped. So did we all. It grew suddenly colder, and stiller than any moment I could recall in all four years. Even the horses caught the silence, swallowed, and held it. Six men quietly detached themselves from the line, while the rest of us—the General, the body, the men of XIV Corps, me—all waited. All we could hear was footsteps: the six guards going to the rear, then the eight Rebels they were returning with.

I noticed the General watching me. "Sir?" I said.

He said, "Hooker. Potatoes. Memories. Ink."

"I never got it," I said.

He grunted, then frowned. "I apologize," he said. "I assumed it'd been taken care of."

"It's a little late to worry about it now," I said. "But thank you."

"The men in your outfit," he said. "They're all fine? That one-eyed boy? He's fine?"

I didn't feel like going into it all. "They're all fine," I said.

"That's odd," he said. "It was my understanding one of them found himself strangled one evening on a copy of the Special Order."

I felt my feet shuffle and my face flush. "That was my understanding too," I said.

"Any idea who did it?"

"Well, of course. I mean . . . it was the war. It wasn't like he was sitting there eating his Sunday dinner and a brick slipped off the roof and split his skull. It was a war injury. That's what I reported."

"I know," said Sherman. "I read that report. Pure hogwash."

"Look, General," I said. "We both know you can change the official record however you want to. Maybe you already have. But you ought to know that's also what I wrote his family, and I very much hope that it won't be censored too." I decided I'd better add "Sir."

"Oh, it won't be censored," the General said. "It's totally wrong but it won't be censored. But the war didn't kill him, Captain. The South did. And it wasn't war. It was murder."

I was suddenly weary. "Ah, Christ," I said, "who's keeping score?" The General turned away.

The guards arrived then with the eight Rebel prisoners. They were skinny, slouch-hatted, and deeply tanned, and they some-how looked hungry and tired and beaten and deadly, all at the same time. Not one of them wore gray—in fact, most of them weren't even wearing uniforms. Three were barefoot, and one's arm was bound in a bloody sling. Two were shirtless beneath the blue jackets someone had obviously lent them . . . or maybe not. Maybe the jackets came off the backs of the boys they'd bush-whacked. Who's keeping score?

"Well, hell," somebody said, "they look just like us."

"But who knows what their souls look like?" said the captain whose man had been hanged upside down.

The prisoners stood staring at Sherman like prairie dogs fixed by a rattlesnake. The General motioned to one of his aides. I couldn't hear a word of the conversation, but the aide abruptly saluted and walked away. Walked to me. Saluted. Walked to the other three captains. Saluted again.

"Gentlemen," he said, "the General requests that one of you oversee the burial of our friend, um, our friend here . . ." His voice faltered as he realized he had no name, or even rank, to drop into the expected slot. ". . . and fellow soldier," he con-tinued. "He wants this burial detail performed by these Rebel prisoners. He chooses you because all four of you have person-ally suffered losses in your command directly due to the recent guerrilla actions of Secesh irregulars."

My head shook "no" before I had time to speak, or really do much more thinking than picture the possible consequences of refusal—which for instance might include following up this fu-neral here with my own court-martial and execution. Then one of the other captains, I thanked God to notice, did exactly the same; so did the third. The fourth captain, the one who had questioned the look of Secessionist souls, raised both arms to the sky.

"I accept!" he cried.

One of the Rebel soldiers promptly fell to the ground in an epilepsy of terror.

As for the other seven—well, they went a long way toward explaining how come this war had already gone four years. They marched into that field the same way we'd heard they obeyed Pickett at Gettysburg—the same way I *knew* they'd marched into the Hornet's Nest, defended Arkansas Post, struggled for Vicksburg, died at Atlanta. They obeyed an enemy general with the same resigned compliance they obeyed their own officers. Obedience unto death.

Let me say right away, nobody died. Perhaps not surprising: a minefield is one of the safest places to spend a war, as long as your luck holds up, and this was one of those cases where the numbers held. The body was buried without incident. The prisoners returned to the line; the guards walked them back to the rear. That left only the General, his staff, me, the other captains, and the fourteen thousand men of the corps. Soon the General and his entourage left too, and we broke for camp just as a cold, wind-borne rain started to fall.

So. Tim. Pete. Bert. Alice. General. Let's recapitulate. We've just sent defenseless men into a minefield. Before that, their not-so-defenseless brothers tortured and killed our companions. Before that we ravaged their countryside and burned their homes. Before that . . .

A look at the nearest faces suggested reaction to what was happening was pretty much fifty-fifty. That is, half of us thought it war. Half of us thought it murder.

By the third week of the March, we were really four separate armies—first ourselves, then our prisoners, then our own escaped men from the great Southern prison camps. Behind them all trailed a final army, swelling daily, of liberated slaves.

Feelings concerning this last army varied. The General tried to discourage it, explaining in each new town how speed and discipline were an army's food and water, and refugees slowed him down surer than plague. He was, naturally, ignored, patience being the last thing a former slave has much of to spare, and Sherman being congenitally the last person on earth to sound sincere preaching it. As we drove deeper through Georgia, he became absorbed by other problems, and he left the burgeoning slave populations to his corps commanders. A mistake.

Our corps commander was named Jefferson Davis. No, not *that* Jefferson Davis—another one. Davis is a common last name, after all, and until the war it was popular to name boys after the only U.S. president to both condemn slave-owners and be one. Our Jeff Davis despised the columns of liberated black folk trailing XIV Corps—he didn't like them as people, he didn't like them as free, and he loathed them as a drag on his maneuverability. As the March grew colder, swampier, and increasingly hounded by Rebel cavalry, his mood turned—so it was rumored he'd crabbed to the General—"blacker than those causing it."

Though nobody's mood was what you'd call light. The war had acquired an extramilitary character more lethal than actual combat. Nothing was legal but everything was permitted—which wound up meaning everyone did what he felt like and no one was responsible for any of it. We were all so tired and jumpy and touchy it became nearly impossible to have a casual conversation without giving or taking offense; disagreements blossomed easily into arguments, and arguments into fistfights, a few resolved only at gunpoint. I kept my mouth shut and my thoughts unshared.

My thoughts. Those little devils. Those dreams, those visions, that incessant bombardment of conflicting woes. When I thought back on all the people I'd lost, some through valor and some on account of incredible levels of boobish incompetence, I wanted to howl. Tim's eye, Charlie's throat, Alice's leg . . . Christ! By the time it was over, I'd have a whole body ready for assembly. War is the last thing you ever should think about while serving in one.

By now it was no longer questioned that we were approaching Savannah. The real question was, would we make it? Daily we marched for hours and miles through vast, algal swamps. Shallow and unnamed creeks funneled without warning into floodtide rivers, sucking and drowning. Snakes fanged into legs, killing within twenty minutes. The morning we crossed Mill

Creek, the water rose so high we had to hold our rifles above our heads; by the time we finished, eight men had collapsed, four from heart attacks, four from leeches.

Then one morning it began raining; the skies turned gray and started to leak, and now every hour was longer and harder and wetter than the hour before. We clashed continually with Rebel cavalry—real cavalry this time, Wheeler's men: superb horsemen, armed to the teeth, familiar with the territory, efficient, intelligent, and ruthless. Our cavalry followed them and got so turned around in the marshy darknesses, they charged into our own headquarters. Rumor spread that in the confusion we had shot and slaughtered our own men.

Because we were moving so slowly, we started earlier and stopped later day by day. For three nights straight we made camp after midnight and left before dawn. The next night we halted at two A.M. and started again at daybreak. I asked why. At first I was handed some lies and daydreams, then I was told we were racing—racing the Rebels to reach the bridge spanning the muckish torrents of Ebenezer Creek.

We lost the race.

When we reached Ebenezer there was a creek there, all right, rocky and deep and choked with stones and weeds and the bloated bodies of starved Rebel horses. But the bridge had been destroyed, and water was rising inches by the minute. Wheeler, all of us realized, had to be very, very close by.

"You know how to swim?" I shouted, over the water's roar, to Pete.

"As a matter of fact, I don't," Pete shouted back. "Could you teach me right now?"

"There's nothing to it!" yelled Tim. "Just alternate keeping your shoulders and ankles out of the water. As long as one of them's not underneath, you're okay."

Pete looked at Tim in disbelief. "How'm I going to remember all that?" he asked. We were told to shut up and await orders.

Ten hours later—just before midnight—our orders came. A pontoon bridge had been slung across Ebenezer Creek.

It seemed to take months before it was our turn to cross, and once we started I remembered just what it was about portable bridges that made me not mind waiting to cross one. Maybe weighted down by only one or two people they felt safe and solid, but with four or five hundred men plus horses and mules and even occasional wagons, they swayed like a rocking chair in the path of a blizzard. I couldn't help but look down, and all the reminders I handed myself that I could indeed swim didn't soothe me. I didn't know that I could swim in *that*.

And I didn't know if I could swim while being shot at. A real possibility: Rebel gunfire rang through the air from behind us, and they'd even managed to set up a couple of cannons (probably ours); the cannonballs missed the bridge but caromed into the ranks of our lead regiment. We could hear screams and our own artillery answering. The rain came down heavier and heavier. The bridge rolled and pitched.

It was daybreak before my half of XIV Corps had crossed Ebenezer Creek. By then the Rebels had edged into our rear close enough for sharpshooters on both sides to sight one another. After the army itself came the Rebel prisoners, still under heavy guard; then the ambulance wagons; then the last of the officer corps and the rear artillery. By now I was so soaked my eyelashes sloshed as I tried to blink; my hands were so furrowed they looked like bark. I shifted my feet, and the suction of mud and rain made my knees buckle.

When the final cannon had been painfully trundled across the swaying and splattered bridge, the Rebels were so near the western shore we could hear the snort of their horses. The slaves still waiting to cross must surely have heard them too.

Davis gave someone a signal. The canvas pontoons quivered once, then flapped smoothly as they were tugged back to the eastern shoreline. The slaves stood stranded.

Stranded. The bridgeless creek surged before them, our corps stood safely beyond it, and the cream of the Rebel cavalry raged at their back.

The slaves rushed the creek the same second the cavalry did. Horses, swords, curses, and shrieks swirled in the air and water. Were the Rebels attacking the slaves, the water, ourselves, the war?—it didn't really matter, the results would have been the same regardless. Almost immediately, dozens of children disappeared—ran into the creek, went right under; if they didn't drown, surely their skulls were crushed by the horses' hooves. I saw the flash of a blade and then a hand flew through the air like a boneless bird.

"Alice!" Tim shouted. "Alice! Alice!"

Those of us nearest the shoreline ran to its edge. Some people tried prying logs out of the gulping earth and rolling them into the creek; others of us hit the ground and began shooting, until we realized we couldn't see to shoot the right people. Meanwhile sections of bridge whipped in our faces, and orders to do everything screamed through the air—put back the bridge! pack it up, put it down! bind logs, set up artillery, forget about it and resume marching. The slaves who made it stood staring at us, eyes blazing with hate.

Most of them didn't make it. Most of them drowned. Wheeler's cavalry captured some of them, but most of them drowned right in front of our eyes. It was our fault and should never, never have happened; it was inexcusable, and it was even more inexcusable that nobody offered any excuses. We dragged out what bodies we could and left the rest in the water. I don't know if former slave Alice Cobb even was there when it happened, but her friend Tim Rice was, and he died from a bullet fired from one side or the other.

PART III
ANNIE

SPEAKER:
Annie Saunders Baker
Southern Widow and Refugee

CHAPTER
NINE

I LOOKED UP the road and saw thirty or forty soldiers, all on horseback. Their poor carriage told me they weren't natural cavalry, and their indifference to being noticed told me they weren't scouts. They were the vanguard of Sherman's army.

Four years ago I couldn't have described them so accurately. I wouldn't, for example, have known the difference between cavalry and mounted infantry, not only because I'd never seen either, but because I didn't understand they were two different things. Nor would I have known the words "scout" or "vanguard," except in the sense that Miss Somebody's hat was in the vanguard of Paris fashion. But four years of war is forty of anything else. Now I understood perfectly the meaning of Sherman's army.

For ever since he had left Atlanta, Sherman never tried fooling the South. He didn't have to: he realized the truth of what he intended would frighten us far more than any lie. And our Southern newspapers, always so vague in regard to our own situation, helped him immeasurably; every instance of his barbarism was reported in awesome detail, every burning, every hanging, every torture, every rape.

So when I looked up the road and saw them, just behind Fisher's Mill, just a mile away in the clear autumn sunlight, I knew exactly who they were and what they meant.

They meant the death of my life.

If only my husband were here! Or Bobby—or Richard—or Henry—or Father—

None were, of course. Bobby, my brother, had been missing since last November; Richard, my brother-in-law, was serving with Hood. Henry, another in-law, had been wounded and captured in the battle for Atlanta. Father had refugeed in August, along with my sisters, my mother, and his mother. As for my husband . . . Randall had died in the final hours of Pittsburg Landing. A hero's death, quick, patriotic, and painless. Or so the telegram said.

But this was no time for a roll call of missing menfolk; I was about to have plenty of male visitors in about twenty minutes. I had to start thinking.

I backed onto my veranda. How long would they take and what should I do? Both questions deviled me, equally urgent, till I understood neither was urgent at all: there was time to do almost nothing, and there would be less than nothing to do once they arrived. Sixty thousand Yankees plus General Sherman—how could one woman hope to outsmart any of them? Let alone all.

By now they were close enough for me to hear separate voices. In another few minutes they would be on the edge of my land; a few minutes more, on my doorstep. I blinked into the sunshine. If I could see them, maybe they could see me: brown hair, brown eyes, brown dress, brown fichu, brown shoes. Brown hair ribbon, tatted brown shawl. Twenty-five years old last Sabbath morning—uncelebrated. No longer a beauty, no longer a belle. Average Annie, the sensible one.

Annie, *get moving.*

I first went into the kitchen. A large cedar table sat in the middle, covered with pans of flour; the doors to the cellar spread open wide. I slammed shut the doors, then butted and shoved the table till it was flush with the doorknobs. Then I stacked it with dishes and pots and spoons and sifters, observed it a moment, and added some kindling and a Turkish towel. I scattered a handful of flour over everything. The idea was to make it all look so boring—so everyday, so invisibly familiar—no one would think to look at the cellar behind it. Then I bolted upstairs.

Get everyone's things. No, leave some—maybe they'll think that's everything. Leave Mother's pearls and my garnet earrings, and bury everything else in the pigsty. Bury them good. No, wait a minute. Bury Grandma's pins somewhere obvious, and stick all the christening cups on top. Maybe they'll stop there.

I sped back downstairs and outside. A shovel, I couldn't find a shovel. . . . Where on this poor sorry land had I left it? I forced myself quiet, and remembered I'd buried six stillborn kittens— what a time for kittens! no wonder they'd died—just last Thursday, behind the barn. I grabbed up my skirts and ran over. It took less than a minute to bury the relics of four generations.

I smoothed the hole over with pebbles and dirt. What more had I missed? There were so many rumors. Some promised nothing would happen, others said everything would: the house burnt, the cotton torched, the livestock slaughtered. And what they were doing to women. I'd heard that too, although nobody knew for certain; nobody knew anyone who had actually *suffered* (meaning *what,* exactly?), but all of us knew women who knew women who had been . . .

I hurried to the back garden and began scooping up squash. The harvest had been too good, they were countless as milkweed, and I seized a bucket and began pouring them in. Then I ran to the carrot patch and began grabbing up fronds by the handful. When I added them to the squash I discovered I'd overloaded the bucket, couldn't budge it; I dumped out the carrots and lugged the bucket under the porch.

Wheelbarrow! Where was a wheelbarrow? I could see one out by the orchard, but that seemed too far, or too close: too far from the house, too close to *them*. I tossed an old afghan over the bucket, reached underneath, crammed in more squash. Think, don't panic, think. What else should I do?

I looked once again up the road. The troops had halted, and I could see the sparkle where sunlight picked up rows of gleaming metal; I hoped it was shining off buckles or canteens and not bayonets. Occasional words kept coming up—"water," "horses," "turkeys." I had two dozen hens and four toms— where could I hide them? I scooted to the pen; turkeys cawed and cluttered, gathering around me and nipping my ankles. I kicked them away. I was not having turkeys and Yankees attack the same day.

Suddenly I stopped. I stopped because they'd stopped too. And I stopped because I wanted to see for the last time what they were seeing now.

Ours was a nameless estate. Neighbors simply called it the Fisher's Mill House, after the nearest landmark, or more often just Saunders's place, after my grandfather. Pine-fenced along its western edge and open in back, it sloped from the outer garden into a manmade gully and two large orchards, apples and peaches mostly, bordered by sunflowers. Which always had been an awful idea; every autumn the dying sunflowers would spew their seeds into the naked orchards, and every April the springtime blossoms would be gnarled with fresh sunflower plants. I used to tell Randall, at the rate things were going, one day we'd wake up to find ourselves peachless and surrounded; the house would be circled by huge, smiling, impossible-to-conquer sunflower plants. But it looked like Sherman had beaten biology to it.

The sunflowers had been Grandma's idea. So had the house. She'd never relished the "plantation look"; she had grown up in Arkansas and wanted a home that looked like a farmhouse, "not one of those Grecian temples." This meant a veranda but no pillars; trees but no arbors; flowers but no laid-out gardens with paths and fountains and what she called those "obscene naked archers," by which she meant the white marble cupids beside

which all Southern women receive their requisite dozen propos-
als of marriage, or so all Northerners like to believe. She was an
Annie herself, which meant she got her way more often than
not; our home looked comfortable and hospitable but never
grand, not even when decked out for parties, weddings, or funerals.

What a shame, I thought now, Grandma was raised in a farmhouse instead of a cabin or shack! Our home may not have
looked like Arlington, but it surely was something those soldiers
would never ignore.

A man separated himself from the others; another one followed. They started down the road toward me. Not in much of
a hurry. No need.

Dead sunflowers crunched beneath the hooves of their horses.
Annie, I said to myself, good luck.

Two minutes later I said, "Good morning, gentlemen. Is the war
over yet?"

The first soldier, a lieutenant, lifted his hat. A great deal of red
hair tumbled over his shoulders.

"Good morning, ma'am. No, I'm afraid it's not."

"Then how may I possibly help you?" I asked.

He smiled. Warm smile, cold smile? Real smile? Smirk? "My
men and I need supplies and a place to rest," he said.

"You're welcome to rest where you are," I said, "for as long
as you want. There's not much by way of supplies, but if you
need water or flour, or vegetables—"

"You alone?" said the second rider, a lieutenant too.

"Shut up, Bert," said the redhead. "You were saying,
ma'am?"

What *had* I been saying? "I'd be happy to direct you to water,"
I said. "There's a stream nearby for your horses and of course
the well's at your disposal. There's not much else, but what there
is you're welcome to share."

The second soldier—Bert—echoed, "Share?"

"Share," I said back.

This one's expression required no subtle interpretation. "I asked, are you alone?" he said.

The redhead looked embarrassed but didn't tell him again to shut up; I noticed this. Both of them waited for an answer. I waited too. What answer was best? Admitting I was a woman alone seemed like a bad idea, but saying anything else would, eventually, require actually producing an adult male—a commodity as rare, in this fourth year of war, as Confederate victory.

"I'm alone at the moment," I said.

"But you're expecting company?" asked the redhead.

"I might be."

"*Armed* company?" he said.

I understood then he was worrying about Wheeler. Good. Let them be worried about *something*.

"I can't say for sure," I said.

"I can," said Bert; "she means 'no.' Come on, Dan, let's go ahead in."

Dan hesitated. "Miss," he said, "you obviously know who we are and what we're here for. Water and flour and vegetables would be fine if that's truly all you have, and you'll give me your word not to turn sharpshooter the minute we enter your garden."

I felt a tiny lift of relief. Maybe—maybe, maybe—this was going to all work out. I decided on one lie and one truth.

"That truly is all I have," I said. "As for my aim—well, my brother used to tell me I couldn't hit a crane fly with a cannon."

Dan grinned. "No William Tell, huh?" he chuckled.

"Not really."

But I didn't chuckle back. I realized I'd said something wrong—lost an advantage. A woman who knew how to shoot could be a deterrent. I'd just displayed helplessness.

"Though I've been practicing," I added.

This time he full-out smiled. "Bert, get ten of the boys and go out to the garden. I'll meet you there in a couple of minutes."

"What about her pigs?" Bert protested. "I saw at least two

dozen pigs. I bet she's got hams, I bet she's got sausages down in her cellar—"

"Bert, aren't you weary of pigs yet? You've downed more pork than a Dutchman since we left Atlanta. Leave her pigs in peace."

"Ah," I said. "Peace. Now there's a word that hasn't been spoken recently. Thank you."

"And there's two more," Dan said. "You're quite welcome, pretty lady."

And there were two more: I hadn't heard myself called pretty anything since Randall's death. Still, I didn't really shine to those couple of minutes this Dan was proposing to spend with me while Bert raided the garden.

"I'll show you both the yard," I said. "And the well."

Dan looked disappointed but said nothing; Bert stepped into the road and whistled. Ten soldiers slung rifles over shoulders and began shuffling over.

Who knows why it happened then and not sooner? Maybe it was just the passage of time, or maybe the shift in the ratio, them versus me; but watching their quiet amble was like watching the sun being sucked into twilight by vast blue clouds. Eternal night and ceaseless destruction: I felt my slim self-delusion of hope reveal itself, illusion only. The wrong move, I thought, the wrong comment, and I would be one more rumor: Annie Saunders Baker, victim; another whispered-in-horror statistic with the details never quite right.

My eyes widened and smarted; I was too frightened to blink.

"Don't panic," somebody said.

I looked for the voice. It was Dan once again, and he was patting my shoulder. How long he'd been patting I had no notion.

"Don't panic," he repeated. "Panic is the enemy. Not us. Just treat us like guests. We'll be gone before you know it."

My mouth surprised me by what came out. "I believe," I heard myself saying, "I believe when you're gone I'll manage to know it."

"That's the spirit!" he said. Then either he moved his arm or

I moved my body. "Why don't you escort us to your garden now?" he said.

He made it sound as though I were giving a tour. I peered at his faded insignia. "Lieutenant . . ."

"Mayhew," he said. "But just call me Dan. And you're—"

"Annie," I said.

"Well, Miss Annie," he said, "if you'll do us the honor?"

I started off the porch. Bert already had joined the ten soldiers and was whispering to them; they looked at him, nodded, then looked at me. We began walking to the garden. Every story I'd heard and half-heard surfaced to mind; I struggled to quash the images. I noticed Dan still was beside me. Panic, I thought: panic is the enemy. Not them. Not the war.

"So which one of them has the matches?" I asked.

He laughed. "No need to worry," he said. "We burnt Atlanta because they had weapons there. We only need food. I give you my word."

"Well, as long as you're giving your word," I said, "let me offer a few. If you take everything I have, it won't matter one pin if you *do* burn me down, because I'll starve anyway. I realize I'm in no position to bargain, but if you could just leave me—"

"We'll leave you enough to get through the winter," he said.

"I was hoping," I said, "that by then it'd be over."

By now we had reached the yard. For a moment we all stood there, gazing at my destruction: the uprooted carrots, that damnable squash. Dan was right, I *had* panicked, and in my panic I'd forgotten to weight the afghan I'd covered everything with; it was telltaledly flapping, exposing all. All that panicked harvesting, and all I had done was help gather things up.

Bert and the soldiers sprang into action. They each carried flour sacks, and began shoveling in everything in sight. One man crammed all I had gathered—which had seemed so much to me, and taken so long to grow, and represented so many dinners, and so much barter, and so much work—into one large bag; and when he was finished the sack wasn't even full, and he started pulling up carrots, row after row, stuffing them into his flour bag until it bulged in a bundle almost as high as his waist. Another he was praying for. Then I saw his face and realized he wasn't watching the body at all; he was gazing at the ground, and following his eyes I saw he was measuring the distance between the road the entire XIV Corps was huddled on and the field, where a thin line of smoke from that last explosion wavered palely in the stiff, cold breeze.

Abruptly he leaned over and picked up the head by its hair. Standing there staring at it, he looked like an executioner—an executioner with the leftovers of a badly balled-up assignment.

"Get a bag for this, somebody," he said.

One of Nichols's men stepped forward and removed the head from the General's fingers. "Wrap up the rest of him too," he said. "And find out his name. I want him buried right here."

"Right here where, sir?" Nichols asked.

"In this field," Sherman said. "Where he *pro patria mori*'d. Where they killed him."

Those of us near enough to hear this looked at each other and shuffled our feet.

"Um, this field right here, General?" Nichols said.

"No, a field two thousand miles from here," Sherman snapped. "Yes, Major. Right here."

Nichols said nothing. Nobody else spoke either; we were all too busy picturing ourselves, tiptoeing, scraping, creeping, mincing: taking that one fatal footfall on the path to Heaven, or oblivion. As for me—well, let me put it this way. I no longer could say for certain my mama had borne no idiots. But she definitely had not raised any volunteer suicides—particularly not in four different counties simultaneously. I took several steps back, trying to arrange my face to assume the look of anyone save a potential gravedigger.

"Major," said Sherman, after a few moments' inaction. "Let's make that burial today, shall we?"

"Yes, sir."

"I mean right now," Sherman said.

"Yes, sir." Nichols reluctantly turned to our line. I felt his eyes seeking to meet my own as I desperately tried to find any other face to fix on—the General, one of the captains, even the corpse.

took out a knife and began whacking the squash off their stems. A third grabbed two turkeys and plunged them, still squawking, into a knapsack.

Another soldier grabbed another turkey, and it bit him.

"Goddammit to hell!" he roared, and tossed the turkey across the yard.

Before it was halfway to earth, something whirred by my face, and the loudest bang I'd ever heard shattered the air. Someone had fallen to his knees and was shooting—shooting my turkeys, one after another, shooting with one of those Spencer repeaters they told us the Yankees could load up on Sunday and fire all week. The killing was totally pointless: hit so close, the turkeys exploded, shredded far beyond edibility, just feathers and guts and claws.

"Cut it out, Al!" Bert barked. "We're supposed to be saving ammunition!"

They stripped bare the garden in less than five minutes. What wouldn't fit into their bags and knapsacks they left in a heap by my feet. Then Bert began pulling up handfuls of red-earthed seedlings. The others paused, watching Dan.

"I told you not to do that," Dan said. "You do that, there goes the next harvest."

"That's about the idea," Bert said. But he stopped.

They all did. They stopped just like that. A second ago they were ravaging devils, and now they were just grocers; they stood looking around as if waiting for someone to pay the bill. It was hard to feel I needed to thank them, but toting the choices, I deemed I did. I was safe; I was whole; I still had a roof and pigs and a cellar. The war was now four years old, and I'd just won my first battle.

"Time to move on?" one of them asked Bert.

Bert looked at Dan. "In a minute," Dan said. "Miss Annie, you said something earlier about flour?"

"I was baking bread," I said. "I'll fetch it."

"I'll come with you," he said.

"That won't be necessary."

"I don't mind."

Well, *I* minded, of course, but what could I say? Calculating how swiftly this fragile victory could shatter by haggling, I smiled with what I hoped looked like pleased hospitality and said, "Fine. It should be just about ready."

"Fresh bread! God, what a treat," he said. "Bert, you boys gather that stuff up and locate the well." He turned to the man who had shot the turkeys and said, "You, Al, keep a lid on that Spencer or I'll see you're in front of it one of these days."

"You and who else?" the Spencer man muttered.

Dan, ignoring him, smiled at me as we walked to the kitchen. Soldiers' voices retreated toward the well. He opened the door for me, gestured me in, then carefully shut it behind him. I reached over and opened it again.

"Do you just want the bread," I asked, "or the flour too?"

"I want you to sit down," he said.

"Is that an invitation or an order?"

He sighed. "It's whatever you want. Tell you what, you stand and *I'll* sit." He settled into the closest chair and loosened his cartridge belt. "You think you could find me a glass of water?"

There was a pitcher of water beside the oven; I poured him a glass, handed it over, and retreated back to the stove. He drained the glass and wiped his mustache.

"Fantastic," he said.

"It's not very fresh," I said. "The water, I mean. I drew it last night."

"No, it's fine. It's been a dog's age since I drank water out of anything besides a tin cup or my own hand. I've missed it."

"After four years away from home," I said, "I should think you'd miss something more basic."

He shook his head. "You're wrong there, Miss Annie. You stop missing the basics real early on. My family, my friends—I hardly ever think of them, except when I get a letter or meet up with someone I knew before. But I do miss the details. Those I miss all the time."

I started to wrap the bread. One detail I'd miss was these tea towels I was wrapping it in. "Such as?" I asked over my shoulder.

"Oh . . . mostly things I could do by myself. You're never alone in a war. Even when you're sleeping there's dozens of people sleeping beside you. I miss reading. I miss daydreaming. I miss whittling without having people ask what you're making. I miss watching a sunrise without somebody telling about a sunrise he once saw. I just miss the quiet."

I stacked three loaves and shook a fourth out of its pan. "What do *you* miss?" he asked.

"I'm afraid my missings are more theatric," I said. "I miss my husband."

"Is he—?"

He didn't finish the sentence. Nobody does, during a war. The odds are too good you won't like the answer.

"It's been over two years," I said. "He died at Pittsburg Landing. What you people call Shiloh."

He got all the quiet he wanted then.

After awhile he said: "I'm sorry."

I looked at the bread and laid it on the breadboard. I was sorry too. And what I was sorriest about was I wasn't much sorrier than he was.

When I first heard about Randall's death I thought I was going to die. I didn't know until then that a broken heart isn't just an expression; your heart really does break, you feel it inside, you hear it, it cracks, it hurts, you can't breathe. Where once there was something special—your love—now there's just air, which everyone breathes, and tears, which everyone sheds.

But there just isn't time, in a war, to mourn correctly. For civilians too, there's never a moment you're really alone. The war is so constant a subject, so demanding, so ever-present in what you do, read, speak about, think of, it becomes a guest, then a boarder, then a roommate; finally it becomes your lover, and you and the war become one; it's now as much a member of your family and a part of your life as your real family and your real life. You become used to it, and you put off your mourning to meet its demands. And the moment for mourning passes.

I wanted to miss my husband. Every morning I wanted to think about him. But my sorrow was too common to share, and

my moments of solitude were too exquisitely rare to spend sor-
rowing. I just didn't have the time; and in time, I didn't have the
sorrow, either. Now I felt when the war finally ended, I'd miss
it instead.

"Do you want more water?" I asked.

Dan held out the glass. "I wasn't at Shiloh," he said. "Though
I suppose that doesn't matter."

"No, it doesn't. Somebody was."

"I guess wars are harder on women than anyone else."

I banged down the last loaf pan. "Guess again," I said. "War's
hardest on the soldiers who die. And it's probably nearly as hard
on the soldiers who don't. All your friends out there—"

"They're not all my friends."

"Your associates. I don't lay claim to seeing what's in their
heads, and for all I know they're each one having a high old time.
But one of these days they're going to be old men—*if* they
live—and they're going to find themselves wondering how one
minute they were fighting a war and the next they were doing
battle with a flock of turkeys whose only sin was to practice a
little natural self-defense. I've lost a husband and maybe a
brother and I can't even count the friends; but at least I don't
have to ask myself why I'd let a general whose own people think
he's crazy give me permission to act like a savage. Worse than a
savage—a bully. So why don't you take this bread and the flour
if you're taking it too and throw in that glass if it makes you so
happy. Just stop wondering what it's like for women and widows
because you're really not the right person to guess."

He stood abruptly and put down the glass. "We're leaving,
Miss Annie," he said. "We'll leave right now. I can't give you
back what we already took—"

"That's true, you can't."

"—but we won't take any more. I'll tell the men."

The door was suddenly flung wide open. Bert ran in, four men
behind him, all yelling.

"She's lying! I knew she was lying!" he screamed. "Her
pigsty—"

"I told you to stay out of her pigsty," Dan said.

"Her pigsty's a goddamned jewelry store! Look at this!"

He held a dead piglet and my topaz hatpin in one hand. The others were carrying everything else I'd buried—Grandfather's cuff links, Mother's gold miniature, Grandma's wedding band, Randall's razor. His watch. My nephew's silver teething cup. My sister's brass-plated charm bracelet, a gift from her first proposal—why had I hidden that? it wasn't worth anything—a small wooden box, laden with marbles.

"Put that stuff down!" Dan commanded.

"Like hell I will! I knew she had more than squash and turkeys! I'll bet this whole house is crammed—"

"I said put it down!"

Bert hurled Randall's razor directly at Dan's forehead. Hair and a sliver of skin fluttered through air.

Dan staggered and moaned. One hand rose to his face, the other fumbled for his revolver. Bert grabbed a skillet and smashed it into Dan's wrist. The gun fell to the floor, and I tried to grab it; Bert shoved me aside and kicked it to one of the men.

"Give me that gun!" Dan yelled. "Give it back, or you'll be up for a court-martial so fast—"

"Court-martial! What for? 'Forage liberally,' the General said; that's what he said and that's what we're doing! Sam, Thurlow, look in that cellar. Frank, you get the others."

But the others already were there, looking back and forth—first Bert, then Dan, then Bert again.

"I promise you," I said to Bert, "I promise you there's nothing down there but preserves and a ham—I'll get them for you, you can come with me—"

"I don't need your promises, lady! What else you got hidden here?"

I answered him because he held the revolver: Dan had become useless to me.

"I'll give you everything," I said.

But the moment when giving was still an option had ended. Thurlow and Sam were emerging from the cellar, their arms bulging with bacon and jams and jellies and something I truly hadn't hidden, just forgotten—an ancient barrel of huckleberry wine. Bert whacked in the lid of the cask with his revolver and grabbed Dan's water glass. He took a deep draught, then another.

"Hey, not bad," he said.

He passed the cup to the one named Thurlow. He took a drink too. The man called Sam scooped his hand into the barrel and licked his fingers.

"Don't do that," said Dan in a dead voice.

He might just as well not have spoken. Bert stuck his head out the door. "Hey, Kennedy!" he yelled. "Come in here!"

A tall, bald man stomped into the kitchen. He looked at the wine and grinned; looked at Dan. His grin vanished.

"Sir?" he said.

"Seems Dan here's been slightly wounded in the course of performing his duties," Bert said.

The bald man gawked. Blood was running into Dan's eyes, and he seemed to be crying. If I'd had any thought he still might be able to rally himself and help me, it vanished then, when I saw those tears—tears made out of the first water he'd drunk from a glass since the start of the war. Still, I had to ask.

"Are you going to just sit by and let this happen?" I said.

"Ain't up to him," Bert said. "This is all legal." He reached into his coat and withdrew a ragged piece of paper. General Sherman's name was on the bottom, and on top in large letters were printed the words "Special Order Number 120."

I didn't even bother to read it.

"Sherman's the last person on earth," I said, "to make *anything* legal."

Bert jerked his head at Kennedy. "Take her outside," he said. "Dan too. Find a kerchief and make him a bandage. C'mon, hoof it. You too, lady," he said to me.

I didn't budge. I don't know why. It wasn't heroism; heroism requires fear, and I was no longer really frightened. And it wasn't bravery (once defined by Randall as heroism without an audience), for I had an audience, all clearly waiting for me to get a move on. Nor was it resignation, for I still wasn't sure what to expect, although I was curious . . .

That's it. I was curious. This invasion, this horde, this armed intrusion was the most interesting thing that had happened the whole war long.

"I'm not going anywhere," I said.

"Suit yourself. Stay here, though I can't be responsible for your safety."

"As if you are now," I said.

At that he said nothing, just kicked open the door. Kennedy looked at Dan. *Resist, resist,* I silently begged him; resist this, you know it's wrong. But when Bert lifted Dan's revolver and started to point it toward Kennedy's head, Kennedy grabbed Dan's arm and shoved him outside.

Besides Thurlow and Sam and Bert, there were a dozen other men, all still bunched in the kitchen. Three of the men had removed their canteens and were dipping them into the wine; another unwrapped one of the loaves and took a large bite. Bread, wine: for a second it looked almost biblical—sacramental. One of the men peered into the dining room, took a few steps, then turned to Bert. Bert nodded, and two of them walked into the main part of the house. A few moments later two more followed.

Bert took another swallow of wine.

"I'm warning you, lady," he said. "I don't kill civilians but one more dead Rebel really won't break my heart. I'm taking this house down."

"I'm staying," I said.

"I'm serious."

"I'm serious too," I said. "I'm serious as cancer. I'm staying and if you want me out of here you'll have to kill me."

A crash boomed from the dining room and glass shattered. Four of the others ran after the sound. A soldier standing right next to me seized a bread pan and slammed it into a pile of drying china. Shards of porcelain fluttered like dusty snow.

"Now might be a good time to reconsider," Bert said.

I shook my head.

"You take care of this kitchen," he said to someone. "Go back into that cellar and clear it out. Everything you can't carry, burn it or break it. And I mean everything. Start with that sack of flour."

The man looked at the flour—my last—and picked up a bucket. He sank the bucket into the sinkful of water. Then he scooped up a cupful of lye, tossed it into the water, and stirred it, using one of my loaves for a spoon. As soon as the lye, hissing, dissolved, he tipped the flour onto the floor and threw the water on top of it. The flour contracted in smoky blotches.

"Where's the sugar?" Bert asked me.

I just hadn't had enough time. They found the sugar; they found the pepper, the honey, the precious few packets of salt. They threw pepper on the sugar and slipped the salt into their pockets. They opened the jars of honey and dipped their hands into the jars, sucking their fingers. Then they broke the jars against the windows, breaking them too. Sam and Thurlow went back into the cellar and came back, grunting, with two years' worth of yams. They hauled the burlap bags into the yard, dumped the potatoes, and returned to the kitchen, the bags neatly folded under their arms.

"Finish it up," Bert said, and nodded toward the firewood. Then he grabbed my wrist.

"I don't believe in keeping ladies tied to the stove all day," he said. "Show me around."

We walked—he walked me—into the dining room. Marched me. Into what once was a dining room. It was nothing now. The long mahogany table was smashed nearly in half by the collapsed china cabinet; shattered dishes were inches deep. The silver drawers were empty. The cushions had been torn from every chair, and the chairs, stacked in a corner, smoldered. Underneath them was a pile of burning daguerreotypes. Every frame was missing. Even the curtains were gone.

I could hear footsteps running upstairs. Mother's pearls, my earrings, I thought grimly; that should start off another riot. Never mind that the pearls were age-scratched and splotchy, the garnets a final present from a now-dead suitor. These people stole children's marbles. They wouldn't stop to measure my memories.

Bert still held my wrist.

"Show me the sitting room," he said.

We entered. It took only one look for me to say, "Well, it's a little too late to offer a seat."

For the fact was, there was no place to sit, not even the floor. The chairs and couches had all been gutted, and someone must have been outside and back, because there was a bucket of horse—I hoped—manure in a corner, and some of it had splattered onto the carpet. This was a spin that even the wildest rumors had failed to mention, so audacious and unexpected it was almost thrilling. Even Bert had the decency to look astounded.

"Once things get started," he muttered, "they're hard to stop."

I gazed at the stinking, ruined carpet. I had learned how to read in this room; my mother said I had learned to walk here. I had been courted here. Now it was utterly clear that even if they did not burn me down I could never live here again.

It was not only what they had done. It was the fact they had been able to do it. Home, with all its multiple meanings—safety, security, an enclave from a harsh world, from even a good one—had failed me. I'd always thought that as long as I lived in this house I was protected; I could count on its shelter to shield me, seashell-like, from the tides of the world outside. Now I saw my home was vulnerable, penetrable. An event so small as a war could undo it.

My home had failed. I had failed too. I'd been unable to save anything, unable to stop anyone. Unable to halt it for even one minute. Helpless.

My curiosity melted. I was embarrassed and angry and giddy with impatience for them to get out of there. Get out, so I could go too.

I took out the piece of paper Bert had given me in the kitchen, his Special Order Number 120.

"That's interesting," I said. "Even Sherman doesn't suggest defecating in the sitting room. I wouldn't have credited your men with that much imagination."

Bert said, "You know where the door is, lady. You can still leave."

"I can't leave," I said. "I might write up my memoirs one of these days. I need to see everything."

He smiled. And his smile, at that moment, was truly daunting. If only it'd been a leer, or a threat, or an imitation of those grim, slick smiles of Sherman's I'd seen in the newspaper drawings! For had he smiled like that, I could have hated him and smiled back. But no—his smile was daunting because it *wasn't* Sherman's; because it brightened his eyes and softened his face and made me realize that beneath his mustache and dirt, under the dust and grime of four years of carnage and battle, the soldier in charge of pillaging my home, destroying my life, was a boy even younger than my youngest sister.

"How old are you anyway?" I asked.

Upstairs something crashed.

"What's it to you?" he answered.

"I'm curious."

"You're curious in more ways than one, lady. And it's none of your business."

"Tell me anyway."

He shrugged and said, "Twenty-two."

"So you've been killing people most of your adult life."

He said: "It don't change you."

"Really? It would me, I think."

He spit on the carpet—no need now not to—and said, "Nope. Wouldn't change you at all. You'd be the type who'd charge to the front every time. Not like Dan there—the sort who just kind of drag along. Those're the ones who always get killed—the ones who don't want to do any killing."

I wondered. Randall had hated the war—feared its coming, loathed being in it, despised his abilities, pitied his targets. And died. Now I was hearing that all the chaos, all the slaughter and bloodshed I always pictured when I thought the word "Battle!" would be something that, rather than shirk, I might actually welcome.

Something above us tumbled over, and Bert ran up the stairs. I followed.

Six men were in my bedroom. Two had ripped down the canopy and were slicing it into ribbons; two were in my closet, tossing out dresses, hats, my bridal veil. A box with all my letters and two diaries I'd kept as a child were on the floor, the letters in uneven halves, the spines of the journals broken. Soaked with cologne and half-ignited, the War Department announcement of Randall's death blazed in one corner; letters my parents had sent each other before they were married flamed in another. Everything private. Everything that had ever mattered.

But it didn't matter. Memories, privacy, hidden hopes, intimate plans and expectations—all those things that define oneself, those secret desires one fears exposing—once exposed, instantly lose their meaning: turn out to have had no meaning except their secrecy itself. Another man popped out of my closet. He'd stuffed himself into my wedding dress. Seams snapped and buttons flew; acres of lace caught on the floorboards.

Bert scowled at him and walked to a pile of burning letters. He started stomping the fire out with his boot.

"Let it burn," I said.

He stared at me, opened his mouth, closed it, shrugged. He kept stomping.

Outside, down below, there was fresh yelling. I walked to a window. It was grimy with smoke. I picked up a broken music box and smashed out the glass to get a better look. A man was standing by a half-dug hole and shouting to Bert.

"We found something more!" he cried.

The men in my bedroom ran down the stairs, whooping; the one in my wedding dress tripped halfway down and fell to the bottom, landing in a lacy heap. He limped out to the yard. Bert started to follow.

"You better come too," he said. "There's fires in half the rooms here."

I said: "Half's not enough."

Then I picked up my bridal veil, dipped it into one of the fires, and tossed it onto the bed. I walked down the stairs. The last of the soldiers ran out behind me. By now there was fire in every corner.

Outside the men were gathered around a mound, digging with hands and buckets. The smell of burnt linen wafted from the broken windows. Looking up I saw flames suck up my bedroom.

One of the squatting men stopped digging and reached into the hole. I watched his hand disappear into the dirt, feel around, dig a little deeper. Then his hand jerked, and he jumped up, dropping something back to the red earth. It was the corpse of one of my buried kittens.

I saw Bert stiffen, then frown. Somebody chuckled.

Down the road the horses were nickering, rested by now and ready to start. The men began shifting, stretching their shoulders and stomping their feet and checking canteens and rifles. Bert kicked some dirt back over the tiny body and smoothed out the grave. Then he stuck out his hand.

"See you around," he said.

CHAPTER
TEN

FOR A ROAD I had known my entire life, a road I had looked at, walked on, ridden down, taken as much for granted as my own voice or face—a road common to me as water, as Southern defeat—for a road so familiar, the road leading out from our house was as alien as a road from somebody else's dream. Boots had trampled the earth soft as velvet and furrowed it into waves; it was like walking within a vast, dry riverbed. The posts of every fence had been removed and ignited. Bushes burning, straight out of Exodus; trees on fire, dripping with tar. My breath felt heavy, encrusted with dust, and the air was mottled with streaks of smoke edging like gangrene toward the heart of the sun.

I began walking. I felt hot and cold at the same time, flushed with excitement, fevered with anger. And I felt light, almost bouncy, as if something were missing or cut away. I realized I had never once walked with so little at hand. Never once walked without a scarf or gloves or a shawl or a hat; never once walked without the weight of Destination. I had told my folks that if worse came to worst I would join them in Charleston, but the truth was I had no idea how to reach Charleston—no idea, in fact, whether Charleston still existed or if it too had been put to the torch. I was *going*—that's all I knew.

I walked and walked. The sky darkened and lightened as fresh clouds of smoke popped up along the horizon and slowly unraveled. The road became covered with cinders, and every few yards the texture of cinder changed, depending on what had most recently burnt: a house, a garden, a dress. It took me nearly two hours to reach the home of our closest neighbor. It wasn't on fire anymore. It just wasn't there.

I stood gazing at the emptiness. We used to play tag in those fields, we used to rig swings from those trees, measuring who could go higher. Once Randall had leapt, upside down, off his chair and into the fragrant branches. And now not only Randall was gone, but so was everyone who had stood on that turfy earth watching him soar feet-first toward heaven, and the tree itself was gone, and the earth and the sky were so changed they were almost gone too. That whole world never existed, except in my memory.

It was just before sunset when I saw my first refugee cart. It stood outlined against the dying sunlight like a movable bed, its wheels entangled with pumpkin vines, and as soon as I turned to observe it another one rumbled up. Evening quickened and the rigs multiplied, bouncing over stubbled fields, rolling in over the tops of hills, lurching from forests. They all looked similar—thin horse, thinner mattress, swaying lantern, water jug. One woman would hold the reins, another would hold a child. More children huddled behind them, some tossing beneath camphor-smelling blankets, some shivering with exposure. Others didn't move at all, not even to cry.

I looked around me. A dozen or so wagons were drawing together in two half-circles on either side of the road. Voices murmured; horses whinnied and stomped. Babies whimpered. A young girl was walking from wagon to wagon with a burning twig, which she carefully plunged into each outstretched lantern. Each time the light flared into her face she looked like an angel; and each time it happened she coughed up blood.

Soon people, especially children, began climbing down from the carts. The road became crowded with refugees. A brave handful purposefully mingled; the rest strayed at most only a few fearful feet from their wagons. Some women were wearing coats; most of the others at least had shawls; a few wore officers' capes. But all were basically the same person: homeless, directionless, planless, and empty-handed, fixed like pinned butterflies within the rigid encasement of war.

"Miss," somebody called to me from one of the wagons, "you, there, miss. You got something to eat?"

The voice sounded Southern but foreign—Tennessean, maybe.

"I don't," I said. I knew somewhere around here was an apple orchard that was probably still standing, as it was fairly hidden and I hadn't seen any recent smoke. But I wasn't sure how many apples remained—or, more precisely, how many *would* remain, should this many people share them.

"I'm sorry," I added.

"*Need* any, then?" the voice asked.

"Any what?"

The woman calling to me prodded a boy sitting cross-legged behind her. He slipped off the wagon and scampered over to me, taking my hand with familiarity. His own hand felt blistered and smelt of horses.

"I'm Andrew," he said. He was about twelve years old.

I said, "I'm Ann."

"You can call me Andy."

"You can call me Annie."

"My full name's Andrew Jackson. No relation. Don't ask. My ma wants to talk to you."

"What for?"

"Just does. You got something better to do?"

He was right: I had absolutely nothing to do, better or otherwise—I couldn't even keep walking, as it would have been madness, walking alone at night. Andy guided me to his wagon. A woman about thirty-five, wearing spectacles, boots, and a Zouave jacket, stuck out her hand. It felt just like her son's.

"If you don't just take the cake," she said.

"I beg your pardon?"

"We've been watching you over an hour. We saw you from over the hill. I said to Andy here, 'Andy,' I said, 'that lady walking alone down there, you should thank God that lady isn't your mother.' "

I dropped her hand, fast. "Her name's Annie," Andy said to his mother.

"Well, Annie, I'm Sarah Jackson. And I'm not a betting woman, but if I was, I'd bet you didn't get burnt out more'n eight hours ago. And if my husband was still with us he'd make me a side bet—five hours tops. Am I right?"

I backed away a few steps. Nobody likes being insulted and nobody likes being watched; and most of all nobody likes being watched without any hint it's happening. Sarah had managed to drive in all her nails with one blow.

"That how you pass the time?" I asked. "Eyeballing refugees?"

"Honey, we're refugees too. Been such ever since that skunk Bragg abandoned the field at Murfreesboro. That'll be two years this Christmas. We're experts on passing the time."

Andy climbed up the side of the wagon in two leggy strides. He started rummaging under a plaid wool blanket that was itself blanketed with fine red dust; he sneezed, and his mother turned to him in concern.

"You're not catching cold, are you, Andy? 'Cause you know there's nothing I can do if you—"

"Ma-a-a-aa!" Andy whined, in four elongated syllables. "I'm *fine.*" Sarah turned back to me.

"What Andy and I were wondering," she said, "was whether you're just dumb as all get-out or trying to court suicide."

The old Annie—that is, before this morning—would have answered that question with a verbal slap and a flounce into the next county. The new Annie, equally annoyed, remained where she stood. For it felt good, this talking—not the insults, of course, but the talking itself, after so many hours of being alone, with only my doubts and my answerless questions keeping me kin. I was starting to realize the heartache of solitude isn't loneliness, like everyone says. It's silence.

There was much silence here. Even the wagon-to-wagon visiting was done with downcast eyes and lowered voices, the way old people talk at funerals. The questions I overheard were all negative: "Haven't seen any firewood, have you?" "Can't spare any salt, can you?" "You don't have a dose of figwort, do you?" And even when the answer was yes—when a stick of wood would be exchanged, or a tiny and precious salt packet, or a cluster of dusty foxglove—the thank-yous were negative too, both parties knowing nothing had really helped, nothing had really changed; the cold were still cold, the hungry still hungry, the ill still sick and probably dying.

But mostly people didn't speak at all. A woman in one cart sat staring at nothing. In her lap was a dead cat, and by her side sat a little girl, sucking an unlit candle. In another wagon a pregnant woman was vomiting steadily over the side. A white-haired man who looked older than my grandfather plucked at a sore that covered his face from neck to ear and bathed him in pus. An unmoving baby lay in an open violin case. Its mouth was outlined in dust.

Sarah Jackson looked around her and shook her head. "These folks and you," she said, "have a lot in common. For one thing they're all ladies, even the men. For another it'd require a miracle of Red Sea proportions for most of them to make it to the end of the month, and I doubt even the Second Coming could pull 'em through New Year's. The same could be said of you."

"Thank you," I said. "I always knew we Southern women would pull together in a crisis."

Sarah spat.

"Southern women!" she said. "Honey, you better stop thinking of yourself as a Southern woman and start seeing yourself as the lowest of the low—a person who's *losing*. None of these folks can help you. They might want to, but they can't—they're full busy sending invites to their own funerals."

She pointed a grimy finger at the pregnant woman.

"Look at that cow over there heaving her guts all over the

road. Where's her brains, to get jammed at a time like this? And don't tell me her husband was home on leave and who knows when they'd meet again; if he loved her he'd have stopped by a whore on the way home and relieved himself. Hell, if she loves him so much she'd've kept her knees locked, just so he doesn't come back to his everloving and all that's left is a couple of gravestones."

Now she looked at the scratching old man.

"I don't care how much it itches," she said, "I always tell Andy—"

"Sarah," I interrupted, "if you've got such objection to other folks' problems, why bother talking to me?"

She smiled at that. It was, I realized, her first smile.

"Oh," she said, "Andy asked me to."

"How come?"

"He thought you were pretty."

Even in the darkness, even in this nest of despair and exhaustion, I blushed. Andy's movements in the wagon froze.

"He's at an age where he notices," said Sarah. "And he worried because you didn't have a shawl or a basket and didn't seem to have anything to eat. He said you looked like you were out taking the air and it didn't seem to have sunk in how dangerous all this was. So he asked me to help you."

She shrugged.

"I've lost my husband and my daughter and two brothers and three brothers-in-law," she said. "The chief crop my farm grows these days is skulls and tombstones. Andy's all I've got left out of this whole damn business. I do what I can to make him happy."

She patted the seat next to her.

"Climb up," she said. "You can't travel with us because it's hard enough finding food for two. But I'll tell you what I know about how to survive."

It was hard climbing into her wagon, because she went out of her way not to extend her hand, and Andy was still too immobilized by embarrassment to offer to help. I heaved myself up to the bench—and it really *was* a bench, hacked neatly in half and covered with a Union officer's greatcoat. Sarah noticed me no-ticing and shoved her glasses up into her hair.

"I didn't uproot it from some public park, if that's what you're wondering," she said. "It was just lying there. I suppose some miniature Sherman tried torching it but it must've been wet—maybe from all the blood spilt."

"That's a nicely poetic way of putting it," I said.

"It's nothing but truth," said Sarah. "Andy and I passed through Resaca awhile back. I never can keep these battles straight one from the other but Andy's hot for it, and according to him this one we won. Well, it took place about six months ago and the Oostenaula River's still running so red it's dyed all the fish gills pink. And you go back in the trees far enough—you know, into those places the sun never reaches—you can find boots filled with blood half a year still hasn't dried. This whole state—this whole country, this poor sad Confederacy—the soil's so full of bones it feels like you're walking on eggshells. Our boys'—their boys' too. You know how they're going into battle these days? They're pinning their names on their coats, so the gravediggers know to write the right families. And on our side there's so little paper they're making do with used envelopes, and it's got so confused they're listing the same dead twice.

"Which reminds me. Haven't you seen any soldiers yet? Dead ones, I mean?"

"No," I said, "the ones I ran into were all too alive."

"Well, give it time. You'll get lucky. Dead soldiers've turned out to be me and Andy's main sustenance."

"Theirs," I asked her, "or ours?"

"Not ours, honey. Ours can't offer a thing, save lice and a sad expression. But theirs have it all. Shoes, cooked food, green money, dry blankets—one time we even found us a map, only it turned out to be missing a couple of states so we decided we'd better chuck it. I got these spectacles off a Union—what was he, sugar?" she called.

"Lieutenant-colonel," growled Andy.

"Lieutenant-colonel. A weak-eyed lieutenant-colonel. But that's the first lesson, honey. Well, the second lesson. The first

lesson you've already botched. You should never have just hit
the road like you did. You should've taken whatever you could."

"There wasn't anything left to take."

"Really? You went room by room? You checked every inch of
your garden and your shed and your root cellar? You sifted
through every pile of ash on your whole property, and you
couldn't even manage to come away with one single turnip?"

I studied my dusty palms. She was, of course, right: I hadn't
gone room by room or inch by inch, let alone ash-pile by ash-
pile. I fretted the hem of the Yankee uniform tacked to the
bench. There was something profoundly alarming about Sarah's
goods-laden cart—something the swaying lanterns and mil-
dewed blankets of the other wagons only reinforced. For even
the worst-off refugees—even the dirtiest, poorest, most crowded,
most sickly, most meagerly outfitted family in this entire encampment—were infinitely better provisioned than I.

I shredded some more material. This March through Georgia—it wasn't some scene from a history book, with right and
wrong already settled and a clearly determined finale. No one
was watching this, no one was judging; nobody knew how it
would end, or if it would end at all or just turn into everyday life,
so that this became what was normal and not losing everything
became the unusual. I should never have gotten excited by what
had happened: I couldn't afford to. I should take this dead
seriously, as seriously . . . as seriously as death.

Pumped up as I'd been by everything, neither cold nor thirst
nor hunger nor exhaustion had touched me the whole afternoon.
But now I felt cold indeed, and thirsty and hungry and all the
rest. And scared. That too. That most of all. I realized I had
absolutely no idea what to do about anything. I shivered. I felt
the lacy shudder of early panic.

Sarah reached behind her back with one hand and into a
pocket with the other; when she straightened back up both arms
were extended, a stained flannel shirt draped around one wrist,
a bloody muffler around the other.

"No cure for pneumonia, far as I know," she said. "Take
them."

I did, buttoning the heavy shirt over my cotton dress and tucking the itchy muffler into my bodice. I now looked exactly like Sarah, with her men's boots and soldier's jacket; I now looked exactly like everyone here. A person with nothing, an invisible person: a person who lives off the land. No. Sherman's soldiers lived off the land. We lived off the dead.

Sarah passed me a turkey sandwich that someone had taken two bites from, and started to munch another. Hers was still whole. After a few minutes Andy joined us. Looking everywhere except into my face, he accepted half of his mother's sandwich and downed it in one swallow. I offered him mine. He ignored me. Sarah, sighing elaborately, gave him her second half, and took half of mine.

"You plan on sulking the rest of the night?" she asked him.

He munched the second sandwich without answering.

"You do what you want," said Sarah, "but Annie's going her own way in the morning and if you don't talk to her now you won't be talking to her period."

He took a last swallow.

"I never said you were pretty," he said.

"Well, I wish you had," I said. "You're not so bad-looking yourself. For a non-Georgia boy, I mean."

He squeezed out a slit of a smile. Sarah rolled her eyes.

"Everybody friends again?" she asked. "Good. Now, Annie—I told you I thought you could do with a little advice. First is, it's real important when you travel these days to dress like you are now. You don't *want* to look good. You don't *want* to look pretty. You don't want anyone to want anything you've got—not your body and especially not your clothes. I emphasize clothes because if they take your clothes they may go after the rest of you even if that wasn't their original intention."

My hand automatically rose to adjust the muffler.

"Who's this 'they' we're speaking of?" I asked.

"They're every single person you meet," she said. "With the exception of me and Andy, *everyone* is a threat and you better never forget it. Most of it's desperation but some's sheer meanness. That's on *our* side. As for their side—well, they're the enemy, they're supposed to act like murdering jackasses. If you're lucky they'll only act like the second.

"Next, never leave one of these camps without enough food to last two whole days. If you can't trade for it or beg for it, go ahead and borrow it—who knows, you might actually get around to returning it, if the war keeps going. Should you find more food on the road—and you should, that's what you're there for—eat what you got in the morning and take along what's new. Don't eat any canned Yankee food without boiling the whole tin first, and stand to the side in case it explodes. And don't open it right off the bat or it'll blow up in your eyes.

"Third and most important, I want to give you something and ask you something and then we'll call it quits. I asked you before about seeing dead soldiers. Don't be so pert about whose side they're on: they're on nobody's side anymore. Check their rucksacks and their pockets and their hat brims—sometimes they store jerky up there. And don't ever take anything military—orders, passes, signals. It's too late for something like that to aid our side, and their side'll shoot you for spying if they find it on you."

"Ma," said Andy, "you're talking too much. Give her the thing."

"I've had about enough 'things' for one day," I said. "What 'thing' are you talking about?"

Sarah ignored me.

"You can give it to her, sugar," she said to Andy.

Andy reached into the darkness behind me and emerged with a package large and heavy enough to fill up and weight both his arms. Whatever it was was wrapped in a moldy, embroidered tablecloth.

"I'll need the cloth back," Sarah said hastily. "All I'm giving is what's inside."

Andy held out his arms, and I took the package. It felt, somehow, soft and stiff at the same time. I slipped off the mossy tablecloth. It was the chevroned jacket of a military uniform.

But from what army! For it wasn't a Rebel uniform, and not Union either—and not Zouave or navy or butternut homespun.

It was the bright robin redbreast of a British soldier's topcoat from the days of the Revolution.

"Ain't that a hoot?" Sarah said. "The good old days, when we both were fighting the same enemy! But it's thick and it's whole and at least nobody'll mistake you for being on whatever side they aren't. Go on, try it, see how it suits you."

It was a gift of incredible generosity, one I couldn't possibly accept—although, on the other hand, I really longed to. For which Sarah herself was to blame. For if you weren't to leave an encampment without food, how much more so were you not to leave without clothing! And if someone were so naïve as to give you—

"I can't possibly take this," I said. "It's too valuable for you to just hand it away like this."

Sarah nodded. "Couldn't agree more," she said, "I could accomplish some pretty fair trading with it, no question. On the other side, I don't want my last-born perishing of heartbreak, or worse yet talking about it from now till hellfire. Now first thing tomorrow morning you dump wax all over the front and rip off one of the sleeves. You'll be a lick cold on that side but folks'll be less likely to steal it if they figure they can do better picking the strays off Sherman or Hood."

Andy took the coat from my arms and held it for me, his bearing imperious as a headwaiter. I slipped inside.

Oh it was warm! It was like fur—no, like flannel, like baize, like cambric warmed by a fire in winter, the way my mother used to warm up my childhood nightgowns. And so protective, so solid a barrier against all elements, natural and less so. I hadn't realized how cold the night had become until now, when the parts of me not covered by this marvelous coat turned suddenly chilled and resentful; but with this memory of a long-dead Redcoat guarding my arms and back and flopping over my wrist bones, I felt I could stand up to any degree of coldness. A surge of confidence darted its way through my warming heart.

"Wherever did you find this?" I asked her.

"Where I find everything," she said. "On the ground, in the rivers, off people's backs. One time we found a whole heap of hams stuck in a tree—Yanks must've intended to come back for 'em later. We couldn't possibly eat it all so we swapped for a comforter, two quarts of quince honey, and a packet of pins. Though sometimes I trade just to pass the time. Refugeeing's not bad once you know how, but it does get boring. Nothing ever changes. I wish I could find me a kaleidoscope."

"I keep telling her she should learn how to read," Andy said.

"Nah, I'm too stupid for that," said Sarah. "Speaking of which." She turned to me. "I'm not so stupid where it counts. I asked you awhile back if you had any food. Where is it?"

Snuggled inside the crimson jacket and anxious she might snatch it back, I tried to remember exactly what it was I had said.

"I don't have any food," I said cautiously.

She made a face. "I can see that," she said. "Only I also can see you know where to find some. Am I right?"

The apples! Of course after this gift she was welcome, more than welcome, to all of them, only . . . only how had she known?

"You took too long saying no," she explained without smiling. "So—what is it and where?"

"An apple orchard," I said. "About a mile or so away. It's sheltered in a little hollow—not easy to find. I bet even *they* missed it."

"An apple orchard," Sarah repeated. "Andy, sugar, you want to go with Annie and bring back some apples?"

Andy eyed me with apprehension. I knew our being together alone would shatter the shell of his spell in nothing flat, but who could resist his mother, her face now abeam with the satisfaction of a successful gift-giver? He grabbed up a basket with the words "Property of Atlanta Women's Lying-In Hospital" stamped on the back, and we slipped off the bench. We already were on the road when we heard Sarah calling.

"Andy! Listen! If you find any apples, be sure to give Annie the first bite! They might be poisoned!"

I was surprised she'd neglected to tell him, should anything fatal befall me, to take back the coat.

.   .   .

After about five minutes Andy said, "You still hungry?"

I wasn't, but Sarah had me convinced I'd best always eat when offered a chance. "Why, what've you got?" I asked.

"I don't have anything," he said. "I'm just still hungry, is all. I'm so hungry all the time now I can hardly remember being anything but. I bet I spend most of my daylight hours thinking about food."

I looked at him sideways. He was just skirting that age when boys normally start their five-year eating jag—the one ending when either they fall in love or have to start making their own arrangements for dinner.

"That's a bad habit," I said. "You better quit it. You'll drive yourself crazy."

"I can't help it," he said.

"Well, try to. You're making me hungry too." He looked instantly contrite, which made *me* contrite. "Talk about something else," I said. "Tell me about your home. I've never been to Tennessee. To me it's as foreign as China."

He huddled himself a few inches further into his jacket (a lumberjack coat belonging to no current army and no prior war). "It's cold there this time of year," he said. "Colder than here."

Now I felt chilly as well as hungry.

"Go on," I said. "What happened to make you leave?" I already sensed, after only one day, that this was a standard question in the wake of great armies.

"Well, I'll tell you," said Andy. "Only it's about food, so don't get mad. Promise?"

I promised.

"It was just before Christmas," he said. "Tobacco was selling treble, even with both the blockades, so Pa went to the coast and managed to move some. He came home with the first fixed money we'd seen for quite a spell. Ma cooked up boar for supper, with peas and relish and dried radishes and store-bought coffee—I'm sorry, Annie, but it's part of the story—and she made a nut-cake for dessert. Right after she'd served it somebody knocked at the back. Pa guessed it was his brother, my

Uncle Jack—the one who was always claiming he could smell my ma's nut-cake clean over the valley. So he opened the door.

"It was a Yankee soldier. He stood rearing his arm back a good half-yard. Then he sank an ax-handle straight into Pa's forehead. It was Pa's own ax too, which Pa seemed real umbraged by and kept trying to point out. Only he couldn't talk much on account of the blow kind of confused him, so he soon quit complaining and just munched on his nut-cake till it got too full of blood and what-all else he was leaking for him to much care for the texture. Then he died."

My fingers twitched toward Andy's, but his remained still.

"The funny thing is," he said, "I miss my father like Sunday blazes but I miss that nut-cake almost as bad. 'Cause every time I think of one I think of the other. And afterwards of course we left so fast we had to leave it behind, and you know my mother, she's still complaining about it. She's also been kicking herself the past two years on account of she didn't take the ax. But she was a sweeter lady in those days so she made lots of mistakes."

"She doesn't make many now," I said.

"Nope," said Andy. "She's got it down cold. And she'd take an ax to *me* if I told her this, but if peace ever comes, she's gonna be bored as heck. She'll have to go find herself another war zone. Mexico, maybe."

By now we were nearing where I thought I remembered the orchard was. Though I wasn't sure; it had been nearly six years since I'd been here, and daytime too, and I'd been with Randall, who knew the way. We had come here so he could propose to me. It was supposed to have been a surprise, but wasn't: I'd sneaked up behind him earlier that month, intending to kiss him hello, and overheard him practicing: Annie, we've known one another ever since childhood; Annie, my parents and your parents always assumed; Annie, I've never looked at or thought about anyone else. I'd gone home and practiced too: Randall, you're the only boy in the county who's got both brains and a soul; Randall, I always wanted you too; Randall, what'll we do if everyone's right and a war breaks out?

The orchard was still invisible, but by now I could smell it, tart and sweet, half its fruit assuredly rotted but enough still hanging for Sarah to respect me. The remembered scent made me miss Randall—miss him more sharply than I had for a long, long time, and I grimaced, hating the familiar, forgotten pain. I glanced over at Andy, who was peering into the aromatic darkness.

He said, "Shhh!"

"Why? What's wrong?"

"Shhh! Wait! There it is again!"

"There *what* is?"

He was standing as strained and panting as a dog at a foxhole. He waved me silent.

I listened too.

There was definitely something out there, something besides trees and fruit and leaves and the night wind. But beyond that certainty, nothing definite at all. We stood like two athletes awaiting the signal, poised and aching. I could hear a slight rustle and a faint, pausing shuffle, and I tried to classify it—animal (which animal, what size, how close?) or human (which sex, how armed, *whose side?*).

"Annie," hissed Andy, in a low, unfamiliar voice, stiller than whisper, more like a growl. "Annie, we're being watched."

My desire for apples, now and forevermore, instantly vanished.

"Walk backwards," I commanded. "Backwards and out of here. Don't turn around. Just walk back."

I could just see the outline of Andy's head, shaking back and forth.

"No good," he mouthed. "They could just as easy surround us. I better go in."

"Forget it!" I snarled.

"I'll be all right. I've got a knife. I want you to stay out of the way."

"Andy," I said grimly, "you leave this place and I leave with you. You go into that orchard, you don't go alone."

"Ah, c'mon, Annie . . ."

"No! You listen to me! Your mother'll kill me!"

"Jesus Christ!" roared a voice from out of the orchard. "What the hell is this—the Children's Crusade?"

Andy dropped his knife. I dropped to my knees.

"Don't shoot us," a voice that came out of my mouth but was surely not mine kept repeating. "Don't shoot us, don't shoot us, don't shoot us, don't shoot us. . . ."

An arm dragged me up and somebody lit a lantern. The first thing I looked for was, is there a uniform? The second was, which color?

God smiled on Annie. The color was gray.

"Rebel soldiers!" gasped Andy.

Two other bodies emerged into the lantern's circle. One of them coughed. The other said, "No longer, sonny."

I shook my arm free.

"Deserters?" I asked.

"Well, that's one way of putting it. How about you folks?"

"Just refugees," I said. "They don't let civilians desert."

Andy said, "You fellas got any food?"

A hand and an apple extended themselves, and whoever was holding the light started walking. The rest of us followed, moth-like.

By now I had my bearings enough to study their faces. It was difficult telling anyone's age—war had sandpapered them all into the same weary adulthood—but one of them barely looked older than Andy. He reminded me a little of Bert, this morning's bonfirer. I told him so.

"Thanks heaps, lady," he said, "but I didn't quit Johnston to go bumming with Sherman."

"I just meant your age," I said. "I can't believe how young some of you are."

One of the other men cleared his throat. "You wouldn't believe how *old* some of us are either," he said. "I'm Fred Bauer and I'm fifty-one. Got a three-year-old grandson and twin six-month-old granddaughters, or so I'm told. This gawky consumptive"—he pointed to the coughing man with the lantern, who seemed both uninsulted by the description and resigned to it—"is my son Rob. Age twenty-eight and my youngest son in the service. The infant there's Micah Hopeland. Joined up as a drummer boy, only he feels he's got nothing left beating for."

I gazed at them all, my mind flowing one way, my heart another. Deserters! Part of me pitied them so, part of me was enraged. And part of me was still so astounded and embarrassed by my recent "Don't shoot, don't shoot" performance I stopped thanking God they were Rebels and simply gave thanks it was dark. Andy was stuffing apples into his mouth and darting admiring glances at Micah.

"Drummer, huh?" he said between crunches. "I bet you've seen everything!"

Micah shrugged.

"Which one was best?"

This time Micah shrugged so elaborately he nearly popped out a shoulder seam.

"The Hornet's Nest?" asked Andy.

"No, not that one," Micah mumbled.

"Hell's Half Acre?"

"It was okay."

"Vicksburg?" Andy suggested. "Chickamauga? Chattanooga? New Hope Church, Pumpkin Vine Creek, Pickett's Mill? Atlanta?"

"Say, you know your battles, sonny," Fred said. His son Rob coughed. Whatever he spat was so heavy I heard it land.

"For my money," Fred continued, "I'd say you hit the nail on the bale with that Vicksburg affair. You know we were eating lice by the finish? Sure. White lice for officers, brown lice for men. Red lice for cavalrymen. Civilians ate rats and cockroaches.

"Nor would the Yankees permit their withdrawal. 'Unconditional surrender,' you know—just a prettified way of saying kill civilians. Which they did: just left 'em in place, side by side with the army. Women and children, wounded and dying, hiding out in coffins and caves and under rocks, perishing if not of starvation then typhus or pox. Mothers crawling into piano boxes to deliver dead babies, while that son of a bitch U. kiss-my-ass S. Grant sat drunk on the deck of a gunboat for *forty-eight days,* with his hell-blown assistant Tecumseh Sherman dancing attendance.

"One of my men got shot in the stomach. He spewed out so much intestine we were tripping on it. We couldn't even spare a bullet to kill him so we said our good-byes and with his permission—which he couldn't give fast enough: Lord, nothing on earth turns a Christian man's thoughts to suicide faster than a bullet in the gut—we tossed him over a cliff. There were so many Northern ships in the river he landed on one of their engines and blew up the whole boat. Killed more people dying than the rest of us did while alive."

He scratched at his neck.

"And we *still* would've won," he said, "we *still* could've fetched a victory, if goddamn Jeff Davis hadn't stripped this poor army to skeleton strength for the Gettysburg campaign. Not that *that* did much good. How that goat-brain got to be president I'll never understand. And Lee! R. E. Lee! Royal Easterner Lee! I know in Virginia they think he's the Second Coming but the war back there and the war out here ain't the same war—theirs is heroic—ours sucks eggs—"

I'd always heard everyone south of the Delaware thinks Southerners suffer a mortal tendency to go on and on about things; Randall in fact once declared this to be the primary cause of the war: "They just don't care for our narrative style, Annie." Now I lifted my hand to staunch the flood of Fred's words.

"Let's sum up," I said. "After you spit out the roaches and stitch back the stomachs and patch up the soldiers . . . well, Vicksburg was just another battle we lost."

The three of them stared at me, almost—but not quite—too outraged to bother to set me straight. Even Andy bristled.

"Annie!" he moaned.

"Don't 'Annie!' me!" I snapped. " 'Annie' what?"

"Annie," he whispered, "show a little gratitude."

"For what? Some glorious battle we didn't even win?"

"Lady," said Fred, "some people might say it was glorious *because* we didn't win."

"Well, those people would be fools."

Micah had turned so furious he trembled. Staring at Andy, ignoring me completely, he hissed:

"Listen. Your friend. She's right. Everything Fred just said about Vicksburg's a lie. It wasn't glorious and we could never have won."

He ran his hand along the stock of his rifle.

"The only good thing about Vicksburg," he said slowly, "was it gave civilians a taste of what war's really like."

Now he was looking directly at me.

"Problem was," he added, "they all died. So they couldn't bear witness."

Andy, confused, plucked at his jacket. Rob Bauer coughed his slow, throaty rattle.

"Shut up, Micah," Fred said.

"No, I won't shut up," Micah said. "Who the hell are we doing this for? Not for ourselves, that's for damn sure. It's for *civilians*—know-nothing, know-it-all civilians. People like her."

I stood up. Micah stood up too. He grabbed my arm. I noticed he was quite a bit taller than I, and quite a bit angrier. I couldn't do anything about his height, but I didn't have to stand for his anger.

"Get your hands off me," I said.

"You listen to me," he said.

"I said let me go."

"I don't care if I hurt you," he warned.

"I'm sure you don't. In fact a Yankee soldier told me more or less the same thing this very morning."

"Maybe you bring it out in people."

I threw off his arm.

"Then arrange the world," I said, "so the people I bring it out in don't cross my path every five minutes! I don't want any more war and even less do I want any more war stories."

"You listen anyway. I was at Kenesaw Mountain. You know about Kenesaw Mountain?"

"I know about Kenesaw Mountain!" said Andy.

"I bet you do." He turned to me. "Do you?"

"I bet I'm about to," I answered.

He stiffened. Fred chuckled and nodded to Andy.

"Son?" he said.

"Sherman's biggest defeat was at Kenesaw Mountain," Andy reported.

Micah nodded. "That's the ticket," he said. "We kicked Sherman's ass. Just about everywhere else he outflanked or outshot or outran us, and usually all three. But at Kenesaw Mountain he elected to attack us directly, and we destroyed three thousand Yankees in less than four hours. If we could've kept up that pace we'd've killed one million men in under two months."

"Imagine that," I said. "You could've wiped out New York, Philadelphia, and Boston before the end of the summer."

"For a couple of hours I thought we had."

He reached out and mussed Andy's hair—an old man's gesture, unsettling to see in a boy scarcely older than Andy himself.

"They strolled up to meet us," he said, "as calm as smoke. Somebody signaled an order and they fixed bayonets. Real slow and lazy, though, drowsy-like; it was a hot day and they were moving the way cats do in sunshine—no bother, no hurry, no thought of shelter. Just taking their own good time. So we naturally seized advantage of that one quiet moment in the whole war. We yelled our Yell and we loosed our howitzers."

Fred sighed. Rob shifted his legs. Micah said:

"We start shooting. They start falling. But they don't know how to retreat, 'cause they never had need to. They keep on marching till they reach our trench line. They jump in the same second we jump out. They're swinging their bayonets left and right, only it doesn't help, 'cause the slowest rifle kills faster than the sharpest bayonet.

"It gets so it's impossible *not* to kill them. We just kill them and kill them and kill them."

By now I had sat down without realizing it. All of us had; Micah too. He was gazing into the orchard as if a cyclorama of the battlefield had been affixed to its whistling branches.

"I couldn't take it," he said quietly. "I couldn't take the killing going that smooth. It hadn't bothered me taking the dying every minute for thirty-eight months, but it turned out I couldn't kill like this, up close and so silky. It was too simple, too easy. It didn't feel like war. It felt like . . . cheating.

"I figure I owe an apology. To *them*—can you believe it? But that's how I feel. Only I'm no Jesus; I can't restore life, and I'm no longer sure He can either. Which leaves only one clear way for me to tell 'em I'm sorry. And that's to surrender."

He glanced at the four of us.

Nobody spoke. The word "surrender" hung high in the air, stained as a battle flag, private as death.

"There's so many Yankee wounded it takes nearly two hours to find someone healthy enough to accept my parole before he dies too. Finally I locate a group of about eight living Northerns. They're burying bodies and bitching to beat the band. They talk about General Sherman as if he's God on a stick but the rest of their leaders they wouldn't waste a swallow of spit on. Which about tabs with how I think about General Johnston—that he's a genius but calling the rest of them morons insults the morons.

"I tell them I want to surrender. They look at me like I said it in Greek. 'I surrender!' I say. 'Take me North and show me around! Throw me in jail, present me to Father Abraham, carry me off to one of those camps where you starve our soldiers and say it's account of we're starving yours! But get me out of here. I want off this mountain and out of this war.'

"They stand there staring for a couple of long minutes. I'm thinking, 'This is the fearsome host of Tecumseh Sherman? These scarecrows? Why, they're about as fearsome as mice in a cotton gin!' Finally one of them says, 'You say you want *what*?'

"Least that's what I guess he says. I can't really make it out. At first I think it's his accent, then I realize he's got no teeth. I repeat what I want.

" 'I need it over with,' I say.

" 'I need it over with too,' he says.

" 'Well, I need it more,' I say.

" 'No, you don't,' he says.

" 'Yes, I do,' I say.

" 'You started it,' he says.

" 'Well, you made us get started,' I say.

" 'Says you,' he says.

" 'Says me what?' I say.

" 'Whoa, boys!' somebody else says. 'Says you, says me—you sound like a couple of goddamn senators!' He walks up to me and puts out his hand. I figure I'm supposed to shake it. Pretty civil, I'm thinking—maybe that's why they call it a civil war. I stick out my paw. Turns out he just wants my Enfield.

"For a second or so I hesitate. That rifle's been with me longer than most of my brothers, and saved my skin one hell of a lot more often than any poor bastard living-or-dead human soldier ever did. But only dolts and civilians get sentimental over hardware, so I hand it over. I take out the bullets first. I may not be sentimental but I don't intend being shot with my own musket.

"They pass me a shovel and a couple of dirty looks and I join them burying bodies. I try to imagine which ones I personally corpsed but that's pretty joyless so I stop. We bury whole bodies for two or three hours, then we bury limbs and organs so the wolves don't come and uncover it all. Then they say to me, 'Okay, let's do that surrender.' We start to walk.

"We walk. And we walk. *And* we walk. We're one week into full summer, so it doesn't get dark for a long, long time, but eventually the sun lowers, and we stop. They've each got a tin of canned pork and a tin of canned potatoes. They offer me some. One of the Yanks chews the potatoes for the one with no teeth and gives it to him all porridged up. I find this so touching I almost cry. We resume walking.

"It's finally true dark. Way, way off in the distance I see a light. It's probably a lamp in a cabin but it could just be starlight hitting a rock. We keep walking but we never seem to get any closer to the light. It occurs to me that maybe we're going in circles, but I don't say a word. I'm thinking they may be intending to kill me. I don't say a word about that either.

"Instead I start thinking of everything I remember from church about death. Heaven is angels and harps, but never anything definite; it was hell they were always specific on. Hell is stakes in your eyes and nails in your ears. Hell is talons of eagles ripping your throat open and wild dogs drinking the blood. Hell is seeing your own broken fingers stretching for food that keeps moving further away, and watching your burning and blistered feet bathe in a cooling stream that turns to a river of fire. Pain and starvation and eternal degradation.

"I start in laughing. Sounds like an average day's work in the war to me! Not even a day of battle. Less dangerous. Less interesting.

"A light jumps up. It's right in my face. It's sharp, bright orange and it seems real familiar, and I realize it's the very hellfire I've been thinking about. Only it's a whole lot hotter and less amusing when it's so close it's burning the metal of my buttons right into my chest.

"Somebody speaks my name. Of course Satan knows your name from your birth, doesn't he?—so that's really not such a surprise. Still, you don't expect Satan to use your nickname, and the boys have been calling me Mitch since the fall of Donelson. I struggle to see and then, suddenly, I can see everything.

"Everything except for the sons of bitches who brought me here.

"Who've high-tailed it, naturally. But before they did, they've marched me right into the rear of my own goddamn army. Yep. Slipped me right in with the rest of the drummers."

Andy said, "Oh!" The rest of the apples lay whole in his lap, nervously polished.

Micah said: "I look around. It's like I never left. There's nothing to eat, as usual. Three friends are missing and nobody even bothers to tell me whether they're dead. Somebody's sitting on my drum and when I ask him to move he's so deaf from the shelling he can't even hear. I realize I'm the only man here who's eaten since daybreak or who's seen or done anything new since the start of the war. I realize I'd rather they'd killed me than sent me back.

"And I see the hell of the whole situation is this: those bastards assume they did me a *favor*. They're out there right now, heading on back, and telling themselves what heroes they are, exposing themselves to the hills and the guns and the dark and the risk, all for the sake of setting straight this poor, sorry Reb—both saving his life and reminding him of his duty.

"For I know what they're thinking. Knew it from the minute they gave me a shovel instead of a bullet, and pork and potatoes instead of a bayonet thrust. They're thinking we're all on the same side here: we're all soldiers. The war's our friend. It's our people we're enemies of."

Micah was lying down in the grass now, watching the wind surge through the trees.

"So to be true to the soldierly brotherhood," he concluded, "I deserted again. And this time I asked no permission of Yankee or Reb. I quit on my own."

He looked briefly at Andy, longer at me.

"You two," he said. "People like you. You squeezed more out of me than I ever was born with. You decide from now on. Fight it or end it. Leave me out of it. From now on I go to the wall for Northern soldiers, and I kill Southern civilians."

Fred rolled his eyes; Rob smiled. Both of them looked like they'd heard this story so often they no longer heard it at all. Andy looked like he wanted his mother. I looked—like what? One day into the March and I'd lost my home, bad-mouthed the war, and been threatened by both sides' armies. Probably I just looked tired. My eyes were blurred from the burning applewood, and when I lifted them to the sky and the stars, the night's dark beauty seemed like an error.

"It's difficult understanding," I said, "why if we all want it done with, it still goes on."

"*Micah* said he wanted it done with," Fred corrected. "I didn't. And *you* said you wanted it done with; the boy didn't."

"Well, if you don't want it done with," I said, "how come you're sitting out here with us and these apples instead of your men?"

Rob cleared his throat. "He's here for me," he said. "He's keeping me company."

"Hush up, son," said Fred.

"Why? You talked. Micah talked. Why shouldn't I put in my

two cents? 'Course in Confederate money, that's about three hundred dollars."

"I hear that's enough up North," Micah said, "to buy yourself a substitute."

"Well, I hear that's enough down here to buy yourself a pound of sugar, *if* you're good-looking and maybe related to the person you're buying it from. But I'm telling you this. You look proudly at Vicksburg, Father; you like how the men died there. And Micah, you look with horror at Kenesaw Mountain: you don't. But I'm dying of consumption and nobody's looking one way or another at that kind of death. Vicksburg may lift folks onward and Kenesaw may inspire to peace, but at least they'll do *something*. I've got an illness people get in war and they get in peace. I'm coughing my life out with every breath and it bores even me because death in a war is supposed to mean battlefield death."

He cracked his knuckles and coughed his familiar cough.

"I feel left out," he whispered.

"Ah, son," Fred said softly. "Don't fret it so."

"Yeah, Rob," said Micah. "We're all being left out one way or the other. The survivors miss being heroes. The heroes miss being alive. The only ones not left out are the ones who never went in."

Rob sputtered what sounded like sobbing. "There used to be rhythm and pacing," he said. "Someone was dying, there was time for it—time for the person himself to get used to it, time for his family too. Now death seizes its victim and boom!—a minute of noise and blood and unbearable pain and he's out of there: no chance to adjust, no opportunity to think it all over. And when the family hears—well, they're sad, but it's a story they've heard before. But to die at an old man's pace in a young man's grave-yard: it's humiliating. It's unfair. Nobody'll remember."

Micah dug his shoulders further into the earth and stared at the sky. Rob coughed. Fred rose to his feet, nudging my shoulder.

Andy and I rose too. My knees felt locked and chilled from sitting so long on the cool dirt.

"Rob," I said.

He looked up. His face was shiny with sweat, but he looked even colder than I was. The kerchief he clutched in his hand was splattered valentine red.

"What," he said, inflectionless.

"You'll be remembered," I said. "You'll be remembered by people who never even knew you. They'll look at this war and they'll think of the bodies and yours will be the only death anyone will be able to bear. It'll be the only death anyone will be able to understand."

Micah opened his mouth, then closed it; Rob didn't say a word. Fred scooped up the lantern to guide us out, from the private war of the orchard to the other war. Andy was silent, hunched in his coat. When we reached the main road, Fred handed the lantern to Andy and told him to check a few yards in all four directions.

"I appreciate what you told my boy," he said to me. He kissed my cheek, and when Andy returned he kissed him too. Then he took back his lantern and returned to the woods and his son.

We reached the camp and tiptoed to Sarah's wagon. Sarah was sleeping. Every so often her breathing snagged on a sob, then released itself with a long sigh.

"She's not as tough as she thinks she is," Andy whispered.

Who is?

Andy was sound asleep when Sarah shook me awake, long before daybreak. I repeated my thanks for the coat. She patted me into its folds, adjusted my scarf, checked all my buttons, then eased me over the side of the wagon. Whether she intended to tell Andy I had left on my own or at her request I never found out; for like so many others along the road, I never saw either again.

I began walking. It was one of those cold, late-dawning autumn mornings where fog hangs entrapped in leafless branches and rivers of dew sog the ground. Mud sucked at my feet and snaked through my shoes and stockings, and the dirt-stiffened hem of my skirt pounded my legs like the smack of a ruler. When the sun finally rose, the color of jellied peaches, it added no warmth and almost no light.

It's surprising how easily chaos becomes familiar. Yesterday's ruins had spasmed my heart with anginal pincers. This morning's seemed nearly normal. The only element still surprising was how rapidly Sherman was moving: for whichever direction I looked, he'd been here already, burning and emptying out. The smoldering wood made the air smell cruelly like Christmas.

The pale sun continued rising, illuminating the destruction, its sheer scale, its thoroughness, the *thoughtfulness* of its thoroughness. Frost-scarred lettuces lined the road, and I gathered them up and munched as I trudged along. With the future so undecided, I did what all victims and refugees do: I daydreamed and recollected.

Since yesterday morning I'd met five soldiers—two blue, three gray—the varied representatives of two great armies. I had discussed the meaning of war with them all. But Bert was the soldier whose discourse I most remembered; and what I remembered best was his discourse regarding me. I spit out some spoiled lettuce. Bert had said—and he seemed to be someone who ought to know—he had said I would make a good soldier.

I wondered if this was true.

What was being a soldier like? Seen from without, it appeared sluggish and feudal—compulsively formal, bedeviled by rank, laden with precepts and strictures and prohibitions. Yet I had glimpsed, lolling interstitial amongst all those rules, massive pockets of freedom—whole vast empty rooms of it. The life of a soldier seemed like a climb up a stairway without any stairs, only the wooden supporting spine of preagreed ritual. Step away from that spine and anything might happen—to you, by you.

So . . . what was it like? Leaving your home, family, friends, all you were used to, to go to war: how would it feel?

Well, how did it feel right now? I missed everything—missed it all, all I had lost, and strongly enough that the simple *thought* of missing it saddened me. On the other hand, the wide-open diciness of what had replaced it bedazzled me. This sense of throwing it all away, of starting anew among faceless others, faceless yourself—was this what going to war was like? Had it been for Randall? Was it for Dan—for Bert? For Sherman himself? Was it?

Hey: it didn't sound so bad.

Yes, but what about what soldiers *do*? Forget those tearful departures and yearned-for families and those daily encounters with strangers and strangeness; what about what they *do*? How do they do it? Could I do it? *Would* I do it?

What would it feel like to kill someone?

I'd seen people die. My grandfather died while sitting beside me on the front porch, my feet in his lap and a pitcher of lemonade by his elbow. My neighbor's child had died of rabies while she and I sat by his bedside, rubbing his hands and easing him out of his sweat-soaked pajamas. Later my neighbor herself died, one week after childbirth. Randall's brother, missing two days, was found drowned in a flooded gully. All genuine deaths, all sad, all—even Grandfather's—much too early. But, at least, all *natural*. No one had died at the hands of an enemy. No dead Randalls. No killing Berts.

What would it feel like to hold a gun in my hand and aim it at someone?

It was hard to imagine. Hard—but not impossible.

For one thing, you probably actually didn't fire directly at somebody all that often. You were part of a pack, firing into another pack. All around you were shells and bullets and dust and powder and what really had rattled Randall, incessant and brain-numbing noise: booming, screaming, roaring, bellowing; orders and counterorders; charges, explosions; the yip-yip squealing soprano of our infamous Rebel Yell. It was probably so noisy and confusing you fired without really thinking. Maybe.

But what if it *wasn't* like that? What if it only was you and one other person? What if you and your enemy, both lost or confused or abandoned, or simply because somehow in the bleating cacophony your eyes and his accidentally locked—what if it became just you two? Two soldier-citizens, legally duelling—in fact, legally compelled to duel. Would you pull the trigger?

Annie, would *you* pull the trigger?

It might be your-life-or-his. But then again it might not: he could be another you, wondering whether to shoot or just close his eyes and pray for the battle to break on another shore. So . . . would you?

I swallowed the last of the lettuce and tugged myself closer into my coat. I was still cold and still hungry and still tired, and there was nothing for me to do but keep walking and become colder and hungrier and more tired yet. And enough of seeing both sides of this imagined contest: *he* isn't you, *you* are. You lift your weapon. You shoot.

All I knew for sure about what happens next was it was different from any disease but just as deadly. I would drop my arm and look at the body. For want of another identity, I pictured the body as Bert's.

He appeared, dead, younger than ever. But otherwise no less dangerous—nor any less likely to do exactly what he had done while living: threaten me, turn me out, burn me down. He'd looked like an enemy then and he looked like one now. And he had been right: I *would* make a good soldier.

I felt absolutely no remorse.

My walking assumed a pattern as the day wore on. The first thing was always to listen. Refugees travel with horses but so do Yankees: hooves meant hide somewhere and wait for what came down the road. Dead birds also hinted of soldiers, since having a gun in one's hand seemed to lead automatically to shooting the sky. Barking dogs meant abandoned houses. The howl of a cat meant acres of foodlessness. The rumble of thunder meant an excuse to sit down.

I watched too. Footprints, wagon wheels, boots, dust—all told who was ahead of me, and in what strength. And the detritus scattered across the road had its tale too, for refugees never drop anything; all is too precious, too irreplaceable. Armies, on the other hand, are slobs; I could, and did, eat off what they'd not even realized they'd spilled. It occurred to me, as I gnawed an abandoned heel of bread, that it might be my own stolen bread I was eating, and the feathers from my own comforter whose path I was following.

By the time I reached Benbow Crossings, a tiny village marked by two roads and a church, it was late afternoon. I could smell smoke and animals, fire and sulphur. I approached the church, hoping for food. Its steeple shimmered within the yolk of the still-unset sun.

It was clear Sherman's men already had been here. Pews and crosses and a charred pulpit littered the yard; the front door, wrenched off its hinges, was scarred with epithets. A row of windows along the side of the church had been expertly broken, each in the center, as though pierced by arrows, or baseballs. It was equally clear they were gone—clear more than anything else by the silence, but clear also by a feeling in the air itself, an exhausted feeling, a lack of tension. The Union army sparkled, it exuded energy and strength. And there was no energy here.

The sun fell into the horizon, and the yard turned blue. I walked into the church.

"Somebody there?" cried a man's frightened voice. "Somebody there? Who are you? Get out! There's nothing left!"

"I'm here for shelter," I said, trying to see where the voice was coming from. "I'm not with anyone's army."

At the sound of my voice, a man moved out of the shadows at the back of the church. He walked as though he were blind.

"A woman?" he said. "You a woman? Say something else!"

I said, "Tommy Stepple? Is that you? It's Annie Baker!"

"Annie?"

We rushed to each other's arms. Tommy Stepple, Randall's childhood friend and an usher at our wedding, felt cool and thin beneath the scratch of his homespun uniform. But he glowed with the same flame I knew from his smile I glowed with myself—the glow of the familiar, the glow of a face from Before.

"Oh, Tommy," I said, "it's good to see you. It seems like a thousand years."

"It's good seeing you too, Annie," he said.

Something in his voice—a hesitation before the word "seeing"—made me look up. His eyes were closed and tears rolled down his cheeks.

"Tommy," I said, "are you—did they—can't you see me?"

"I can see you," he said. "Only . . . it hurts. There's too much light."

Except for the moon, half-full but beclouded, there was almost no light at all. I shuddered.

"What happened?" I asked.

"Nothing," he said. "I mean, the docs say it's not permanent."

"What's not permanent?"

"My eyelashes," he answered.

I looked at his face once again. It was absolutely hairless: no lashes on upper or lower lids, no mustache, no beard. Cheeks scaly and dry as a lizard's, except for the twin paths of tears.

"What happened?" I repeated.

"Oh, just the per usual. Some officer dreamt up a brilliant idea nobody'd ever tried. 'Course I realize now the reason nobody'd ever tried it is it wouldn't work—the trouble with most brilliant ideas, it appears. But we were stuck in the Atlanta trenches with low ammunition, going nowhere, starting to thirst and sicken and starve. And the Yankees just seemed so *healthy*—they were the invaders, but they seemed to be doing so much better than us. So this officer had an idea to shake them up a little by catapulting Greek fire into their lines."

"Greek fire? What's that?"

"It's from the Crusades. They'd pour it over the sides of castles. It's green and it glows and it gets on your skin and just burns and burns. If you try washing it off, you make the burns blister. Try brushing it off with your hands, you ignite your fingers. And if you just leave it on and pray for the best, it'll eat off your skin right to the bone."

I already could see where this had to be leading. Tommy said, "I guess we'd of made lousy Crusaders. Because unfortunately there was a brief summer squall while we were launching it and this officer forgot water makes it go off. Damn stuff blew up in our own faces."

Tommy opened his eyes, tested the darkness, and smiled at me.

"Too bad old Rand wasn't still with us," he said. "I bet he'd of known his chemistry well enough to recall naphtha isn't waterproof."

My own eyes started to sting, although not from pain. I said, "Hard to say. He could have known or not known, or known and forgotten. But how can you fight if you can't see?"

"I can't," he said. "They cashiered me out. Only by the time I got home, I didn't have one—the house was gone and my family with it. Maybe if I'd of made better time I could've found 'em, but I can't really travel except after dark on account of the glow."

"So you're just staying here?" I asked.

"I move around at night. I figure it won't be much longer. Davis has had it, Hood, Johnston, Beauregard—hell, if it weren't for Robert E. Lee, the whole mess would already be over and done with. Who'd ever expect the worst curse on an army is a general who never loses?"

A chill wind blew through the doorless chapel.

"You hungry?" said Tommy. "The Yanks dropped a couple of cans of something or other. See if it's anything you recognize."

He reached into his pocket and took out two tins. Each had a drawing of an ear of corn and a grazing cow on its battered label.

"I think it's stew," I said. "Illustrated stew."

He took back the cans. "We do that too," he said. "Not all the boys read." He plunged a knife into the top and twisted back the lid.

The can rocked so hard it nearly leapt out of his hand. Trembling and vibrating and shaking, and all the time belching a keening hum, it quaked and bleated and gurgled like a fevered teakettle. I peered inside. The tin was swarming with twisting, glistening worms, packed in as tightly as bees in a beehive.

"Uh-oh," said Tommy. "I recognize that smell. We can't eat that stuff. It isn't the little worm fellas—they can't hurt you none—but that stink means they canned it wrong. Trust the Yankees to screw up their own leftovers."

Exposed more and more to the cold night air, the can bobbled and whined and whistled. Tommy reached for the second can. It was wormless, and stewless as well. It had been canned with dozens of tiny stones.

I was outraged. Tommy just smiled.

"You know, this is why I can't hate the average Yank soldier," he chuckled. "At least when we got no food we know it. But imagine toting this crap around from dawn to nightfall in the expectation you're carrying dinner, and it turns out somebody stiffed your own commissary department by selling canned rocks. You know what Rand used to say about all this? He'd say the Yanks should come down and kill without mercy all the planters, and the Rebs should go up and kill without mercy all the bankers. Then we should all go home and pull down the shutters."

"He was about two years late with that prescription, wouldn't you say? There's no more shutters and no more home and no more Randall."

The church was now shrouded in moon-nipped shadow. Tommy opened his eyes and this time kept them open.

"I miss him too, Annie," he said.

"Yes," I said.

"He left a void."

"Yes," I said politely, "he did."

"He was an odd one, our Randall. When I picture him as a kid I don't see him saying much of anything. Seems to me I provided all the chitchat. And when he and you started courting, my recollection is you mostly talked and he just listened. But now that he's gone, whenever I think of him, all I remember is things he said. Nothing he did. Just what he said."

I nodded. It seemed to me very natural no one would have paid much attention to anything Randall said until after he died. It only was then that you noticed that his observations, which all seemed so common coming out of his living mouth, were observations nobody else ever made.

"Tommy," I said, "seeing you makes me think . . ."

"Don't think," he said.

Suddenly I was staring into his lashless eyes. What I had started to ask was something I'd often wondered: just what was the best way to understand Randall's death, in a war he'd predicted would come, predicted we'd lose, and predicted we'd lose even if somehow we won. But Tommy's abrupt "Don't think" kicked off a question far less exalted, far less philosophical. Far more specific.

"You must have been with him that day," I said.

"What day?"

"That day. Tell me."

"Tell you . . . ?"

"What happened," I said. "Tell me. How Randall died."

"He died like a hero," Tommy said instantly.

"Don't tell me that. I know about heroes whose deaths—well, if that's how I thought Randall died, I'd have to drive a pick through my brain to blot out the picture."

He patted my hand.

"I didn't mean it like that," he said. "I just meant, he died exactly like everyone else."

"And what does that mean? I've heard of more ways to die in this war than I knew there were corpses. I've heard there isn't a battle where both sides don't shoot their own men—sometimes on purpose and sometimes for mercy, but most of the time by mistake. I've heard boys on both sides are killing themselves, so they don't burn or smother or drown or starve, or pass whatever they're dying of to others. I've heard about guerrillas and murders and firing squads. I've reached the point where I don't know if anyone ever just dies from the other side's bullets. The other ways all seem more common."

"Randall," said Tommy, still holding my hand, "died from the other side's bullets."

"What happened?"

"Nothing," he said.

I dropped his hand and gave him a look.

"Annie, I'm not trying not to tell you," he said. "It's just . . . nothing happened. He died, that's all. He was shot. In the chest. By a Union soldier."

"When?"

"The next day. The first day we won—I mean, the South did. And we expected to win the second day too; I don't know why exactly, but this was the first battle in the whole war to last more than a couple of hours, and we just didn't know any better; we figured the odds one day would be exactly the same the next. I know that's what Randall thought. He told me the two of you used to play dice and you'd told him the chance for rolling a seven was always the same no matter what you'd just hit.

"We were in a wooded area, kind of pretty and still and green. Just east of Shiloh Chapel. We'd already won, like I said, on the day before, but we'd lost about half our boys doing so, which is pretty much average for us. And Grant: well, he'd lost his whole army but it never fazed him—he just ordered out for another.

"It was the middle of the afternoon when we started to see them coming. Then we just never *stopped* seeing them coming. If we stayed there we'd be slaughtered and if we charged, well, they were so many they wouldn't even notice. So we did a little of one and they did a little of the other, and after I can't tell you how long, Beauregard gave the order to withdraw.

"It was a slow retreat and an early sunset, light on the stars, heavy on cold and mud. It started raining. Then it started hailing. A lot of the boys—their boys too—were too hurt to move and too far gone to be saved. They were lying there bleeding in the wet red grass and not crying or saying a word, until the hail got so hard it started bouncing off bodies. Then *we* started crying, because seeing and hearing something like that was pretty hard to take. So me and Randall and a couple of the other boys offered to go back to the field and just try to cover the wounded—not save them, just try to make it not hurt so bad. And some of their men did too.

"We filled our canteens and picked up what few extra blankets and jackets we could spare. Then we started across the field.

"Most of us pretty much stuck to our own boys, because there were plenty to go around without playing Saint Francis. But Randall started heading in the direction of the Union lines."

It was like watching a play: I could picture it, hear it all. The rain, the hail, the blood, the tears; men calling to one another across a carpet of human flesh. And strolling along this path of a thousand crucifixions, my own husband, his step jaunty, his eyes narrowed, his face as interested as the day he heard sea in a seashell; watched a predicted comet; listened to my entreaties; enlisted anyway.

"It took me a couple of minutes to notice he wasn't beside me," said Tommy. "Then I saw him heading away like that. I figured he'd got himself mixed up which way he was going, so I called to him. He didn't turn around."

I remembered Micah.

"Maybe he wanted to surrender," I said.

"Maybe. Or maybe he wanted someone's surrender to *him.* Maybe he hadn't had enough killing. Maybe he'd turned out, after everything he said, to like all this. Or maybe he'd had too much killing. Maybe he wanted to die. Or maybe he figured there weren't sides anymore so it didn't matter where he wandered or who he helped. Who knows? I never knew him. You never knew him. The man who shot him knew something we never knew. He knew that sweet, strange, friendly, smiling, unwilling Randall had the makings to be the deadliest enemy. He could say more about Randall than you and I ever could."

I said: "How long did it take?"

"Ten minutes. A short ten minutes. Me and a couple of other boys dragged him back. He said he was in a lot of pain but not as much as he would have imagined. He told me to try to find you. He told me to tell you not to be sad. He told me to tell you to cut back the sunflowers. He said you'd understand."

CHAPTER
ELEVEN

IT TOOK ME nearly a week to outmarch the Union army, but sometime in mid-December I finally did it. After six midnights in churches and cellars and barns and abandoned schoolrooms, I stumbled into a place I no longer dared to expect existed: a segment of Georgia untouched by war.

It wasn't, of course, *completely* untouched. In expectation of Sherman the entire area had been evacuated of all living creatures, and some dead too: rumors of desecrated graveyards had led survivors to dig up and scatter the bones of their grandparents before the Yankees could do it for them. And when I tiptoed into the public hall at the center of town, I saw the offices had all been stripped mapless. It was clear the war had shunted the life out of this township. It was equally clear it had been Southerners doing the damage.

The homes at the edge of this nameless town (someone had filched all the outlying road signs) had been deserted in leisurely fashion. I wandered from house to house and in each one saw the same evidence of the luxury of time: neatly stacked carpet tacks;

unpaired socks; well-sorted bookshelves with no matched sets; tarnished silver and chipped dishes only. After a half-hour's tour of five or six vacant houses I nearly whinnied with pleasure and greed. What a haul! What had been left behind might have been dregs and oddments to these houses' occupants, but to me they were cornucopia—unbelievable manna, unconscionable waste.

The very last house was my favorite. It wasn't the largest, and certainly not the grandest; in fact, with its thatched roof, wattled bricks, Dutch-shuttered windows, and frost-begotten lawn sprinkled with dusty cupids and iron deer, it looked like an English farmhouse, or at least the way English farmhouses look in American magazines. Which was precisely what drew me to it—I admired its owners' zeal, so like my grandmother's, to build in the South the very obverse of a typical Southern home.

The house sat on a hill facing east, toward Savannah, and overlooked miles of green-seamed gullies of flooded rice. I tried the doorknob. Its locks had been left unbolted, as though its departing residents knew locking a house against Sherman was like locking Canaan against the Flood. I opened the door and made straight for the kitchen.

The owners had taken much. But left behind even more: for with no Sarah to guide them, no Andy to advise, they'd foolishly spent more energy packing porcelain and family portraits than they had curing and smoking and drying and tucking into any spare corner every last nugget of the Refugee's Only Currency—food. Their larder alone contained more potatoes and onions and jam than the entire Confederate commissary. I opened cupboards and drawers and closets and breadboxes. Then I started to eat.

I ate for nearly an hour. There were obvious gaps—no bread for the jellies, for instance, no salt for the corn—but the opportunity after all this wandering to have *selections* was a treat more dear than the richest missing cream or the creamiest absent butter. To have to choose whether to consume those almonds on the spot or carry them with me was a fascinating dilemma; to complicate the problem by having not only almonds but peanuts and hickories almost hurt. I ate and sorted and ate.

I was just about finished when I noticed a large painted can, stuck behind a set of nested pewter mixing bowls and weighted with bricks. I removed the bricks and prized open the top.

It was a fruitcake.

It weighed about what all fruitcakes weigh—too much—and smelt how they all smell, brandied and peppered and overbuttered. It looked like they all do too—wizened chunks of unrecognizable species, suspended in batter the color and consistency of waxy mud, crosshatched with gilded nuts. Even to me after six nights of hunger, it appeared almost inedible. Then why . . .

Why did looking at this misshapen chunk of sweetmeat bring tears to my eyes and the slowing heartbeat of sorrow to my breast?

It was not a reminder of home. We didn't bake fruitcake at home. Nor was it a reminder of neighborly hospitality, for if ever a neighbor should bring one over, it never got eaten; we'd put it aside till it ossified, then toss the whole mess to the pigs. This cake, in other words, and this sorrow, had nothing to do with me or my memories; it was *this family's* memories. It was their cake I had discovered, and it was their sorrow I was suffering. I had unwrapped a happy and hallowed tradition and cruelly exposed it to the withering air of an outsider's derision.

I was becoming a forager myself.

The cake had been draped in an oiled newspaper, which I now unfolded. It was dated July—just five months ago and already so stale it could just as well have come from medieval Florence as modern Savannah. SHERMAN IMPALED ON KENESAW MOUNTAIN. ATLANTA PROUDLY INTACT! BAREFOOT SCHOOLBOYS FROM THE VIRGINIA MILITARY INSTITUTE ABANDON CLASSES TO FACE AND DEFEAT AN ENTIRE YANKEE ARMY! ROBERT E. LEE HARRIES THE UNION SUCCUBUS THROUGH THE VIRGINIA MOTHERLAND.

I read a few stories, then refolded the paper. Half of these headlines had never been true, not even in July; now not even the true ones mattered. I wrapped back the cake. They had baked it in summer to eat it this Christmas Eve. Who would be eating it now? Was not even the fate of becoming dessert for Northern soldiers preferable to just being left here, to harden forever under a shroud of outdated victories?

I strolled into the dining room. The aging wallpaper, brown against beige, showed oblong boxes of yellow against bright white; nails hung from the center of every oblong, and I realized portraits or paintings had been removed, revealing the paper's original pattern. I touched the clean, newly exposed wallpaper with my fingertips. It felt nubbly, like nutmeg seeds, and crumbled beneath my hands into glue and dust.

I walked on, into a tiny study tucked under the stairs. It held a desk, a chair, and a waist-high globe mounted with copper prongs. I spun the globe; the world rushed by my fingers in a spray of color and parallel lines, and when it stopped I was looking at Asia: hundreds of rivers and mountains I'd never heard of, crossing borders of countries whose names rang only the vaguest bells. I nudged at the orb with my fingers, turning it west and east. Who lived in these unfamiliar nations? What did they speak, think, feel? How many dwelt in a state of peace? I wondered if those who did ever gave thought to it, or whether peace in those lands was like peace had been here—accepted, unquestioned, the unexamined background against which Real Life existed.

A series of cubbyholes ran along the back of the desk. All were empty, cloudy with dust. The drawers set into the desk on both sides were empty too, except for occasional pencils and a needleless compass. The center drawer was jammed tight, and when I managed to tug it open, I found it stuffed with kerchiefs and gloves and a heavy muffler. You always can use a spare muffler when your country is under siege; I decided to take it. But it was wedged into something, stuck fast, and when I gave it a pull, it only resisted.

I pulled harder. It loosened and unfolded. Something fell to the carpet.

It was a revolver.

I picked it up. I'd seen revolvers before. I'd even used them— my brother had taken me out once to shoot jelly jars. First he had carefully placed each jar inside an empty birdcage, so the glass wouldn't scatter if I managed a hit; then he had passed me the gun. At the end of the first hour I'd winged two jars, and at the end of the second hour I could no longer raise my wrist to squeeze the trigger. Now I placed the revolver on top of the desk and looked it over, remembering that row of jelly-jarred birdcages and the two at the end, raining glass.

Was it loaded? I checked. It was loaded. The next question was, who would I use it on?

About forty-five minutes later the war burst in.

I had just left the study. The day had become so silent I was starting to wonder whether it might be snowing; if so, I would be wise to find paper or cardboard to line my boots. I walked to the window to check the sky, and a man dashed into the yard. He looked behind him and raised his arm. His arm remained up even as his legs buckled and his chest erupted in blood and smoke.

Then the entire hill seemed to surge. The yard turned into the war's newest battleground.

For the first few moments, it all seemed without reason or pattern—just a mass, pointless ruckus of horses and men and guns and screams. But before long it clarified into a series of separate, reasonable actions, some obviously practiced, some being invented even as I watched. There were, at most, thirty or forty men, each somehow appearing frightened and cool simultaneously. All had rifles, one with a bayonet; a few had revolvers as well. One was flashing a sword.

Within seconds I saw there were two basic principles, shelter and high ground. Men huddled beside the iron deer and clustered behind bushes, and wherever the yard rose, however infinitesimally, was where shooting was hottest: at the raised edge of a bricked flower bed, at the mounded feet of the cupids, at a circle of rocks surrounding a leafless tree. I watched a Confederate soldier on horseback swing by the tree, then leap off his horse into its lower branches. He shot six Yankees. The seventh shot back.

The Rebel fell from the tree. His waiting horse, anxious to be remounted, cantered, kicking him in the head. His face disintegrated, hoof, flesh, mud. Somebody grabbed his rifle. Somebody else grabbed the grabber's hand and forced it backward. He dropped the dead horseman's rifle, jerked himself free, and reached once again for the gun. Shots from across the yard hit his knees, stomach, and heart. The horse, panicked, bit at his writhing legs.

By now at least a dozen soldiers were motionless—mostly on the ground, but a few draped across the spine of the deer and one leaning against a cupid's head, as if receiving advice from its stony mouth. More men were hit but not dead, some trying to crawl to cover, some staring with disbelief at emerging freshets of their own blood. The unwounded men kept firing, firing—though it got to a point where it appeared that only the *same* men, maybe five on each side, were actually hitting anything. The rest set and aimed, set and aimed, but nothing happened; nobody moved, nobody fell. The five true shooters on each side curled into their rifles and shot and shot.

It was appalling, exciting, exhilarating, bloody beyond belief. What it had to do with North versus South beats me. For this wasn't our war, it was War—any war. War the bludgeon of history; War, history's boldest hour. I watched with revulsion and fascination.

I wanted to run.

I wanted to join.

And then, suddenly, it wasn't a matter of choice . . . of running or joining, of either/or. A soldier jumped onto the porch and began firing. He was less than six feet away from me, on the opposite side of the window.

He was in blue.

He crouched for a moment. Then he threw himself flat, aiming into the yard with unhurried accuracy, the rails of the porch hiding him perfectly from the others below. I could see the faces of some of his targets; they looked startled and puzzled—not surprised to be shot, but surprised it had come from this unexpected direction.

My first thought was that he'd done exactly what I would—sought cover and high ground. My second was, this was one case when smartness wouldn't matter.

I ran to the study and grabbed the revolver.

I ran back to the front room. He was still on the porch. But by now he was standing.

He had edged himself upright along the shank of the main baluster and was still shooting. His concentration on the yard below him was so fixed he looked carved—back braced, face still, except for the flash of his eyes as he blinked away smoke. His mouth and throat were ringed with black powder. His arms were like an extension of his rifle. His fingers, twitching against the hammer, made the same movement over and over again, like a pianist testing pitch.

I stepped outside, my revolver extended. I pointed straight at his heart.

He saw me. Or heard me. Or felt my presence—too late to defend himself, just enough to shift his position. He kicked up, toward the outstretched revolver. I fired. He fell. Only, goddammit: he wasn't dead.

It was his leg kick that must have done it. He was down on the floor with blood pouring out of his thigh. He must have hit his head falling, as that bled too, down the side of his face and onto his hands. I stared at him for a few seconds, stunned less by the fact I had shot him than that I had to shoot him again.

I stepped further out. He was fumbling at the gushing wound on his leg. Blood started to stain the stairs of the porch. I raised the revolver and saw his rifle. Angled up from the floorboards, aiming right at me. I heard a click.

I pressed down on the trigger but not hard enough; he jumped, but nothing happened. His eyes widened and he looked up, right into my face.

Then the stock of his rifle jerked just as though I had shot him. It lowered itself to the ground.

I gripped the gun harder. This time would do it. He stared at the revolver. He was making no sound, not even to breathe. Blood dripped from his eyes. He already looked dead.

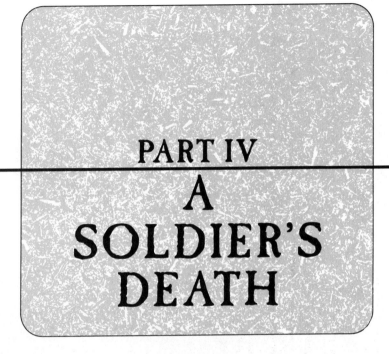

PART IV
A SOLDIER'S DEATH

SPEAKERS:
Nick, Annie, General Sherman

CHAPTER TWELVE

NICK

I LOOKED UP the barrel of her unwavering silver revolver. I pictured the waiting bullets, bundled neatly as beads. I'm going to die, I thought.

It could have been her lying here and not me. I'd had enough time—not much, but then it doesn't take much—just that one quarter second of overwhelming relief, when I realized I'd have enough time to shoot back. That whoever had hit me was about to die. And then I saw her. Her face. Her dress. Her hands. Her shoes. Her . . . her . . . her . . . a woman.

A woman. A civilian woman. A civilian woman with a revolver.

I couldn't do it. I just could not shoot her. I couldn't live with that much dishonor, that much shame; it would hurt more than dying itself. What a bitch it was, being born with a conscience! Too late to return it, ask for another . . . I lowered my rifle.

Nick, I said to myself, you are a real idiot.

The pain was different—worse—than the other three times. The range had something to do with that; she was so close.

Although maybe it just was seeing her—actually seeing the face of someone who wanted to kill me. Everyone else who had shot me had wanted me dead, but not dying. I could see in her eyes she wanted both.

I tried to concoct some consoling thoughts for these last few heartbeats, only my head hurt so much from my cut I could hardly think. I wondered if I had done my brain some permanent damage falling like that. Permanent in the relative sense, that is; what was about to happen would be much more permanent. I had a terrible feeling she was going to try to shoot me in the chest and the gun would jerk and she would shoot me in the face instead. I guess it didn't really matter except the second way made such a bloody mess. I was sorry now I'd spent so many years sketching cadavers; the effect of my death on my body was all too easy to envision.

She was certainly taking her time. Something no soldier would do, and I didn't appreciate; I was starting to go dizzy, and I feared she would kill me while I was unconscious. Which you might think is just how you'd want it, but believe me, when the moment comes, you'll take one more second of conscious thought over proof of the existence of God. Stay awake, Nick, I told myself. Lady, for Christ's sake, get a move on.

It sounded to me like the skirmish was about finished; the shooting was dying down, horses were trotting away, all the familiar sounds of battle were receding into a numbed background, leaving me with this reciprocal throb in my leg and my head. A voice from somewhere behind me, a man's voice, Southern, spoke to the woman over my body.

"Don't," it said.

I was lying on somebody's couch. Behind me a window bathed me in low, gray sunlight.

I lifted my head. Through the glass I could make out a corner of porch, a glimpse of sky, and a long stretch of mud-pitted yard. The yard was empty and the sky was scudded with cloud.

The porch looked familiar. I realized why. It was here she had shot me.

My head buzzed. I lowered it, feeling it fall into pillows. My leg was resting on pillows too. I touched it. It was bandaged. So was my forehead. Both ached. I'd live.

That is, if they'd let me.

I could hear two voices from somewhere behind me. One voice I recognized—the soft-spoken man from the porch. The other belonged to a woman. She sounded aggrieved and excited. I meant to stay silent, in the unlikely event they were discussing anything else but my future, but they must have spotted me moving about. They both came into my field of vision at the same moment.

He was a Confederate officer. She was the woman with the revolver.

Only she wasn't holding it any longer. He was.

I eyed him first. He was about my height, maybe a little taller, and younger than me—say around twenty-five. He had blond hair and a blonder mustache, and wide green eyes, tired and strained with sun. He would have been very handsome if he hadn't appeared so exhausted, and if he hadn't appeared so exhausted he might not have seemed so extremely dangerous. But the only threat worse than an armed enemy soldier is a *tired* armed enemy. He seemed threatening indeed.

I looked at his uniform. His boots and trousers were crusted with mud and dying leaves; his belt hung loosely, like the belt of someone who hadn't eaten all summer. A tarnished sword dangled from his left hip; on his right a New Model Remington swung from a battered holster. The buckle of his belt was so badly scratched I hardly could read its fading but oh-so-familiar legend. CSA. Confederate States of America.

I kept looking upward. It got worse. The scuffed gray coat hanging over the sword and revolver was piped in yellow, which meant he was cavalry—the men we'd been chasing, and vice versa, since early Atlanta. Wheeler's men. The men who had murdered Charlie.

I sighed. It figured. I looked at her.

She was wearing men's boots, women's gloves, a tattered waistcoat, a dress, two vests, and a couple of dirty scarves. Her jacket looked like a prop from a *tableau vivant* about Valley Forge. Indeed, her whole outfit looked like it came out of some-body's attic, and she didn't look too happy looking like that. Although it was hard to read her precise expression. It certainly wasn't friendly, but it seemed—or maybe I merely *hoped* it seemed—a little less hostile than earlier. I decided on second glance it was no less hostile than earlier. It was merely the absence of lead in my face.

We stared at each other. She had brown hair and browner eyes, and she never stood still, rocking back and forth on the heels of her boots as she stood watching me. She looked tense and angry and wide awake—far less tired than he looked or I felt. In fact, if I had to choose one of the three of us to win this war at this minute, she'd get my chit. I cleared my throat. I said to her:

"Sorry I kicked at you back there. You planning on trying again?"

"I surely wouldn't mind," she said.

"Look," I said, "go ahead. Do it. Shoot me. I'd much prefer getting scythed here and now in relative peace and quiet to death by starvation in one of your famous prison camps."

"Yours aren't much better," she snapped.

"Maybe not," I said. "But I'm in no position to help you find out."

She looked pointedly at the right hand of the officer holding her weapon. He noticed her glance and stuck the revolver into his waistband.

"Nobody's shooting anybody," he said. "Everyone just relax."

"Don't start giving me orders," she told him. "Just because we're on the same side doesn't mean we're allies."

"I apologize," he said. "It wasn't an order. Just a suggestion." He touched the butt of her revolver with the edge of his finger-tips—a gesture both delicate and menacing.

"Had we been invading *them,*" he added, "I would have suggested the same to a Union lady."

He appeared calm. She appeared furious. She already had shot me once; he already had saved my life. But they both were Rebels; they both were enemies; they both, in the long run, were equally likely to kill me, she in anger, he out of habit. The only difference I could make out was, with him it would probably take less bullets: cavalrymen pride themselves on minimal shooting. On the sheer-cliffed walls of Eternity, that wasn't so hot a foothold.

And I wanted a foothold, badly. I wanted a break. I wanted, at that moment—hurting more than I'd ever hurt in my life, and feeling closer to dying than ever before, and captured and helpless and scared, and embarrassed to boot—I wanted desperately—so desperately I was suddenly close to weeping—I wanted desperately, frantically, hungrily, madly, to live.

All the thoughts that supposedly come in your final seconds came to me now. All I would miss: reading, talking, ice skating, fishing; dozing outside on summertime evenings; cats; ice cream; bookstores; trees. Jokes—hearing them, making them. Laughing. Running. Sitting in kitchens discussing the weather; sneering at almanacs; rain, wind, snow. Being fitted for boots. Buying things. Cracking the spine of a new sketch pad, fanning the rich, empty pages. Working. Being paid. Spending money. Walking down streets with dollars and friends and anticipation, and nothing but time. Sleeping. Dreaming. Imagining.

And the women. Those I loved, those who loved me. Those I was meant to love but hadn't yet met, and now never would. All those loves and flirtations and temptations, which had all seemed so real, and mattered so much, and that I now saw lived only within me and would die as quickly as I was about to, blocked out image by image by the bullet bombarding the yielding brain. I pictured next Christmas, my brother reminding my niece how the first time they left me alone with her I became so befuddled I put socks on her hands and mittens on her ten-week-old feet. Tiresome Uncle Nick, always talking to her about history. Only not anymore.

"And you know what probably bothers Nick most?" my brother would tell her. "What's eating him up, wherever he is? He didn't even get to find out who won."

Say something, say anything, I said to myself. It can be funny, it can be obscene—just don't let them start to talk to each other, or the next thing you know they'll become best friends, facing their common enemy. Remind them you're here—that you're somebody too. Don't let them let you become a *thing*.

"Umm, names," I said. "Names. My name's Whiteman—Nicholas James Whiteman. Everyone calls me Nick. Miss?"

She didn't answer. The soldier prompted, "Yes, miss, you're—?"

"Annie Saunders Baker," she snapped. "Everyone doesn't call me anything."

"Well, we'll call you Miss Annie, with your permission," he said. "Unless you'd prefer Mrs. Baker?"

"I'd prefer neither," she said. "I hadn't planned to engage in this much chitchat."

"And your name?" I asked, launching my voice over her bitter glances.

"Lindley Holland," he said. "Just Lindley is fine." He turned to the woman. "Is this your home?"

"It is for today," she said. "My real home's a pile of stone and bricks one hundred miles west of here. Possibly thanks to him."

"I never burnt out any innocent civilians," I said. Then I thought about Charlie and Tim and Alice—two dead, one God alone knew—and a spurt of anger admixed with my desperation.

"I considered it, though," I added.

Lindley winced. He looked like somebody wending his way through a rocky quadrille; only good manners, I felt, kept him from dumping both these unruly partners. He asked, a little forlornly, "And where's *your* home, Nick?"

"Decatur," I said. "Right in the middle of Illinois. Pretty part of the world. You?"

"Not far from here. Milledgeville. Also quite pretty. Capital of Georgia, as you might know."

Annie rolled her eyes.

"If it's still standing," she said.

Lindley smiled politely. I wondered how politely I'd smile if someone had just suggested my hometown had been felled by invasion. I wondered if I'd be smiling even if I intended to shoot one of the invaders.

"So . . . what are you?" I asked.

"A teacher," he said.

"No, I mean in the army," I said. "What's your rank?"

"Oh! I'm a major."

"Then you outrank me. I'm only a captain."

He smiled again. His eyes were an extraordinary color, that green you see in country horizons just before sunset (or used to, in the days before country horizons always came smothered in flame). He said, "Well, great. Only I don't think it counts if we're not on the same side."

"Oh! I thought you *were* on the same side!" Annie murmured.

Lindley started to say something, then shook his head and slowly sat down, his thin body sagging into the cushions as though he were having trouble balancing. I wondered when he had last seen a chair, a cushion, or the inside of a house. I wondered when he had last closed his eyes. I wondered if sleeplessness clawed up his mind the way it did mine, making thought more trying than action, and action more soothing than thought. I decided I'd better not ask.

But I'd better ask something. Silence was descending over this room none of us belonged in, and silence scratches the nerves of people with guns. I didn't want any sudden moves or sudden emotions. Teatime decorum, no matter how bogus, was the key.

"I, ah, I wonder what pictures they used to have," I said, pointing. "I see they've been taken down."

Lindley swiveled his head painfully to stare at the empty walls. He looked like he hoped he might find, imprinted into the wallpaper, some suitable response to my comment. Finally he said:

"Probably family portraits. That's what's on our walls. My parents. My wife's parents. My children."

Christ! His parents and children. His wife. Nice neutral topics: gee, Major, when's the last time you've seen your family? That long, huh? How come?

"You're probably right," I said. "I guess that's what's on most people's walls. Unless they're rich, and then they collect art."

Annie heaved a loud sigh. The sigh said, I have no walls to hang *any*thing on. I sighed too. Lord, what I wouldn't give for more of a flair with small talk! Mother was right—I *did* wind up wishing I'd paid more attention during Deportment. Every subject that I could come up with had to do with the war.

I moved my bad leg. I said, "So! Anyway! How long have you been involved in all this?"

"All what?"

"This business. This activity . . . this, you know, this thing here . . ."

"You mean the war? Since it started. You?"

"The same."

"Long time," said Lindley.

"You said it."

"I didn't expect it to drag on like this."

"Who did?" I said.

"Some people did. I remember one of my men . . . he's dead now . . . saying after Stone's River—"

Suddenly Annie exploded, bounding so quickly across the room that just watching her crossed my eyes. She planted herself in front of Lindley and said, "Look, what's going on here? I know what happens when soldiers start talking—they parley for hours, like it's already over. But guess what, Major? It isn't. So could you possibly can the war stories and decide whether you're going to shoot this Yankee or declare him a prisoner? Unless maybe you're planning on taking him home as a trophy for the family gallery on the parlor-room wall."

"It's already decided, Miss Annie," Lindley said softly. "No shooting, no prisoners. No trophies either. We're all just going to act like it never happened."

The pain in my leg and my head evaporated in a warm blast of purest relief. But Annie was livid.

"Goddamn you," she whispered.

She swore as if speaking a foreign language. Lindley flinched.

"I'm sorry," he said. "I know you want something more. Something to make what you've suffered have some—any—meaning. But you have to believe me: it doesn't work out that way. What you want to do to this man—you do it, it's done, you turn around and still nothing's right—still nothing makes sense. Only by then he's dead, so you can't change your mind."

He stood up and touched her shoulder; she shrugged him off.

"I'm leaving now," he said. "I've hidden my horse and I don't like to make her wait. Plus it's time I catch up with my men anyway. Nick, I want you to rest here as long as you want. You'll find your army: *we* always do. As for you, Miss Annie, I'd like to give you an escort somewhere—somewhere out of the action, where you might be safe. We won't need to exchange a single word. But I know folks around here, I have relatives, friends, I could find you a place to stay. . . ."

"Don't bother," she said.

"Please think about it before you say no."

"I can take care of myself. I already have."

"The past's no guarantee of the future. I'd feel better if I knew you were out of harm's way."

"Major," she said, "I'm not really interested in making you feel better. And to tell you the truth I don't trust you—not any more than I trust"—a nod to me—"him. In fact, less: you remind me of one of the men who burnt me down. He too started out as a real nice guy, but in the long run he didn't do a thing for me either. Anyway, I'm packing some goods I found in this house and then I'm leaving. The same way I got here. Alone."

She turned to me.

"As for you," she said, "you better not count on another Confederate archangel saving your life. If I ever see you again, Captain just-call-me-Nick-from-Decatur Whiteman, I'll tell you this: you'd better shoot first."

She stomped head-high out of the room, slamming the door behind her at hurricane force.

. . .

For several moments neither of us spoke; Lindley, still standing, was watching the door; I was flexing my leg back and forth, making sure everything still worked. Above my head I could hear the pounding of her boots. A few seconds later something hit the floor with a thud. Lindley shook his head.

"You scare her," he said.

"*I* scare *her?*"

"We both do. Soldiers, gunfire, a battle right in her own front yard . . . she was probably wise to shoot. She had no idea what you might do if you saw her."

He sounded as though he were making the apology she never would.

"I wasn't going to hurt her," I said.

"Maybe not," he said, "but she doesn't know that. Only you do."

"*You* know," I said. "*She*'d know too, if she'd bother to think it over. I lowered my rifle—I gave her the chance to shoot me again—what the hell else could I possibly be thinking? Jesus! You people!"

He turned from the door, which had finally stopped vibrating from the energy of her slam, and gave me a level stare.

" 'You people,' " he repeated thoughtfully.

"Okay, bad word choice," I said. "Only I just don't get how anyone watching me could have so totally misinterpreted—"

He smiled briefly.

"But that's the big problem with war, isn't it?" he said. "Not knowing what's on your enemy's mind. Not having much time to find out."

"That's one of the problems," I said. "I wouldn't say it was the main problem."

"No," he said, "of course not. Death is the main problem."

His words struck me as both bad luck and bad taste, and I shook my sore head, in case Anyone were listening, and brushed the still air with the tips of my fingers. I wished I could shovel this whole conversation back into both of our mouths and start it over: you scare her, I didn't mean to, she doesn't know that; good day, good-bye, good luck, and he could be out of here. Instead of this tentative, quicksanded camaraderie . . .

"Actually I think the main problem with war is time," I said.

"Time?"

"There's so much of it. And then there's so little. Take me. I've been in the army for over three years. I've been in all of the famous battles; also the less-famous ones. Also feints and scrambles and scrapes and skirmishes no one can name because nobody knows where we were when they happened.

"But I've been *at war* about seventy-two hours. Three days of real combat, where there's actual shooting, out of forty-three months. The rest is just marching and sleeping and having conversations with people you like or you don't but basically wouldn't ever know if the war hadn't thrown you together. When this is over . . ."

"Yes?" Lindley prodded.

"Oh, I just sometimes wonder how well I'll handle myself. My sense of time is so skewed. Sometimes I see myself careening about, jamming everything I've missed—or imagine I've missed—into one massive party. And sometimes I think I may just spend the rest of my life untying my boots and trying to hang up this uniform, because when I'm not being shot at I no longer remember how to do anything fast."

Upstairs another door slammed and thumped. Lindley walked to the chair across from my couch and leaned his hands on the back.

"I believe we're saying the same thing," he said. "Time *is* death in war."

I glanced at his arms. They looked tanned and tough as leather. A wedding band, loose, circled his finger like the illustrated orbit of a textbook planet.

"Time somehow acquires its own special schedule," he said. "A brand-new measurement, time during war. Death moves so swiftly. The major event of your life, and it's over in a few seconds.

"And killing! So quick to do, so simple to figure out how. It took me ten times longer to learn Latin than to learn how to shoot. I can wipe out a hundred Yankees faster than teach one student to spell his name. You could kill both my daughters in less time than I took to name them. You blink and either you've killed or you're dead. How can anyone win a war against that kind of enemy?"

He sat down, looking over my head, beyond the window and porch and out into the yard where the battle had taken place. I said:

"They keep saying this war is different. They keep talking about technology. Supposedly this is the first war where the technology's gotten beyond the human ability to survive it."

His eyes remained on the lawn.

"That's ridiculous," he said calmly. "Name me one time when humans ever were stronger than human technology. Arrows pierce flesh. Gunpowder blows you up. An everyday stone's stronger than the human skull. There's always been some superior technology, because the body wasn't designed for anything much riskier than taking a walk and hoping it doesn't rain—because if it does you'll get pneumonia, and you probably won't survive that either. Technology's just an excuse. Nobody in any war has a prayer of surviving. The losers just run out of time sooner, that's all."

I jiggled my wounded leg. I've never been all that enamored of my personality, but I was at that moment: I would not—*would not*—want to go through this war with his thoughts. I decided to try changing the subject.

"So you're a teacher," I said. "Teaching what?"

"Everything. It's a small school. Geography. Arithmetic. Mathematics if they stay in long enough. Greek and Latin. History. English grammar and literature. The works."

"You enjoy teaching history?" I asked hopefully.

"Not especially. I never liked studying it—never saw the reason. Now even less."

"Oh," I said. "Right. Right. I see your point."

He looked embarrassed. "You aren't a history professor, I hope," he said.

"God, no," I said. "Illustrator. Self-taught. Just squeaked through eighth grade. I never liked school."

"You're not supposed to like it. I didn't like it much myself. You're supposed to like the subjects."

"Do you?"

"I like the students," he said. "I like watching them learn. It's like watching my daughters, only I get paid."

"How old are your girls?" I asked.

His eyes hurried back to the yard.

"Just old enough," he said, "to realize I'm missing. Not old enough to remember why I was there in the first place."

I said, "I'm sorry."

"No, I'm sorry. I'm sorry we ever had them. I'm sorry I fell in love. I'm sorry I married. I'm even sorry I enjoyed teaching. I've got so many happy memories, and so much more happiness to look forward to, and it's ruined everything; it's changed me totally. I used to want to be a good man, a compassionate man—a *kind* man. But I sacrificed goodness and compassion for happiness on day one of the war. I don't care anymore if I'm kind. I just want to see them again. I just want to live."

"You saved my life," I said. "That was kind."

He blushed—a reaction so unexpected I blushed too—and stood up abruptly.

"I didn't save your life," he said.

"Well, I didn't save it and she didn't save it," I said. "That only leaves you."

"I have to go," he said. "I should have left a long time ago. My men'll be in the next county by now. Yours too, probably."

"At least give me the chance to thank you," I said.

He straightened his jacket.

"I'll keep her revolver," he said. "Keep an eye on your own; your rifle too. The leg and the head any better?"

"They're fine."

Already he was halfway across the room. I sat up and twisted around to face him.

"I enjoyed talking," I said. "Thank you for staying. And thank you for saving me. I'd like to think it was more than an act of random kindness."

He stepped onto the porch.

"It wasn't," he said.

It took only a moment for the quiet gallop of Lindley's horse, swallowed by distance and wind, to vanish.

Though the world didn't exactly turn silent the instant he left. Annie was still upstairs, stomping around, and it didn't take much concentration to hear her moving from room to room in a pattern of mumbles, harsh footsteps, and slamming doors. But by now she was so deep into the house, her exertions arrived to me muffled, almost pleasant, like good-nighting guests from long-ago Christmas Eves. I picked up two of the pillows supporting my head, and was pleased to see that even without their support my head remained properly stalked to my neck.

I wedged the pillows behind my back and swung both legs to the floor. The good leg, all pins and needles from inactivity, felt worse than the wounded one. I stretched and twisted and flexed: hips, knees, shins, calves, ankles, all reporting in. Only the thigh of my shot-up left leg twinged and protested, but nothing worse than—well, worse than a close-range bullet hole. There's nothing on earth to compare with that, but it was already, minute by minute, feeling better than the minute before.

I surveyed the room. On the table before me lay a stack of lists, held down by two cracked paperweights. I glanced at a couple: Earrings, bracelets, rings; Stamp Collection—Daniel; Stamp Collection—Barton; Blankets, pillows, canteens; Bonds. In small letters under "Bonds" someone had written "Confed." and "real." There was a candlestick on the table and three silver spoons. Other tables held silver and pewter frames, with no pictures; silver and pewter vases, with no flowers. Everything looked unpolished and dusty: abandoned, even by its owners. Valueless.

There was a pen on the table. I reached for it, and it rolled off the edge and into the room—too far for me to be bothered chasing it. I reached into my pocket for my own pen. The army was yet to supply me my ink, but Pete had—he'd needed some help sending his wife anniversary greetings, and my price had been the means by which to convey them. The ink and its bottle were both pale pink and probably came from a child's pastel set.

I doodled a bit on the back of one of the lists. It took some getting used to, the feel of ink on this sort of paper—the ink was normal enough, but the paper was very low quality, spongy and almost wet, as if instead of wood pulp it had been rolled out of straw or soggy grass. The ink bled so fast it was like painting on sand, or flesh. I shook the pen a couple of times. I wiped off the nib. Then I started to draw.

I thought I might sketch today's skirmish while I still could remember most of its details. I began with the hill we ran over and my first glance into the crowded yard. Then I added the deer and a couple of cupids. Then I drafted the porch. Then I started on one of the faces of one of the bodies—shot, dying, smiling, still not aware. But then, as so often happens, I ended up drawing something I was half finished with before realizing what it was. I blotted the ink and took a good look.

It was her. It was Annie.

In my sketch her hair appeared longer than in real life. Of course it was also pinker, on account of the ink, and looser, because of the blotching pulp. Her eyes came out different too, looking more lost than they actually were, sadder and more confused, and her clothes matched better all painted the same cheerful rose. She also looked taller and less inflamed. It was not, when you come right down to it, really much of a likeness— except for the one thing about her I'd succeeded in reproducing. She was the kind of woman you don't understand why other men don't find beautiful. I'd managed to give her that.

I leaned back on the sofa, suddenly and irremediably tired; I wanted, needed, immediate sleep. I put the pen on the table, pounded the pillows, lowered my head to the heavenly, cottony softness. I was almost . . . then I remembered Lindley's warning. I struggled back up and slipped my revolver between the last pillow and the first cushion, then lashed my rifle to the thigh and ankle of my good leg, refluffed the pillows, and laid back down. It just doesn't do for a soldier—or anyone else, for that matter— to be killed two times in a single day.

I awoke on the couch, encradled by pillows, to the pink light of dawn. Outside I could hear soldiers and horses, whispers, commands. My body stiffened with fear and annoyance: I really could not believe it already was all starting over. I reached underneath me and took out my revolver.

Then a familiar voice spoke my name. Not called it, spoke it—sadly, almost respectfully, with a weird, unfamiliar admiration. Still tangled within my harness of rifle and cushion, I rolled myself off the couch, noisily staggered across the room, and threw open the door.

On the porch's first step, his face peony and eyes turning wider than dollar hotcakes, stood Pete.

Four of my men were scattered behind him throughout the yard. One of them looked up, saw me, and chuckled. Pete was aquiver with mortified shock.

"Of all the screwed-up—goddammit, you stupid son of a bitch!" he whispered. "You're dead!"

I said, "Well, that would explain this headache, all right."

"Headache!" he said. "I saw—Nick, I saw your whole head *blow up*! I was out by one of those angel statues, and I looked up and saw you on the porch and there was so much blood you didn't even have a face!"

"Optical illusion," I said. "Very common during the pitch and hue of slaughter. Are *you* okay?"

"Yeah. Sure. Couple of scratches. Couple of casualties, couple of deaths—you really all right?"

"I really am." Then I noticed one of my men trying to squirrel something behind a tree—something long, and heavy, and metal. I squinted. At first I thought it was some sort of rifle, only . . . maybe something was wrong with my eyes. I stepped off the porch and into the yard.

"What's that you're hiding?" I asked.

"Uh, nothing," he said.

"It's a shovel," I said.

"A shovel," he repeated carefully.

"Look, I'm not telling you what it's *called*, I'm asking you how come you're carrying it."

The man looked at Pete. Pete shrugged: the old Pete, already back, already fed up with everything I said.

"Now why might he carry a shovel, Nick?" he asked.

"Beats me. To bury his booty?"

"It's to bury *you*, dummy."

"Ah."

There followed a lengthy and delicate pause. Two of the men sat down; one lighted a pipe. Pete's blush was fading slowly, like cooling coals, though his eyes were still bulging and his expression suggested that were I to thank him out here, in front of everyone, I might still wind up dead. I rubbed my face in the cool pink air. The man with the shovel said:

"No one could find you. We guessed you'd crawled off somewhere to die. Except Pete said you couldn't have, shot like you were. So we left. We figured it wouldn't really matter—I mean, not to you, not anymore—"

"I'll always be happy to see any of you," I said, "dead or alive. So . . . what have I missed?"

"Not much," Pete said. "While you were relaxing and getting killed, we marched seven more miles and bedded down around midnight. We broke camp four hours later and the boys all went east, except for this little volunteer burial squad. So we ought to get going—we got some riding to do, and they say Sherman's getting twitchy being so close to the ocean. Wants to get there by Christmas."

"What's today?" I asked.

Nobody knew.

We were out of the yard when I felt for my pen and ink. Had the latter, must have forgotten the former. . . . "Hold on a second," I said. "Everyone wait here. I'll be right back."

Pete looked as though he already regretted my resurrection. "Make it snappy," he said.

I made it as snappy as possible. I hurried across the yard and onto the porch and into the house. My pen wasn't there. Nor was the pen that had rolled away. Nor was the stack of lists, the paperweights, the candlestick, the vases, the picture frames. The room had been sacked by an expert. She'd taken her portrait too.

CHAPTER
THIRTEEN

ANNIE

I TOOK THE SKETCH for a number of practical reasons. The first was the value of paper. He had drawn me in pink, with a delicate hand, easily overwritten either with black ink or blue; I was sure I could trade it to some correspondent naïve enough to think letters were still being delivered and people still there to receive them. The second was the utility of paper—you could make it a funnel, for nutmeats or rice; you could use it to pick up hot coal or potatoes; you could wrap it around the neck of recalcitrant jellies or oversealed bottles of fruit. It also could serve as a barrier between your hand and the hand or the foot or the face of the dead.

And there was always the portrait itself. Oh, yes: I paid attention to that too.

It was quite inaccurate. For one thing, he'd made me too pretty; for another, he'd made me too scared. A third flaw was though I hadn't once smiled (the two of them giving me nothing to smile over), I did in his picture: not much of a smile, granted, but a slight parting of lips, slope of neck, tilt of head—a light in my eyes that I knew for a fact had long since gone out and could not be relit, neither by Yankee soldier nor Rebel savior.

It was, nonetheless, an *interesting* portrait. I should probably keep it, I thought. It would serve to remind me of everything I had to keep watching out for. Looking pretty. Looking frightened. Looking happy. Looking directly at all into anyone's face. I should just keep looking away.

One more thing the drawing was good for. Next summer, when the Southern sun would be pouring its syrup of steamy sweetness and limitless heat over the mangled countryside, it would be useful to look at this wintery picture and always remember: throw nothing away. For why should I think next summer, next winter, the following spring, it would ever be over?

I had left the house yesterday evening, an hour or so after Lindley. I was upstairs, in one of the children's bedrooms, when I heard him depart—the neigh of a horse, a murmured command, the rattle of hooves on the icy earth—and I walked to the frost-slickened window and watched him head east. For some reason, seen from above like that, and separated from me by glass, curtains, height, and the comfort of ever-growing distance, he seemed very different than he had standing calm and armed in the twilit parlor—much less imposing, much less persuasive. In fact, he appeared almost frail—so thin, so alone, so just plain tired, riding so fast on so haggard a horse toward so open a future. He looked, far from threatening, threatened by just about everything—Yankees, pneumonia, starvation, snow.

His horse cleared a fence and disappeared. Major, I said to myself, you're not going to make it.

When I finished the bedrooms and attic, I tiptoed downstairs, checking and rechecking—kitchen, dining room, hallway, and study. I mostly took thread and buttons—extremely valuable, and so simple to carry—and small silver items that would easily fit into pocket or hat. Then I slipped into the parlor.

Nick was stretched out on the sofa, profoundly asleep, his arms flung over his eyes and his rifle so thoroughly roped to his thigh he looked like a sailor lashed to the wheel of a very small ship. As for his revolver, he must have hidden it; if I was going to try it again, I'd have to whack him over the head with one of the vases. Which of course I was not. Vases had value. No one was trading for Yankee corpses.

I moved quietly along the room's outer edges, measuring worth against weight as I examined valuables. I took an old patterned candlestick. I took some spoons. There was a pen on the floor, a pen on the table; I took both. I took the sketch and the rest of the paper too. Nick never budged. His breathing was soft and steady as the purr of a sunning cat.

Out on the porch, I wrapped all my stolen buttons into the drawing, walked back into town, and slept on a bench in the city hall lobby. I chose such a bed deliberately: I *wanted* to sleep somewhere wooden and hard; I wanted nobody, soldier or not, surveying my sleeping body the way I had crept around Nick's. I awakened this morning, long before sunrise, when a bell in a nearby steeple struck five times before chiming—of all things— "America the Beautiful," and I started to walk.

By now I'd been walking at least six hours. The long, cold morning slithered toward noon, about to be followed by a short, cold afternoon. I was so hungry. Not for food, exactly, but for *warm* food—for soup, tea, cocoa, hot coffee, hot rum. I would trade all my jellies for one glass of boiled cider—all my candies for one glass of heated milk. Five of my half-dozen pellets of precious bouillon for a lone cup of water steamy enough to dissolve the remaining one in.

I realized the madness—the sadness, really—in this train of thought, and tried hard to occupy myself with other, more warming considerations. But only one other subject had the power to truly divert me. So I tried deciding whether or not I regretted I hadn't killed him.

Killed myself a Yankee.

Killed Nick.

I realized I didn't. Oh, not on account of anything he had said or not said, done or not done—and that includes both his drawing and my eventual understanding that he could have shot back and he hadn't. No: it was not even gratitude. It had nothing to do with him at all.

It was Lindley. The major. The man who had spoiled my aim, the man I had cursed. The man whom just yesterday evening I had watched from a window and adjudged unlikely to come through alive. *He* was the reason. I just couldn't run the risk that Nick, this Nick-from-Decatur or the next Nick from anywhere else, would turn out on closer exposure to be a fresh Major Holland.

All he had said to me, basically, was "Don't." Don't shoot him, don't want to shoot him, don't expect me to shoot him for you. Don't believe shooting will help. It was, really, ridiculously dangerous advice for a soldier to give a civilian—and even more dangerous for a soldier to give to himself. But the chance that, out there, there might be even one other soldier thinking such thoughts was enough to stay my hand.

Coming to such a conclusion brought little comfort. More the reverse: I felt that the only ace I controlled in all this—my power to kill my enemy—had just been trumped. And not even by another ace! Just some war-weary soldier who wanted to spare my conscience what he hadn't been able to spare his own.

I slogged on. I began hearing thunder. I saw flashes of lightning and realized the thunder was actually shooting. Which was a relief: rain could afflict me far more than gunfire. After awhile the shooting stopped and it really did rain, large single drops that splattered like shaken glue, heavy and oval and gray. The drops smelt of smoke and gunpowder, and broke into ash as they fell.

I stayed dry as I could, huddling under trees till the lightning returned, then running into the open to lie facedown in the roots and grasses till the flashing behind my mud-sealed eyelashes ceased. Time passed, the storm passed. A weak sun returned to the punished sky. The thunder mumbled and died away. The gunfire stuttered and finally stopped.

I was crossing the first of several abandoned rice fields when I saw the bodies. Five dead horses, seven dead soldiers; four Rebel, three Yankee. The horses had all been shot. So had most of the men.

One of the men had been gutted. A knife, or a bayonet, had been run from his neck to his stomach, then across his chest, into his heart and through both lungs. I was able to see all this because he was naked, making him neither—or both—side's victim. His wide-open eyes were sodden, flooded with recent, unblinkable rain.

On the other side of the field was a cluster of waist-high bushes, more trees, and the glint of another rain-weary meadow. I walked to the bushes and shoved them aside. I had half of them still to go when I heard voices.

I froze. I wanted to run, but I froze, froze, froze. It wasn't just fright. It was shock.

They were voices I knew.

I forced myself to move, first one inch, then one footstep, then into a crouch. Then I took a second step forward. And then I could see it all.

There was Bert. There was Dan. There were a couple of nameless Yankees I remembered from burning my house. There were a half-dozen more I had never seen.

There was Nick.

There was Lindley.

For a moment I wasn't sure who was the prisoner. It had to be Lindley, but Nick looked imprisoned too—two soldiers were holding his arms flush to his back, and he was struggling and kicking and whipping his head from side to side while he labored to wrench himself free. He looked far more pained than when I had shot him; far more dazed than when he had lowered his rifle. Far angrier than when insulted regarding prison camps and burning houses and war stories.

Lindley . . . Lindley showed no emotion at all. His arms had been tied so tightly behind him that from even this distance I could make out the press of rope and knots into his hands; but he was standing as calmly and politely as if bound arms and bloody wrists were the usual way one encountered strangers. Behind him a couple of soldiers stood bickering over his rifle, his hat, his jacket, his sword, and his revolver. One was admiring my gun. Mine and Nick's.

"This is a mistake," Nick was saying. "A mistake, a mistake, all a mistake. Don't do this."

Bert stepped forward. "Mistake?" he repeated. "What kind of mistake? He's a uniformed Rebel cavalry officer. He ain't at no costume party."

"It's a mistake we caught him," said Nick.

"Hell, Captain, you know the drill. It's probably a mistake we catch *any* of 'em. But if we started throwing back all the mistakes, we'll be here till Jesus rerises. This guy ain't no fish. We reeled him in and he's ours."

"No, you don't understand—"

"Nick," said one of the men holding Nick's arms. "Nick, be quiet, calm down. You're still feverish. You're making no sense."

"Shut up, Pete—"

Dan snapped his fingers.

" 'Nick,' *that*'s right," he said to Bert. "I told you he looks familiar. That was his man ate the Special Order."

Dan stepped in front of Lindley. I should have poisoned your water, I thought; I should have put cyanide in your freshly baked bread. Only how could I know, on that very first day, how to act, what to say, what to do? How useless is wartime knowledge! Everything you learn only works for the moment that went before.

"Was that your signature?" Dan asked Lindley. "Breaking a poor boy's fingers, then stuffing a military proclamation down his throat?"

Lindley said: "No."

"But now that I mention it, how does it sound?"

"Inappropriate," said Lindley. "Unsurprising."

"You don't approve of it?" Dan persisted. "I mean, if the situation were reversed and we did it to you?"

"That's not a fair question," said Lindley. "We never issued an order advising our men to rape an entire countryside."

I almost moaned aloud at his answer. Nick actually did. I think we both realized at that moment something Lindley already had.

There was no point in his replying to these questions with apologies or explanations or appeals to pity, or a detailed list of reciprocal mutual tortures and reverse atrocities. There was no need to answer at all. This war could have been practiced on both sides with the politeness of Camelot, and it still wouldn't matter. They were going to murder him because there was no reason not to.

"Dan, listen to me," Nick said. "I don't want to go into all the details, but this man is a special case. Killing him would be a terrible mistake, and I can't allow it. I'll bear full responsibility, I'll swear you saved him only at my request, I'll explain to whoever needs explanations, right up to Sherman himself . . ."

"Why tell Dan all this?" asked Bert.

"Okay, I'm telling you. I'm telling whoever I outrank. This man's my prisoner."

Bert looked around with an aura of feigned confusion.

"I don't see nobody here you outrank, Captain," he said.

"Well, there's Dan and yourself, for two right there," Nick said.

"Guess again, Cap. There's only Dan. I'm captain too. Got a bar for crossing the bridge at Ebenezer Creek. Seems I was one of the few to get all my men over the water without killing half the slaves doing so. Not to mention without shooting my own men by mistake."

Nick's face flushed and his eyes narrowed.

"Then I apologize," he said. "You're right. I don't outrank anybody. We're doing what I say anyway."

"Oh, are we? Why's that, Captain?"

"This man saved my life," said Nick.

"He saved your *life*? In the middle of a war your enemy saves your *life*? That settles it then." Bert started to chuckle. "The bastard deserves to die," he said, "for doing something so goddamn stupid."

He turned around.

"Come on, let's get started!" he called. "Where's that damn horse?"

Nick suddenly shook himself free. His whole body jerked, then catapulted into Bert's throat. Bert staggered and fell to the ground.

Nick's fingers contracted—I could see them clamp deeper and tighter as the weight of his fall released him from gravity—and Bert started to choke. His left arm was pushing and jabbing against Nick's chest while his right hand scrambled for his revolver, jammed between both men's twisting legs.

Dan and the man named Pete jumped onto Nick's back and yanked him upright, his fingers still buried in Bert's fast-bruising neck. One of the men holding my revolver rammed it into Nick's ribs and leveled it toward his heart.

"Go ahead!" Nick screamed. "Shoot it! Shoot me! I'll kill him anyway!"

Dan ran up to Nick and kicked his right leg. Then he guessed correctly and kicked the left one—the one I had shot him in. He kicked again, this time harder and higher up. Nick collapsed in a cloud of curses and bloody dust.

"Oh, my," said Pete. "Oh, my. Nick, you all right?"

"He saved my life," Nick mumbled, his face still buried in mud and his own blood. "He saved my life."

Bert was rubbing his neck and grimacing.

"Well, this is your lucky day, then, Captain," he hissed, " 'cause I'm gonna save your life too. There's ten good witnesses to what you just did. I could have you court-martialed and hanged right this minute. Only I don't want to have to file the paperwork should one of my witnesses get a sudden attack of conscience and decide to report me."

He turned to Pete.

"Help him up," he said. "Keep him off that leg. And keep him off me too or I'll kill him even before I kill this traitor savior of his."

Pete and a few other men pulled Nick back up.

"He saved my life," Nick repeated.

"Saved his life? What's he talking about?" Dan asked Lindley. Lindley smiled.

"Beats me," he said.

What happened next happened both quicker and much more slowly than falling takes place in dreams. Somebody ran to untie a horse. Somebody else retightened the bonds around Lindley's arms. A third soldier whacked open a pillow and shook out the feathers. Then he smoothed out the empty pillowcase and eased it over Lindley's head. Lindley coughed.

Somebody tied a belt over the pillowcase. Somebody else wrapped it five times around Lindley's neck.

They helped him onto the horse almost gently, as if helping a blinded and much-beloved uncle, or a toddler, mount an uneven stairway. They had to slacken the belt three times to get enough leather to loop it over the lowest tree branch. The noose looked wobbly, like a child's uncertain zero.

"Ask him if he's got any last words," Bert said.

Dan asked, "Major?"

Lindley murmured something. Nick leaned forward. I leaned forward too. No one could hear him.

"What's that?" Dan yelled.

Lindley's voice came out echoless, muffled by linen.

"Don't," he whispered, "remember. Don't remember me."

They smacked the horse, and it trotted away.

Lindley's head jerked backward. His tied arms quivered. His fingers clutched and unclutched, and his legs began kicking. A noise like kindling just ignited or going out trickled from under the pillowcase. His legs kicked more wildly, and the kindling sound grew harsher and louder. Blood began dripping from under the bag. It was thick and black and covered with feathers and dust.

The branch started to sag. One of Lindley's feet dragged the ground. His breath steadied and he began coughing.

"Look at that," Dan said. "He's still alive."

Bert ran up to the tree.

"Jesus Christ!" he cried. "Four goddamn years in this goddamn army and I've still never seen anyone do anything right!"

He took out his revolver and shot four times. Lindley's chest blossomed and everything stopped.

. . .

They cleared out about ten minutes later. Nick stayed behind, seated near Lindley's dangling body. I tiptoed out of the bushes and walked to his side.

Nick showed no surprise. He said, "It's my fault."

"Not really," I said.

"No. Really. It wouldn't have happened if he'd just ridden off with his men. He'd still be alive if he hadn't stayed behind saving me. Jesus Christ, how I hate irony."

"There's no irony," I said. "If he'd stayed with his men he might have been caught even sooner."

"He only wanted to make it through. To make it home. To see his family. To have it over with."

I said, "That's all anyone wants. He didn't want it more than you do. More than I do. More than my husband did. Everyone wants it. Some of us get it and some of us don't. But we all get peace in the end."

Nick stood up. He picked up his rifle, unhinged the bayonet, cut down the body, and propped it against the tree. He untied the pillowcase and closed Lindley's mouth and eyes.

"Come on," he said, "I'll take you home."

"I don't have a home," I said.

He said, "I don't have a country."

CHAPTER
FOURTEEN

SHERMAN

I DID NOT SPARE Savannah because of her vaunted beauty, as her piss-proud citizens like to claim. I spared her because she was not militarily vital. It was not my habit to save or devour cities on the basis of their aesthetics. I marched through Georgia to eradicate treason, not Southern art.

We entered the city four days before Christmas. The weather was cold, the sidewalks skiddy; wind chorded the leaves of the famous oaks. The air was foggy and weighted with smoke from the latest Rebel skedaddle, in which they repeated their defense-of-Atlanta tactic of burning their trains and bridges before evacuating their troops and abandoning their panicked civilians. It made me wonder how long a Union commander would last were he to surrender New York, or Boston, or Washington, the same way the Rebels unloaded New Orleans, Memphis, Vicksburg, Atlanta.

And now Savannah.

We had reached the sea.

It took two days straight for all my men to reach the city and set up camp. By then I had arranged for linkage with our waiting navy, supped with Admiral Dahlgren, toasted his weary blue-jackets, and received the salute of his cheering flagship. I also sent telegrams to Lincoln, Grant, Halleck, Thomas, and Stanton (had to); arranged for the distribution of five weeks of gathered mail; met the mayor and accepted his surrender; met his alder-men and accepted *their* surrender; established a provost guard; arranged a food depot; and ordered the Stars and Stripes run up the dome of city hall and the U.S. customhouse. Just before dawn on Christmas Eve day, Major Nichols rattled the knob of my headquarters door.

"It's open!" I yelled. Nichols came in.

"I hope I'm not waking you, sir," he said.

"George, I never sleep. Haven't you learnt that by now? While others loll in the arms of Morpheus I design tortures for Jefferson Davis and forge the shackles of Robert E. Lee. While others knit up the raveled sleeve of care I plot the further destruction of the Southern Empire. Don't you read the papers?"

"I do, sir. It was my impression it was *you* who doesn't read newspapers."

"Oh, I read 'em, George. How could I recognize the ball-less little syphilitics if I didn't read 'em first? How could anyone in this glorious country work out the truth if we didn't always have the newspapers writing the opposite?"

George squeezed out an uncertain smile.

"Perhaps they're right once in awhile," he said. "The press, I mean."

"Oh, doubtless. I'd guess many's the time they're so drunk or so bribed or so much in a dither to get a jump on the next rattlesnake they come out with the truth by mistake. But don't let me get started on the press on the day before Christmas or I'll fidget too much during the services. What'd you want to see me about?"

"Well . . . the press, actually, General. The navy boys gave me all the Northern newspapers they've collected since the start of the March. Over a month's worth. I've cut out some articles I thought might be of interest."

George handed over a sheaf of papers, crunchy from glue and newsprint.

"Anything I don't already know?" I asked.

He shrugged. I started in.

The first ten articles described Grant outside Petersburg (bleak). The next four concerned Thomas and Hood at Franklin and Nashville (total destruction of the Army of Tennessee, Hood in disgrace, Davis livid). Then followed some kindly suggestions by Lincoln on Reconstruction; severe criticism of those suggestions; severer criticism of the criticisms; Lincoln's response, et cetera, blah blah. The usual D.C. garbage. On page three, though, it started getting interesting.

It was about us.

The first thing I noticed was the surprisingly large number of stories—surprising per se, of course, in view of the general lack of interest in the war in the West, but even more so considering I had (naturally) banned all reporters before departing Atlanta. The second thing was that the Northern papers were all quoting their information from Southern presses. The third thing was that after four years, they finally were spelling my middle name right. The fourth thing . . . the fourth thing was oddest of all.

The March was being hailed as one of the great military endeavors not only of this war but of all wars of all time.

I kept on reading. One paper compared us to Spartans, another to Romans; another to Thebans fighting Spartans; another to Romans fighting each other. They likened our triumphs to Hastings, to Lützen and Blenheim and Salamanca. We had marched into enemy territory without food, without tents, without medicine; without guides, without headquarters; without even an accurate map. We had blasted a guerrilla army on its home ground. We had moved three hundred miles in the heart of an armed and implacably hostile civilian population. We had done what Napoleon failed to. We had conquered a continent and reached the sea.

We were sixty thousand heroes.

"This is pretty impressive stuff," I said, finishing the articles and lighting my first cigar of the dawn.

"Yes, sir, it is."

"Some of it's somewhat exaggerated, of course."

"Not all that much, sir."

"And some of it's totally wrong."

"Much more of it's right than wrong, in my opinion, General."

I stood up and walked to the window. Daylight was pinking Savannah's two dozen pocket-sized parks; snow fell with gentle kisses. The mounted statues of her (and our) Revolutionary War heroes appeared stunted, so dyed and frosted with snow and sunshine they looked like valentine favors. A few of my soldiers were carefully pacing the ice-slickened sidewalks, ankles wobbly with the press of urban restraint.

Atlanta to the Sea. I opened the glass. I couldn't spot the ocean from here, but that didn't really matter—I knew exactly what it looked like at this very moment; I had been seeing it in my imagination for five weeks straight. Just as now I could see the forthcoming winter: a sharp wheel north, our voyage through South Carolina, a clash with the Tarheels; then into Virginia and into Washington and into peace.

Peace! I turned away from the sleeping city. Nichols was leafing through his clippings collection, shaking his head.

"Imagine what the Rebels must think of all this," he said softly.

"Imagine," I said, "what our own soldiers think."

The Green mansion was the finest home in Savannah and one of the loveliest I've ever seen, even in Europe. It had three sets of doors in the front—one served as an actual door, one was inset with glass to let in the light, and the third was louvered, to circulate air and the ocean breezes. Each room had its own marble mantle and silver doorknob, with Austrian glass in the mirrors surrounded by gold-leaf frames. A skylight poured sunshine onto a curved stairway that itself appeared poured, cascading polished steps from the vast second floor like a walnut waterfall. An ironwork porch surrounded the house on three sides, with fretwork as frothy as Belgian lace.

I spent most of my time on that second floor, where I set up my headquarters and those of my senior officers. There were days I descended only to eat: delicious and formal dinners of oysters and mushrooms and thick red French wines whose years Mr. Green took great pains to identify. His family stayed in the house the entire time we were there, and we treated each other cautiously, the way strangers to one another visit the same sick friend—mumbled, repeated pleasantries, controlled impatience, and an urgent desire for the other person to get out of the room. Occasionally one of the younger children asked for my autograph. I always asked theirs in return.

There was, as usual, much to attend to. I had to establish defenses, in case the Rebels returned. I had to settle and victual my men. I had to consult with the heads of the civil service, to make sure the police and water departments stayed operational, and meet numerous times with the chief of the fire department, to assure him we had no intention of torching his city. I had to write endless letters to Washington, accepting congratulations and answering all sorts of questions—the kind of questions it's truly terrifying—*truly*—that anyone in authority could actually ask.

But I handled everything. By the first Sunday of occupation, the churches reopened. By the first Monday, markets and schools. By the first Tuesday, I was in charge of not only a vast encampment of sixty thousand victorious soldiers but a bustling and functional major Atlantic seaport.

Streams of visitors marched up the skylit stairway to see me; as at Atlanta, I turned out to have an abundance of Southern comrades who made it a point to tell me they had never let something as minor as civil war interfere with my place in their hearts. My own men also dropped by from time to time, some to share letters from home, some to lobby for furloughs. Often they didn't speak a word—just peeked in the door and stood waiting for me to look up. "General," they'd say, and I'd say their name back if I knew it, or their rank if I didn't, and we would just look at each other and burst out laughing.

For we'd done it! By God, we had. No one had ever done it before. No one would ever *not* do it now. I loved those men, every single bloodied, triumphant, heroic soul.

Captain Nicholas Whiteman came to see me two days after Christmas. I was taking a bath. The tub was the size of a carriage, and the room was fragrant with steam. I'd fitted a board across the tub, so as the water rose it did too, lying across my chest and functioning as a convenient desktop. I was writing a letter to the head of our Secret Service, demanding why no one could find me a map of South Carolina any more recent than 1812.

"General?" he said politely. "Is this a bad time?"

"I don't know the meaning of bad times," I said. "Come right in, Whiteman. Nick, isn't it? How're you doing? Beautiful city, this Savannah, don't you think? Plenty of ink."

"Very beautiful," Nick said.

"Sit down, why don't you?"

"I'll stand, sir," he said. But he sat down anyway, on the edge of a velvet chair I had piled with papers and a box of Havanas.

"Smoke?" I offered.

"No, sir. Thank you."

"There's some whiskey around here. Care for a drop?"

"No. Thank you."

"Still keeping that diary?"

"No."

"Oh." I was surprised—maybe even a little hurt. "Well, maybe you can borrow somebody else's. A memoir of the March to the Sea—could wind up being something your grandchildren might get a real kick out of."

"They might."

He looked terrible. His eyes, which had glowed such a bright Union blue the first time I saw him, were dark and hooded; his face was watchful and pale; and his hands were trembling, as if in this steam-filled hothouse he was shaking with cold. Recollecting his grim distress at the special death of his Charlie, I wondered if amongst his unit's accumulated letters he had found one addressed to the poor tortured boy. Or worse yet, from the boy's parents, accusing their dead son's captain of permitting their child's death. Or even harder—forgiving him.

"Anything I can do for you, Captain?" I asked. "Anything on your mind? You look a little tired. Sick of Christmas away from home?"

"I've got something I'd like to discuss with you, General," he said. His voice was both quiet and slow. "Something that took place on the March. That you need to know about. And to rectify."

"Rectify?"

"Make right, sir."

"I know what it means. What do *you* mean? What are we talking about?"

He picked a piece of paper up off the chair and laid it back down. He closed his eyes. Steam roiled across his face. He opened his eyes again.

He said, "I witnessed a murder."

My stomach lurched and my own eyes momentarily shuttered. Damn it to holy hell. This was the one thing I never wanted—the one secret achievement of which I was proudest of all: there had been no rapes on the March, there had been no murders, there had been no actual physical outrage committed on unarmed citizens.

And now this . . .

"A murder?" I said. "Who? When? Where?"

"I don't know the date," he said. "I can't even tell you exactly the place. But it happened. I was right there. I know the name of the victim and I know the names of the killers."

"Go on."

"There was a skirmish. We took a prisoner. A Rebel major. He wasn't a guerrilla—he was in full uniform and captured as the direct result of a military action. It wasn't one of those—like when they killed Charlie, or we killed them—it wasn't like that. He was captured in battle. In legal, legitimized, sanctioned battle. He could have been killed in this battle but he wasn't. He was captured and should have been taken prisoner. Instead he was hanged. By us. By our soldiers."

His hands had stopped shaking by now. But his eyes, fixed on my face, remained bleaker than ever, and I felt he was less watching me than something beyond me—as if he were somehow observing every step taken by every soldier, and absorbing every bullet fired by either side, and breathing every last breath. He looked as though the invasion of Georgia had invaded *him*.

"Keep going," I said.

He looked down at the floor.

"That's really all there is," he said.

"Toss me a towel," I said.

He handed one over. I slithered under the board and stepped out of the tub, rubbed myself dry, and slipped into my dirty uniform. I rolled up a sleeve and stuck my arm into the bathwater, unplugging it. The lowering water gurgled.

"That's it?" I asked.

"That's it," he said.

"You saw this?" I said.

"I saw it."

"You asked for their names?"

"I already knew their names." He reached into his pocket and took out a scrap of paper. "These are the names," he said.

I took the paper and dipped it into the draining water.

"The ink's run," I said. "I can't read it."

He smiled tiredly.

"There's a lot more ink in this world, General," he said.

"And there's even more water. Look, Captain, how can you call this murder? For all you know, this man killed your Charlie. Or gave the command to."

"I don't think so," he said. "Too late to ask him, of course."

"Sure is. The guy's eternally innocent now. Or eternally guilty."

" 'Eternal' seems to be the key word here."

"A good word and a useful one," I said. "It pops up pretty

often, when you're looking at over *six hundred thousand* unnecessary and premature individual tragedies."

"Six hundred thousand plus one."

"Okay, plus one. But they killed us just like we killed them. *They* set the land mines. *They* started the midnight raiding. They even armed civilians. Things slipped out of control. It's not like it happened all that often."

Nick said, "It only has to happen once."

"For what?" I shouted. "For the March not to count? For the war not to count? You want to return to slavery just because we corpsed a Rebel who could just as easily have died by a bullet in the very next action?"

"But he *didn't* die in the very next action. He died in no action at all. Without any honor. Without any reason."

I nearly wept with impatience. "Honor?" I snorted. "Reason? There's no honor and reason in wartime, Captain; there's no *time* for honor or reason. Hell, there's hardly enough time for killing. Once wars get started, anything goes. The most we soldiers can do is try to move quickly, before we go too."

Nick stood up.

"You're not going to do anything," he said. He sounded dazed, like a man waking up from a dream of cancer to learn he has smallpox instead. "You could but you're not. I don't believe this."

I noticed now he was limping. He'd collected a bullet since we met at the minefield. As much as anyone, he had been in the center of action since the March began. Since before it began. He was one of my conquerors—one of the sixty thousand heroes I had taught how to kill. And I loved him.

Loved him. Had to and always would. For all that valor. For all that pain. For that astounding and precious gift he had so willingly, gracefully, constantly given—permission for me to order his death for his country.

"Look, son," I said, "I can't rectify this. I'm not about to condemn my own soldiers for killing the enemy just because their timing's a little off. You've got to put this behind you. We made history here in Georgia. Don't let this one incident make you forget that."

I watched as he walked, with his new, slow limp, to the heavy door. His hand already was on the doorknob when he turned around.

"Doesn't it even bother you," he asked, "that this was a good man—a man doing his duty—a man who could have been your own son? Who could have been you?"

"He could have been you too, Captain. We're all good men. Some are just luckier than others."

"But this isn't a question of luck," he said. "It's a question of morality."

I picked up a fresh cigar.

"Morality?" I smiled. "Good, fine, great. Then let God sort it out."

It took the captain a couple of minutes to limp downstairs and out the front door; I know because I listened, and after I heard the door open and close I walked to the window. Someone—a woman—stood waiting for him, a tall woman decked out in three or four wardrobes' worth of jackets and veils and scarves. I watched as they spoke.

They didn't speak long. The woman shook her head; Nick touched her arm; she removed his hand with what looked like pity, but maybe it just was impatience. Then she walked off in one direction, and he walked off in another.

When they had both disappeared, I lit the cigar and went into the garden.

The sky was dark with sunset and heavy with rain; it dripped with Atlantic fog. I sat on a cold iron bench and watched the December clouds roll in from the sea.

I remembered when clouds like this always meant fire—the flames of burning plantations, of burning railroads. Or battlefield smoke, our proud and bloody and costly poetry:

Bull Run.
Shiloh.
Corinth.
Vicksburg.
Meridian.
Chickamauga.
Chattanooga.
Snake Creek Gap.
Resaca.
Kenesaw Mountain.
Peach Tree Creek.
Ezra Church.
Atlanta.
Savannah.

And I remembered earlier gardens, when skies were actually cloudless—that tender, evocative blueness of early dawn, when Memphis fell in the summer of '62. The North was winning, the South was staggered, peace was visible, it was all nearly over. The war was a young year old.

I was outside then too, perched on a wooden bench in a public square, with a dispatch box in my lap. I had reports to file, complaints to address, officials to challenge—the thousand details of high command. Behind me my soldiers wove in and out of my vision, grinning and cheering and calling my name. I leaned back into the June-scented morning. In my pocket I carried a pen, a codebook, ink, and a four-sentence letter from Willie. Just like today.

How clear that remembered sunlight, how cordial that bench! How fulfilling my soldiers' smiles, how gentle that pale summer air! How dear that letter. How sweet that impending peace. How real it felt. Still feels. How missed.

AFTERWORD

SHERMAN

Now, students of U.S. history—and thanks to the March it *is* U.S. history—let's examine the record. What did we do on the March? What didn't we do?

What did we do on the March?

What didn't we do?

We bit the South in the neck. That's undebatable. We poured through her verdant abundance in two great crescents, sixty miles apart and with no communications, and chipped out a wedge of desert in the midst of some of the richest and loveliest real estate in the New World. We effected a mass migration, black and white, uprooting populations as easily as we uprooted train tracks. We destroyed the plantation system. We exposed the myth of the happy fieldhand. We burnt churches and schools and homes and hospitals. We made sacking an art and looting a science. We could have given the Vandals lessons.

Any reason for any of this?

There was a reason for all of it. In fact, there was the *same* reason for all of it.

We did it to end the war.

You can start with anything, but let's open with the destruction, because that's all you hear about all the time anyway. Here's a synopsis of the main thefts (hell, yes, I'll call them thefts, and proudly too—the language needs a new word for robbing traitors):

> 35,000-plus bales of cotton;
>
> 7,000 horses;
>
> 20,000 head of cattle;
>
> $100,000,000.00 worth of houses, jewelry, slave cabins, winding-sheets, state buildings, cannons, organs, pianos, steamboats, and food.

Okay. Cotton. Why did we raze that cotton? Because cotton was all the Rebels could offer for trade. With cotton they could prolong the war—buy overseas bullets, rifles, bayonets, cannons. Without it they couldn't. Next?

Horses. The Confederate cavalry, both west and east, knew their geography better than we ever did—plus enjoyed general civilian support and turned out to be close to impossible to exterminate. Stuart, Mosby, Nathan Bedford Forrest, Joe Wheeler—those men were born in the saddle, and fought like the very Fiend, even against such Northern heroes as Kilpatrick and Sheridan. When you can't defeat a cavalry corps in battle, you beat 'em at the barn. Hence seven thousand liberated horses.

Cattle. Even simpler. Soldiers eat cattle. Without food, soldiers can't fight. Desertions multiply. Battles grind down, turn into sieges; sieges into truces; truces into armistices. Armistices into binding treaties of peace.

Incidentally, we also destroyed the entire Deep Southern railway system, though you don't hear too much bitching about that, except from some Northern investors who clung too long to their stock. Eighty-five miles of the Western & Atlantic Railroad. Ten miles, Augusta to Savannah. One hundred and fifty miles of the Central Railroad. Depots. Bridges. Tunnels. We did this to prevent movements of troops and shipments of food. Again, to ensure the end.

And what about nonmilitary destruction?

Easy.

There was no nonmilitary destruction.

All destruction was military. All destruction was necessary. All destruction was done on command.

Whether we burnt the fields of a great plantation or plundered the hearth of a modest home or simply borrowed a basket of eggs (and I see I better go back and put quotation marks around that "borrowed"), it was always with military intent, toward the overall strategy of stopping the war.

A plantation in ashes grows neither cotton nor food. A home in ashes throws its survivors on the back of their impotent government. A refugee population spells to the world the inability of their leaders to protect its citizens' most basic human dignities. The world sees the leaders are doomed. The population itself sees it. Eventually the leaders wake up and see it too.

What about freeing the slaves (forgot that already, huh)? The South went mad when that started, which should be enough of an answer right there. Eventually we didn't even have to show up; the slaves heard what was going on and they freed themselves—and by doing so robbed the South of not only her chief source of labor but her chief inspiration for fighting in the first place. No point to perish maintaining your God-given right to buy and sell human flesh when your very commerce is flying the coop.

And the deaths on the March? Well, terrible of course as always, but . . . there almost weren't any. Certainly not compared to a good (meaning bad) battle. We lost about 2 percent overall, sick and wounded and dead and missing—but our dead were only *one hundred and three* out of sixty thousand. Work out the math, and you'll see you can easily lose that many men during an average pneumonic February.

What I'd like to know is how many of those one hundred and three dead soldiers died in battle. It couldn't have been very many, because part of the beauty of the March was we had no real battles, just a few clashes and skirmishes. I suspect (though I can't prove it) most of our dead were murdered, by cavalry, guerrillas, or disgruntled citizens. I very much regret that, as I sincerely believe in civilized warfare and commanded my soldiers likewise.

As for the number of Rebel deaths, I don't have the figures in front of me.

My guess is they paralleled ours.

So ends the March. So begins history. Verdicts are mixed. The South, clearly, will never forgive me; the North appears likely never to understand. To the Rebels I will remain forever their foremost Satan; to the Union, their Caesar, their second Grant. No side will comprehend I was a peacemaker; that after four bloody years of this most terrible of wars, I hastened what both sides most ardently desired—not Victory, but Peace. Those who revere me and those who abhor me revere and abhor for the same illusion. I have become not a general in a particular war, but eternal—the eternal destroyer in an ageless, eternal war.

Oh, well. It's hard to become immortal without being misunderstood. Look at Christ.

ABOUT THE AUTHOR

CYNTHIA BASS was born in Washington, D.C., grew up in Anaheim, and attended the University of California at Berkeley, where she studied history and English. She currently lives in Northern California and is at work on a new novel.

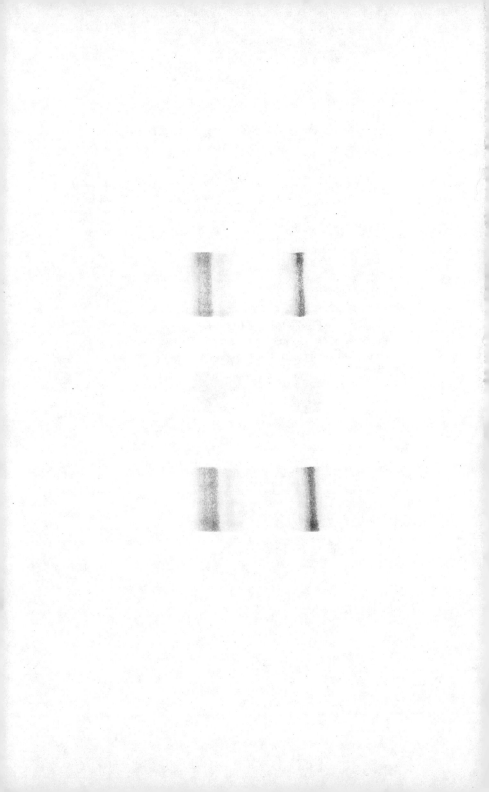